LATE
MARRIAGE
PRESS

.PREPARTUM.

a novel

JULIETE MESMER

translated by
Evalise Pike

LATE
MARRIAGE
PRESS

Copyright © 2008, 2024 Juliete Mesmer
Translation Copyright ©2024 Evalise Pike

Originally released as PRÄPARTUM
in limited edition, privately published by
AVALANCHE - GELBE AUSGABE (2008)

All rights reserved. No part of this book may be reproduced, stored in a retrieval system or transmitted in any form or by any means without the prior written permission of the publishers, except by a reviewer who may quote brief passages in a review to be printed in newspaper, magazine or journal.

COVER ART: Jan van Riemsdyk. "Anatomy of late pregnancy." Copperplate engraving. Plate VI of William Hunter's *The Anatomy of the Human Gravid Uterus*. Published 1774.

COVER DESIGN: Bruno Levine

First Edition
ISBN: 979-8-3303-4310-2

Published by Late Marriage Press

*for my mother and father
and for my children*

.PREPARTUM.

Are not two sparrows sold for a penny? Yet not one of them will fall to the ground unperceived by your Father. And even the hairs of your head are all counted. So do not be afraid; you are of more value than many sparrows.

.Matthew 10:29-31.

Of course you're the only person to tell, my darling. I'll explain as much as I can for as long as I'm capable. I'd tell you everything except there's always something else and only so long left to express it. Less than a month, if things go as they ought. But I've learned to plan for less time than given. You've taught me that.

I'll pick this journal up, set it down, endeavor to keep my narrative in order. I want to relate matters precisely. What I write for you here will be everything despite how much more there always might be. You'll see for yourself what I mean.

I've considered writing nothing. There's no need for you to be burdened with who I am, what I've done, to discover why you're here and how. But I don't think I could bear you not knowing me. Lacking a part of yourself. Even the only part hideous. The one you'll be right to wish away or dream had never been.

I'll never know if you're given this volume. You could be gone by the time I've arranged for it to find you. Taken without knowing a true word of me. It'd be better were you lost in such fashion. Proper you never know this business I'm confessing. If despite my efforts you suffer the fate I hoped to spare you, encounter one far worse, or come to a peaceful end earlier, never being known by my daughter would be an appropriate punishment for me.

I'm pained at how you'll wish you'd known me and were I not to write would go on doing so. By the time you've learned who and what I am, you'll abhor such desires. Prefer I'd gone on being someone else's story of your mother. Despise me for stealing me from you.

If you could've existed without my hand it would've been best. But anything that comes from what I reveal in these pages I accept. Were you to loathe, disavow, disown me I embrace it. Your hatred one more thing I could love about you, your dismissal a response I could cherish you for. I already know it'll be that way. As it ought. Even still I'm too selfish to hold off. I'll make every effort to ensure you know me entirely. No matter how little you deserve it.

As I set myself to this confession, I fear you might be disgusted at having what I tell you as origin. Repulsed by yourself. I'll not be there to tell you 'Never feel that way, sweet Tasha.' Though, were I beside you, I'll have become someone you'd never accept comfort from.

The same as I've known so many things, I know you're strong enough not to succumb to falsehoods, beautiful enough to see the truth, accept it, endure, and to thrive. I love you enough you need never love me. You'll discover you've already loved me too much and for far too long. You're beauty more than a mother can dream. I'm your mother, regardless.

I knew four things. That I'd die birthing you. That in your thirtieth year you'd be killed by four men and a woman. That none of your killers had yet been born. That before I died, I'd execute them in the wombs where they cowered, if need be.

I'd do my best not to hurt the mothers. They'd done nothing wrong. Deserved to be hurt no more than my mother would've had someone known what I'd grow to do. Who I'd kill were killers. I'd be a killer for killing them. Was a killer for knowing I'd try. If I were killed as I attempted to act, it altered nothing. Killers killing killers was as it ought be. But our mothers were the furthest thing from that. We didn't deserve them and they didn't deserve to suffer what we were.

I see I've written 'hurt' when I mean 'kill.' Of course I'd hurt the mothers. I was killing their sons, their daughter. Such deserved a word as irrevocable as Kill. Even if they survived whichever physical assault, had other children, enjoyed rich, full lives in the bosom of friends, they'd always be in part destroyed.

I'd do my best not to kill them. Hoped they'd recover in whichever way such term applied. In the beginning, desired they'd go on to have families, afterward. Might eventually not think of the sons, the daughter I'd killed. Perhaps one day not consider them children they'd lost or children taken from them, simply children they'd never had. Do little more than wonder idly from time to time how their lives would've gone if such children had been. I wanted it to be the same for them as for any woman who wondered of their untraveled past. If they'd had a child with X lover instead of never having one with anyone, become a mother with Y lover instead of Z, how might their worlds be different, how might they have altered, themselves? If they'd had the child they hadn't, would they not've had the others they did? If they'd had that child and then those, would their children not be the children they were? Perhaps all it'd amount to was five women wondering what those lost sons, that daughter would've grown up to be, grown up to do. Never knowing. Never having to.

Part of me must've been glad they'd hurt. How could I not desire it? What their sons, their daughter would do was worth hostility, despite it'd happen long past when they could foot any blame. No matter my certainty they'd be horrified upon learning of your death at the hands of their children, feel betrayed by their own flesh, blame themselves, and would joyfully trade their collective lives for yours, I wanted the mothers to hurt. But I don't, and never did, blame them.

I'm not you, Tasha, and you're you despite me. Your killers were killers despite their mothers. A mother can't be their child. Only do what she must to protect it. I knew that. I know that. I do.

Your father was working on three modestly budgeted, independently produced films, two he'd co-written, one all his own which he'd unofficially have a hand in directing. A step up for him which'd allowed me to take extended leave from my position at the museum. His work uprooted us to an unfamiliar area where we planned to remain throughout the pregnancy then for another few months before returning with you to our permanent home.

We'd lived in our rental apartment for a month when he entered to find me reading. I'd asked him to sit down. He chose the chair across from the sofa, faced me in that way I adored, legs crossed feminine, something between a television interviewer and a coquette. Not more than three hours after I'd come to know it myself, I told him I was going to die during childbirth.

He asked me questions, his face pale, uncertain. Had I been to the doctor, again? When had I learned this? Had there been some change in my condition? A troubling test result imparted? Who exactly delivered so precise, damning, and absolute a prognosis before I'd even entered my second trimester?

So far as he understood it, my pregnancy was trickling along as well as could be expected. Until that moment I'd told him nothing to indicate otherwise. As recently as that morning we'd made love and I'd beamed to him afterward how I felt blissful, powerful, almost holy.

Without my answering a single one of his inquiries, as though there existed no need to give the matter a second thought, he told me I wouldn't die. Crossed the room and told me twice more. First on his knees with palms on my thighs, then sitting beside me, both hands curled around one of mine.

I assured him I would die. Needed him to believe me, whether he wanted to or not, and to disregard any guarantee of my health from whichever party else. Explained I'd not survive your birth but that you'd be born vital. No way around it. He must accept this so we could prepare. In the time remaining to me, much needed to be sorted. He'd be required to tend to you alone, as best and as thoroughly as might be managed. Was all you'd have. It was imperative he comprehend, be braced for necessary sacrifices no matter how resistant to making them he might be or which hopes he chose to harbor. Even if he simply humored me with what he'd consider an overabundance of caution, I couldn't allow my death to be an utter shock, leaving him overwhelmed and utterly ill prepared for what his life would entail.

Without allowing the slightest tremor of mania or excitability to color my demeanor, I explained I'd not been informed of my fate on any medical authority. There'd been no telephone call informing me of a diagnosable condition and it wasn't a question of needing treatments, bed rest, or a regiment of medications. I'd all at once become aware that I'd die and how it'd happen. Three hours previous, while spreading peanut butter over a cracker, had simply known.

At this, his tone became more confidently reassuring. He thought I meant I'd had a nightmare or that some book, article, news story, or anecdote from a friend had spooked me. I insisted to him it was none of those things and upon my doing so he raised my hand to his lips and kissed it warmly. Eyes steady on mine, beard gently tracing against the skin of my wrist, he said "Noor, it was a dream, you know how real and frightening those can seem." Again kissed my hand and with a look of tender alarm added "When you're already anxious, such things can feel like premonition." I wish you could've seen the concern, affection, and confusion on his face as he lullabied that I wasn't in genuine danger and how together we'd do everything conceivable to set my mind at ease. Loved knowing such expression would one day be given to you.

He recalled to me a dream about a house fire which'd deeply rattled him. Practically tactile in its specifics, it'd filled his mind with such pointed terror he'd felt it the harbinger of inevitable tragedy. To this day, could recount the details as though reality. But no fire or catastrophe of any kind had transpired. To the contrary, on account of the dream he'd altered his living habits for the better. Found himself grateful for having endured what he now comprehended were personal misgivings manifested into a jolting specter. The experience had taken him ages to properly shake, but he'd finally exorcised it by writing the scenario into a script. In the end, fear had been retooled into inspiration which he'd greatly profited from.

The film this dream had inspired was one he'd shown off to me when we'd been courting. I understood the tenderness in his mentioning it specifically, the logic and poetics of tacitly weaving the fact we'd found each other and now sat together into the tapestry of benefit such nightmare had paved the way for.

But what I'd experienced wasn't of the same cloth. I hadn't dreamt or experienced supernatural vision. I simply, suddenly knew. I need you to understand me, in a way your father never could. There'd been no flashing jangle of images, I hadn't drifted out of body, time, and space, watched events transpire in front of me as though occurring in real time, and hadn't afterward been abruptly strangled back into myself, gasping, shaking, confused like in the films he so fancied or the ones he wrote. I'd dipped a knife into peanut butter, spread a dollop leftward across a cracker, set another cracker atop it, and as I brought the sandwich toward my mouth had known. It hadn't been any omen or prophesy, wasn't intuition, hunch, or melodramatic burst of presentiment, but knowledge. My death was unavoidable. I wasn't resigned to the notion. Accepted it couldn't be circumvented but was neither numb or at peace. No more wanted to die than anyone. But my death wasn't something I could strike against, alter, or stop. Not without eradicating you thirty years before five others would.

When asked, I couldn't name with precision the hour I'd die or enumerate the specifics of how. Would there be complications during delivery, a toxic reaction, sudden aneurysm, failing heart, would there be a rupture I'd bleed out from while you were pulled free of me and our umbilical severed? I'd absolutely no idea. Neither did I know what means five people would employ to kill you or what cruelties you'd suffer at their hands. Didn't know why they'd target you, in what environment your death would occur, and possessed no insight as to whether it'd be the idea of just one of them who'd bring the others along, was blind to whether all participants in the deed would willingly harm you or if any acted under duress, perhaps regretted some affair they'd become embroiled in and were desperate to extricate themselves from at any cost.

I only told your father of my death, though. Would never have burdened him with talk of yours. Had told him even that much knowing he wouldn't believe a word of it. Couldn't expect him to on the strength of nothing more than my telling him so.

Were I to've insisted the entirety of my knowledge on him, confessed what I was considering in order to protect you, fixatedly made efforts to wrest him into claiming he believed me, it would've only served as a hindrance. Overt displays of emotion or admission of acute distress would worry him, which in turn would limit my ability to act freely. Talk of needing to defend you against a mysteriously preordained demise three decades distant would only put us at cross-purposes. He'd feel obligated to say things he'd know I knew he didn't believe, from which I'd be cajoled into replying with words he'd spend more time wanting to disbelieve than acting on even if he entertained the chance what I'd told him was true.

Full belief in the situation coupled with a complete understanding of my intent didn't guarantee he'd be moved to aid my cause. There was a real chance he might think something else could be done, conjure notions his own concerning how best to protect you, and convince himself to either bar me from acting or to act against me, believing it for the best.

As I'd no idea where your killers were, let alone how on Earth I'd dispatch them, I'd not developed concrete plans. So any effort expended in clarification of the danger you were in and how I'd safeguard you from it was bound to lead to interminable loops of discussion, exhaustion, opportunity squandered before a single step of any method was codified. I couldn't allow myself to be drained of inertia for the sake of rhetorical argument, to endure not only the core of my intention being pecked at, but every step forward instantly interrogated, dissected, no time to think anything through before the consideration was flayed into doubt by the second guesses of someone who'd profess that talking me out of something I couldn't coherently articulate was protective.

Whether he were manipulated into going along or came organically to know what I knew and wholeheartedly resolved to act in tandem with me, no good would come of it. All his involvement could result in was the risk you'd lose us both or we'd both lose you. I didn't need him to join me, simply required he know I'd be gone. To fear it and fear what would come after. So that both of us would. So one of us could to some purpose.

Your father and I talked a long while that evening. I could sense he was anxious, prolonging our dialogue to be certain I'd kept nothing from him. He'd probe me subtly, seeming to drift from a subject only to carefully retread it, commenting on any additional word I used to describe matters previously explored, any tangent or emphasis I'd add. At times, I felt he'd purposefully alter phrasings in order to clock me, but it'd seem awkward to make a direct call out of it. After all, this was a tactic he'd commonly employ during spats or moot debate and one I'd roll out often enough, too. I wasn't interested in causing our discourse to turn argumentative, so allowed it to sprawl, listless and freewheeling. Talked and let him talk to be sure he was calm and believed what he'd said had calmed me. To've cut off what I'd brought into the open with undue abruptness would've unfooted him, left him unconvinced he'd convinced me I'd merely dreamt. From his perspective, he'd rightfully refuse to believe I'd come round to the idea I was experiencing a perfectly commonplace and quantifiable episode of some kind.

During the *tete-a-tete*, I'd argued how necessary it was for him to admit this wasn't the first time I'd simply known something, nor the second, third, or the fiftieth. I referenced many incidents from our lives. Urged him to understand specifically what I meant by 'knowing.' It was demonstrable how often people apprehended matters logic dictated couldn't be known. There was nothing cinematic or out-of-body about such experiences. As explicitly as I was able, clarified how I didn't mean instances of anxieties being unconsciously manifested in dreams nor that we were all free to decode various symbols doled out by our subconscious minds which might coax us to actions of our choosing. People did those things, too. But I was speaking about foreknowledge of events which'd literally transpire in the physical world. Details weren't necessarily presaged beat-for-beat, but enough specifics were sensed that hindsight made it undeniable a divination hadn't been generic.

To prove he understood, your father related occurrences drawn from his life which he'd described to others in much the same terms I was defining. Some he'd shared with me before. It seemed he made certain to emphasize those so I'd not feel myself pandered to with new inventions. He'd many times claimed to've known this or that in exactly the portentous manner I spoke of my coming death, but admitted how, when sober retrospection was applied, he'd more appropriately deem such happenstance "fantastic coincidence or examples of the human mind working to over-romanticize casual observations, transmuting them into proofs of causality by building upon impressions which only after the fact can be presented in mystical terms and thus given undeserved significance."

He explicated an anecdote wherein, out of the clear blue sky, he'd been struck by the impression he'd be given ticket number thirty-three at a sandwich shop he'd never frequented. Remembered with absolute clarity how he'd idly pretended a conversation about being handed such stub as he'd crossed the parking lot and upon entering the shop had approached the counter to be handed a slip with both the digits and the words *thirty three* printed on it. Moreover, the clerk had called him 'Champ' while another worker used the term 'Hun' toward a patron, all precisely as he'd pretended would occur. To give this case due gravity, he made plain it'd been impossible to know the shop'd dispense tickets, there'd be other patrons inside, or that more than one worker would be present. Furthermore, on the stroll back to the car he'd begun humming a tune he'd not thought of in ages and when the radio was turned to a random station in an entirely offhand manner the speakers synced to the very word of the refrain he'd been singing under his breath. "Wildly coincidental, but not outside the realm of banal explanation if one isn't overeager to let their mind boggle." I didn't disagree. To the contrary. Related memories of my own which functioned along the same lines. Minor situations such as he'd chosen to describe. Quirks of occurrence which only amounted to intrigues because it was pleasing not to debunk them.

To display my depth of understanding, I took cues from his favorite example to make clear I comprehended how superstitions could seed, flourish, and get out of hand if indulged too long without scrutiny.

"The clock on the wall displays One-Eleven or Eleven-Eleven no more often than any time else and a given person glimpses a clock displaying Three-Fifty-Two just as often, if not far more often, than they witness either sequence of repeated Ones. But three or four non-repeating numbers aren't a striking sight, so the mind scarcely registers any occurrence nor distinguishes between one non-repeating set and another. Because the average person isn't wont to consciously note how frequently they glance at a clock-face, or to mark it peculiar how often they do so precisely on the hour, they'd not bother arguing if told they look at such top-of-an-hour display five times more often than a display of Eleven-Eleven. Couldn't care less. But the eye is drawn to the symmetry of repetition and the mind recalls the pleasure associated with such observations, further recollecting previous instances of like pleasure each time one is experienced. Thus the sight of a clock at Eleven-Eleven is given a special nook in the memory whereas Three-Fifty-Two or Four-Twenty-Seven get no such distinction. These elements combine to produce the false narrative that one is compelled to turn toward the clock at One-Eleven and, by clear mechanism, each person crafts a fairy-tale out of incidental snippets of observation which is reinforced through hearing other people claiming they've encountered the same thing."

He nodded along to my discourse quite satisfied, then to drive the point home added "Nobody on Earth ever remarks how often they look at an analog clock at exactly One-Eleven, Eleven-Eleven, or even Eleven-Eleven and Eleven seconds!"

My agreement to this pleased him all the more. As did my pointing out how it's only on account of familiarity with seeing One-One-One-One repeated that when someone remarks they'd looked at various clocks showing Five-Thirteen does doing so seem significant. "Precisely because it differs from the more commonplace instance of noting a line of Ones."

We concurred there existed a recognizable path which could be walked back, that along such path one would uncover innumerable reasons X linked to Y thereby informing Z and such connections altered the importance of what amounted to nothing when presented in its proper relief.

Here I maneuvered to disempower his philosophy a bit. Charged him to recall an unsettling incident from our lives, which I narrated near verbatim to how I'd heard him deliver the anecdote.

He'd gone out for twenty minutes to nab us fast food. A solid mile from home, our neighborhood not remotely in sight, noticed a vagrant shambling along the sidewalk and, as he'd driven past, remarked aloud 'That man's the beginning of a horror story.' For the entire errand, had tooled around with conceits for a narrative featuring such figure. Scene after scene of the filthy wraith roaming unchecked, invisible despite his troubling appearance, invading random homes, killing people haphazard, going his way until being arrested or stepping thoughtless in front of a city bus. Per his artistic habit, these cinematic ideas were set to whichever songs played on the radio and while such fancies were so vibrantly entertained that exact man decided to open the gate to our yard and, upon discovering the back door unlocked, entered the obviously inhabited house. Your father'd returned with the hamburgers, tacos, and soft drinks to discover the unwashed, mentally disturbed individual he'd glimpsed not fifteen minutes prior sitting on our sofa while I was hidden in the upstairs bathroom, having been altered to the intruder's presence only by tuneless plonking on our piano keys.

Why this deviant had chosen to make illegal ingress to one of twenty houses, all carbon copies of each other, lining both sides of a suburban drive, could never be known. The odds of him selecting the residence of a man who was thinking of him as a violent dopehead were impossible to calculate. While your father'd been setting a montage of grim fantasies to bubblegum pop songs, the ghoul starring in them had invaded the house where his wife was upstairs showering. There existed no method to reframe such macabre confluence of circumstance as an everyday kink of chance.

Your father agreed this was hardly so benign a coincidence as contemplating the face of a clock and we both laughed even as our blood jointly ran cold at the memory. Though eight years in the past, we'd thought of the event quite often, never able to rid ourselves of the disquiet it'd produced.

I pressed my advantage by reminding him I'd known he'd be my lover from the moment I'd seen him. The sound of the keyring which'd dangled from the belt loop of a complete stranger had prompted a bored glance to the side. While considering which box of hair dye to purchase, I'd observed no more than a flicker drifting by an aisle at the drugstore. My jaw hadn't dropped nor had I swooned smitten at that fleeting glimpse and we'd not met properly until months later, but from that moment forward I'd found myself conversing with a version of him in my thoughts, knowing I'd love the man despite not yet feeling in love. The decision to change my hair color was a whim occurring mere moments prior to selecting that specific drugstore, simply because it'd been at the other side of the traffic light I'd waited through while Bob Dylan sang how he'd been 'wondering if she'd changed at all, if her hair was still red.' Your father'd sung that same lyric, unprompted, during our second conversation, the first wherein we'd said anything beyond my 'Haven't we met?' and his 'Absolutely not.'

I'd not experienced similar 'introductions' with previous lovers. Mentioned as much not to suggest the specific man he'd turned out to be was incidental, but rather to emphasize how our decision to couple demonstrated the difference between sets of coincidence and connections forged of mysteries more substantive.

I'd told him about that day in the drugstore more than once. Each time he'd agreed it was possible I'd known our love was already true. Had on several occasions intimated to me he felt as certain as I that, before we'd ever crossed paths, our daughter had existed. Been waiting. Claimed he believed as much, still. Though I knew his belief was far different than mine, it was enough I used the opportunity of his stating it to sweetly persuade him our conversation had set my mind at ease.

              A week later, I broached the subject of your coming death in a conversation meticulously coded to avoid putting you at hazard. Flatly expressing certainty about your fate would tilt your father cautious, focus his attentions too acutely. Unarticulated concern for my wellbeing might result in questions about my everyday movements. If a drift of suspicion infected our interactions, he'd casually probe for updates on every last thing, attitude subtly cloaked in giddy intimacy or guilt over the hours spent away. It'd be easy enough for him to claim a desire to participate in my pregnancy as much possible, going so far as to request I spend days with him on set. Refusal would come across as worrisome. Were I to invoke a desire for privacy and contemplative comfort, present myself as languorous or brooding, he'd take it upon himself to schedule massage appointments, acupuncture sessions, cooking courses, language groups, go out of his way to befriend me to the wife or girlfriend of an acquaintance, lunches and get-togethers innocuously peppered throughout my previously free time. He was too savvy to risk blunt outbursts of frustration over what'd seem frivolous matters, so any machinations would be eruditely presented as gestures of caring. Direct discussion of your death would strike him indicative of a fragility in my psyche. I'd have to let him talk me down from it as he'd done about my own. Such would hip him I'd only playacted being soothed.

 Trips connected to film projects had been terrific pleasures in the past, the transient adventure of stringing ourselves along gig-to-gig quite invigorating. But I'd spoken of this venture with a tinge of concern. His careful arrangement of three projects in-a-row, all in one place, would benefit us in the long run, but the fact it'd require delivering you so far from our permanent home had unsettled me. I'd been quick to insist it shouldn't make any difference. Hadn't wanted him to take disruptive trips back-and-forth. My physician could be kept in the loop, plus made personal recommendation for a local obstetrician I'd immediately come to adore. Nevertheless, I'd voiced qualms quite candidly. Having done so colored any further misgivings I might voice.

I kept on guard against loving ploys concocted to combat what he might've genuinely believed was an undue burden forced upon me. Perfectly reasonably he'd view the matter through a perturbed aperture, think my pregnancy'd exacerbated the typical anxieties I suffered, and that existing in a *pro tempore* environment enflamed them further. I'd frankly have found it callous of him to view the situation with nonchalance.

Any number of obstacles might crop up to cut me off from seeking your killers if I insisted outright they were an indisputable fact. Indelicate verbiage could result in repercussions beyond tabs being kept on me. A medically sanctioned leash might seem warranted. What would I argue if my doctor insisted regular visits to a counselor were advisable or that I be admitted for inpatient observation? The concern would obviously be your health, so any objection I'd make flew in the face of my avowed stance to take no chances with you. "Would talking to someone two days a week be harmful?" If pressed to answer, what on Earth could I reply that wouldn't suggest I placed your welfare below a point of pride or that my being mildly chagrined trumped medical sagacity and duty of care?

Your father couldn't know what I knew, only hear and disbelieve it. What good was his belief, anyway? You can see for yourself that if he saw the path forward exactly as I did it'd be ruinous.

The man was no more capable of killing than I would've been under any but my current circumstances. Since he couldn't truly share those, to think he'd regard five unborn children as killers was something I couldn't reconcile. The notion he'd feel compelled to act without literally knowing what I did and with his own demise imminent sickened me. It'd be the fulfillment of an insane request, done to please me as much as protect you. A choice made when, for him, there should appear to exist countless others.

Which is how it'd be. Convinced of the truth, feeling capable of action, he'd raze his mind to cinders attempting to conjure solutions which'd both alter your fate and allow me to live. Be driven to risk what I couldn't. To risk everything. Risk you. Lacking the certainty I possessed, he couldn't act in the single, absolute fashion which guaranteed your safety regardless of there being others which only might.

So why tell him anything, speak in disguise? I did ask myself, but don't recall settling on any answer with conviction. Perhaps I sought to normalize my mindset, make my fixation feel less removed from the content of day-to-day life. I might've desired an outlet, as much intimacy as could be procured. Though thinking back, I've every reason to doubt it.

On the pretext of pondering a philosophical article I claimed to've read while waiting on a prenatal appointment, I casually asked what he'd do if he knew someone he loved was going to be murdered. He was to pretend he'd been informed the crime would definitively take place, but only generally when the act would occur. Ought pretend a madman'd strolled up, handed him a typewritten threat which included the victim's name, a vague description of what'd happen, and directions to another dead body. I emphasized how, for the purposes of the exercise, he knew the killer was capable of making good on their threat, could point the fiend out, but couldn't prove to the satisfaction of any authority he'd been accosted as described.

Once he'd confirmed the scenario's parameters, I asked if he'd kill the person who'd made such a vow and proven themselves capable of following through. Wouldn't eliminating them before the date of their promised action be the only sure way to save the person he loved?

Only able to treat what I'd asked like the impetus for some film script, his mind immediately dotted about with gleeful explorations of an intriguing hypothetical to unpack the implications of. Made digression within digression concerning the "interesting things a scenario like that brings under the microscope" while I acted as referee, sprinkling additional nuance here and there to close off semantical escape routes, his thought process thus being hemmed as close to consideration of my reality as possible.

It was a peculiarly beautiful discussion. I smiled until it hurt, guffawed often, and let myself enjoy the sway of his enthusiasm for the boundless What-ifs and But-then-what-if-alsos he'd indefatigably populate with intricacies enough every riff seemed the recitation of an ever-present absolute. This curiosity and unflinching passion for explicating any idea had always both aroused and exhausted me. But knowing it might be the last time I'd bear witness to such thought-play, I only felt tranquil and adored.

Of his own volition, he altered the scenario to concern a man protecting his child. This made the most sense when the 'some point in the future' deadline was taken into account. Allowed "the most interesting stakes into the libretto." Took the further unprompted step of filtering the storylines he spun through himself rather than "offering moot reflections on what some strawman hero-figure might do." Narratives wherein the protagonist represented a universal quality were burdened with limitations, wrested to fit themes within societal mores, and bored him to tears. His technique when developing a script avoided hackneyed conventions of storytelling to focus on the pitfalls a regular person'd face in even the most banal scenario. Tethering an exploration to this methodology allowed for the titillating and unpredictable ins-and-outs of human psychology, regardless of the hypothetical caper the character became mixed up in. The point of any tale was self-examination, not overwrought moralizing with the takeaway pre-packaged, however twisted or nihilistic an author might bend its fictive delivery.

What if after being approached, he'd decided to perpetrate the defensive murder, kept the matter to himself, developed some plan, orchestrated it, and got away clean? The would-be-murderer lay dead. We'd agreed there'd been no cohort. So all seemed tidied away. "But what guarantee?" he asked. "Would the death of the threatening party ensure the child lived to thirty? Wouldn't it be more interesting were I to've killed only to have the kid die at twenty-three? Their life had without doubt been safeguarded from one ghastly end, but they'd remained at the mercy of fate and come up the worse for it!"

A twist of this nature didn't diminish how he'd spared his child being murdered, just threw in a nasty ripple. Being protected from a certain death at thirty opened up the possibility of dying sooner. For all intents and purposes, the driving force behind his transgression had been nullified, despite the extremes he'd allowed himself.

Had he known his child would be slain by a different perpetrator at twenty, would he still've felt compelled to take action against the first, on principle? According to the exercise, the first killer was definitively that, so he likely would've acted against them. Likewise if there'd been a third killer who'd have struck if the child lived to one hundred after the first two were eliminated, though the motivation for doing so perhaps amounted to little more than a pedantic aside to the actual query I'd proposed.

He digressed to the question of what he'd have done had he known of an earlier, natural death and of a murder which'd happen only much later on. Correctly tweaked, such additional element made for an even more gutting thought experiment, in his opinion.

"How would one choose between having their child die painlessly by sudden accident or peacefully from a medical condition at age twenty versus being gruesomely murdered at thirty? Was a decade of life worth what'd be endured at its end? Would having one's adult child pass away with family present to hear their last words and make certain the last words they'd hear were 'We love you' be more desirable than having the same child expire terrified on the end of some blade in the dark with only their killer as audience to whatever last sentiments they might utter, Christ only knowing which words such creature'd insist be the final they heard in this world?"

While such was an ugly puzzle to contend with, it remained entirely rhetorical. Because one might well say they'd do everything imaginable to keep their child free of disease or to circumvent whichever accident and then, if such were accomplished, still have ten years to develop a method that'd prevent the forecasted murder.

"The notion of definitive guarantee, in the abstract, is one matter. In practice, it's preposterous to say you'd pick one alternative but not spend every waking minute working to prevent the still lurking outcome. Therefore, no actual choice has been made."

Pointing out "even more scintillating" offshoots of my proposal, he asked "What if at the expense of the would-be killer, the rescued child winds up responsible for the deaths of six or seven others? How would it be if that child, now age sixty-eight, took a gig driving school bus but, either through negligence or on account of heart failure, crashed a vehicle full of teenagers into a frozen lake? Or at thirty-five became host to an infectious agent they unwittingly spread until thousands of lives were claimed, the peace of mind of countless others destroyed? Suppose at thirty-three they fathered or gave birth to a psychopath who went on to murder umpteen victims in as gruesome a manner as they'd have been killed if not for my intervention?"

Many genres in cinema and literature tackled the central conceit of my speculative scenario. Time Travel narratives, tales of fiendish tricks played by Djinns, fables of reincarnation, bury-my-bones yarns, Promethean allegory. We'd chatted about such media often in our years together and though I was more than conversant in such material he defined terms as though such matters were brand new to me. Bulldozing ahead with such proctoring address often caused friction between us, but this time I'd no urge to curb his spiel. Didn't want him to ever stop speaking. Listened to his repetition of well-treaded subjects, as fresh and alive for him as they'd been the first time. He'd regularly expressed that's how he saw things. "This is the first time I'm saying 'I love you' for the thirtieth time. Every time I say it's the first and only time I've said it that time. I love you, Noor, and never repeat myself saying so. Why repeat 'I love you' when I could say it the first time for the fiftieth time, the fifty-first, the five-thousandth?" So I listened to what might be the first and only time I'd hear him get carried away for the last time and imagined him never repeating himself to you while I did.

"The crux of most of these storylines is an amoral negotiation. Trading 'certainty' for 'uncertainty' due to the belief the latter will become 'something else certain' merely because a choice was made. 'A child being murdered' becomes 'What happens if the child lives?' becomes 'They'll live a rich full life, never harming anyone, and die happily of natural causes.' But this third item seldom proves true. Such entertainments exist to remind contemplative audiences how personal desire muddies the conscience and that conscientious choice doesn't guarantee personal desire. What's reinforced is that one can never know the future until the future happens, even if they know the future, in advance."

He exhaustively detailed how many portraits of circumventing

Fate come round to revealing such conceit as illusory. Whichever achievement the characters win are phantasma.

"Whether or not all things are fated doesn't change the fact no one can alter what's going to happen through any method other than living life as anyone naturally does. We say the world would alter in some dramatic way had a despot died in their infancy, yet fail to ask why the world remains so rote and predictable when a random pedestrian is flattened by a bus or a stray bullet plugs an innocent shopkeeper. Are we to believe only a tiny percentage of rare human beings could change the course of what's happening, living or dead? Shouldn't every murderer claim they'd traveled through time to eliminate a figure who'd trigger Armageddon and berate us for executing them when we ought be commissioning a statue in their likeness, instead?"

Joking aside, he summed up this portion of discourse by flatly proclaiming "Even when you're only acting to save your own life, it's a grave mistake to think dodging one bullet makes you immortal, or even less vulnerable to the next round in the chamber."

In all of this, he spoke as though people were nothing but fictional constructs. Stories needed us to pretend what wasn't real was, thus avatars were written with chance upon chance doled out to them, their existence composed of endless loops within loops. Though placed in sticky situations, such tokens were granted the opportunity to repeat repeat repeat repeat under the auspices of whichever genre device. Narratives were mere starter-kits for further refinements which'd continue forever in an audience member's private thoughts. Even the protector-father version of himself proffered in response to my query had been granted an abstract ability to sand down the edges of his flailing attempts at correcting history, bucking fate, exerting human will over Nature or God. No matter what, such story-self would always pull the short straw in the end, otherwise the exercise was rendered glib.

At the conclusions of their sagas, *dramatis personae* given fate altering choices were to realize self-sacrifice would've been the surest way to save who they'd aimed to or set right the balance they'd tampered with. Undoing their recalibrations required eliminating themselves from the equation. A single human being living outside Humanity's scope wasn't permissible as it sullied the shared humanity of all. Such cursed figures, afflicted by what they knew, found cure in no longer knowing it. The blotting of their inappropriate attribute, in turn, protected the congruous existence of the world, writ large.

"My child living but having to go on without me also puts under discussion whether I could bring myself to lay down my life in return for a guarantee of what I desired. Was I content to achieve it but not bear witness to such? The notions of propriety and volition are probed. Would whoever I saved desire so extreme a sacrifice be made on their behalf or, if given voice, would they feel molested for being robbed of their own chance at demonstrating selflessness? If the would-be savior learned the would-be victim would've rather laid down their life so said savior might live, are they to honor such principle or insist their will upon the endangered party?"

When a speculative story didn't take that route, it'd wend to the sour revelation that the party who'd transgressed in order to slip free of their destiny or save someone they felt worth it was trapped in a version of Hell. The rug'd be pulled from under them by learning their actions had precipitated whichever ill they'd wanted reversed, what they'd believed protective instead was the deed which'd set the stage for however the death of their child, loved one, or humanity itself would transpire. If not for acting in the manner they'd convinced themselves would safeguard whichever circumstance, the conditions resulting in jeopardy would never've materialized.

He admitted the specific scenario I'd presented was a horse of a different color. With the caveat of the would-be killer having no accomplice thrown in, certain avenues of exploration were curtailed. This removal of variables cemented matters in a way he found unnaturally restrictive. Stating a conclusion so bluntly from the get-go eliminated the ever-present uncertainty which defined lived reality. A character might take the killer's word they'd no accomplice, but writing one who'd accept such assertion at face value seemed cheap. Refusing to front-load them with naivety, on the other hand, maintained the moral conundrums inherent in a perpetually fluctuating existence.

"The killer might be eliminated. Perhaps hadn't been working in concert with anyone. But there could yet have been an unknown party, waiting in the wings, who'd been moved to enact the murder of the child specifically because the original killer'd been expunged. A cumbersome set-up, to be sure. Convoluted and largely dissatisfying. But it allowed for intriguing interpretations of the overall trap. Recontextualized the original threat as prophesy beyond the would-be killer's understanding, a glimpse into the future nothing to do with their personal intent to've committed the promised crime. What they'd threatened had come to pass, but with them unaware how being stopped was the crucial event which'd coaxed the act of another. A ghoulish representation of believing the clock showing One-One-One-One was exceptional instead of predicated on the commonplace nature of automatically discarding how often it was regarded at Four-Seventeen."

Winking at me and seeming relieved I reciprocated in kind with a chuckle, he clarified that he understood my set-up was meant to keep devious hoodwinks out of bounds. With the puckishness of fate sidestepped, I'd proposed a solid question concerning one person acting against another person's strictly human agency.

"In such case, were the killer killed, the victim'd be demonstrably safe. But a question posed thusly functions best as an excavation of existential dilemma, a treacherous parable pitting belief against the modulations all life is intrinsically bound by."

With further uptick of enthusiasm and apologies for the forthcoming tangent, he went on how there were similar story set-ups wherein characters foresaw their own death via visions, viewed such chimera as preventative clues, took the warnings to heart, dictated their lives accordingly, employed all manner of restrictive living methods meant to circumvent their demise, only to wind up discovering what they'd been given unnatural glimpse of was how they'd eventually slit their own wrists due to the strain of existing under the stifling conditions they'd put in place.

This was his favorite variant of such tale. He summarized in much detail a novella his close friend had published some years before, ignoring the fact I was well acquainted with it. The slim volume's final reveal found a man learning he'd made a pact with another man to kill him but, due to a psychological ailment, retained no exact memory of having done so, only a vague sense that his days were numbered. Possessed of the notion he'd foreseen his own murder, a third-party was hired to discover who might've wanted him dead. This sleuth got to the bottom of it and, upon learning the truth, the man became horrified. His amnesia had robbed of him of any previous desire to die. But regardless of knowing the full details of his situation and desperately wanting out of his self-made snare, it was too late. The death-contract was fulfilled. "Poor bastard got what he'd desired even as what he'd desired became anything but."

Reigning himself in, your father admitted he'd strayed from the scenario I'd presented. Nonetheless, propounded how any story about 'seeing the future' or 'being threatened with distant horror' was composed in service of reminding an audience how even fanciful characters are only granted peeks at some tiny speck of what's to come. No one is shown everything. Most often only a preview of the 'physical future.' The mechanism beneath it remained something which could only blindly be guessed at. Not to mention the mechanism beneath the beneath.

"Whoever thinks they 'know the future' simply fills in the blanks between broad strokes, themselves. Akin to how brains are wired to correct for visual blind spots with composite information, characters subconsciously cobble up plausible scenarios out of snips of forgotten experience, stories they'd read, or conversations they'd overheard peripherally. In doing so, they utilized to dreadful result what would be recognized as nothing more than the trivial assertion that the grand design of the world can never be manipulated even if it were fully verified. Due to the stressor of 'knowing their fate,' these fictious stand-ins are presented as incapable of accepting that any 'proof' of their foreknowledge is coincidence, unable to see clear to how such coincidence are born of their own selective memory constructing palatable narratives to keep them from having to stare down the barrel of something too horrible to contemplate. But just because we can prove the oxygen in our tank'll run out in an hour doesn't mean we'll ever be able to breathe underwater."

He felt the thought experiment would be improved if the madman didn't physically accost anyone. Suggested I imagine him as a character receiving an anonymous envelope containing two names, one belonging to the would-be-killer, the other being my own. Also included was a threat of murder and the statement such violence would be carried out in whichever number of years. A set-up so direct but marginally outlined allowed for the most potent excavation of the moral dilemma. "I'd be certain I'd not penned the letter and sent it to myself, but couldn't ever be one-hundred-percent sure it hadn't been written by you!"

Perhaps I'd arranged an elaborate suicide pact such missive was integral to. Sent it with no intention of killing anyone, but as a means of exerting macabre control over his life. Been compelled to produce it under duress, luring him down the garden path at the behest of an unknown villain for reasons I'd not been made privy to. So on and so forth.

"Whichever way one might interpret such letter, the experiment becomes a question of trust and belief versus paranoia, a tick-by-tock progression through personal misgivings. Attempts could be made to unravel what was actually going on, who'd be protected by which action, or whether there's anyone to protect apart from myself, but as my mind unraveled itself in such attempts, it'd dawn on me that any choice I might make, and every last thought in my head, was only a reflection on my own psychology. Therefore, any outcome I came up with to avoid a particular fate might be more properly branded a desire I harbored trepidations about actualizing."

Almost blushing from the protracted effort of staying to a single point for more than two minutes, he closed a fist and joyously declared "No matter the story set-up or philosophical exercise, the Future Unwritten is always semantical." Even narratives which concerned characters who'd experienced 'genuine visions' in which they'd 'seen their own murders' would veer from cut-and-dry conclusions. In many, the victims had requested the killers end their lives and remained perfectly cognizant they'd done so. To aid in suicide by peacefully euthanizing them. Sacrificing them ritualistically according to the ancient dictates of an occult clan. "So far as common sense definition, such victims were 'murdered.' Suicide. Killing. Dying. Such terminologies can be swapped out for each other. The laws of a particular society, tethered to a certain time and place, have no overarching authority to define the core meaning of a deed. Therefore, a presentiment of 'murder' would be accurate, despite the fact the death was the dying party's sincerest desire. Any word's as appropriate as any other so far as being used in a prophetic dictum!"

Laughing along as he giddily split these hairs, I flirtatiously needled him to return to the question I'd posed. He held up his hands and popped his lips in a kiss my direction, promising he'd simply wanted to give the best answer he possibly could. To that end, he asked "If I were to kill the would-be killer in order to guarantee my child wouldn't die at thirty, but then my child died at twenty, was I the cause of my child's earlier death or does my child dying at twenty mean they would've died then, regardless? However righteous I deemed what I'd done, had I taken a life for nothing? Let's say Yes. In that case, what's meant by 'for nothing?' What's 'nothing' and what's 'anything'? Is either concept what I say it is? I might blow up a hospital because I believe doing so necessary to stop an atomic bomb being dropped on the city in which the hospital stands. The hospital and all those inside are obliterated. No atom bomb falls. Is there any way to know whether my action had causal link to the lack of incident? No. My belief that I'd saved more people than I'd harmed was all I'd have to comfort myself with but would mean nothing to anyone else."

I pouted impatiently. Snarked how if he didn't want to answer me definitively, I'd not continue to press him. Sighed how I well apprehended that either nothing or a million specific things might be done, but reminded him 'doing nothing and something at the same time' wasn't an option. I wanted to know what he'd do.

With a bratty attitude which at any other time would've prompted me to close off the chat, he insisted he had his answer ready, but felt I'd not really know what it meant if he just blurted out some rudimentary soundbite. "If you don't know what my answer means, how can you know what my answer actually is?"

From this quip he pivoted to a final preamble. Now spoke about souls and possible damage to them. Referenced various deals made with various devils. Bargains in service of honor, love, to secure twelve-tone music, return a child from the grave, or construct an engine which'd run on salt water. Mentioned the danger in being granted a vision for purposes ulterior and fiendish. Quoted Hamlet's requirement for 'grounds more relative than this.' Warned of demons tempting into perdition those who lose sight of the requisite limitations of their humanity.

His ideas were playthings. I concurred with the lot in the levity tinted way one acquiesces to notions of inconsequential make believe, enchanted by the contours of the concepts he tinkered and jiggered with. Loved them as I did the scripts he'd pen or those his colleagues worked on which he'd show me, keen for a verdict on every thematic nook and conceptual cranny. Great fun to soak in the inventions he was marvelous at devising, insidious morality plays, crafty labyrinths of ethics the rules to which could be refined on the fly. Provided they suited the story, what could it matter if they didn't fit flush? They were gossamer, spendthrift, the world and everything in it tools with which he'd tinkersmith events which never could happen in order to shyly poke at whichever things actually did.

The bottom line was "You can't go killing people for things they haven't done, be it God, the devil, the tarot, your own heart, or the science of probability urging you to." He wouldn't hunt down the lunatic who'd slipped him a card, no matter who they'd threatened. He'd sympathize with someone who might, empathize with someone who did, but have more than one mind about them.

I challenged this assertion in a cheeky way, prodding him with "But were I murdered tomorrow, you'd be fine with my killer being put to death afterward?"

Flashing the put upon expression I adored most of all, he assured me he'd be a-okay with that. Grin widening as he spoke, furthered that he'd wholeheartedly succumb to vendetta in my name. But curtly raised a stern school marm finger as he pointed out vendetta was all it'd be. No matter what my killer'd done, wanting them dead was garden variety thirst for revenge, nothing profound or informed by impersonal principle. As to whether a jury of my killer's peers, a judge, or some doctor of the wits declared the beast deserving of imprisonment, rehabilitation, or medical observation? "Perhaps the bastard was and perhaps the bastard wasn't, but I'd desire them dead, without quarter."

Keeping the tone of the question frisky while making it abundantly clear I demanded a straight and succinct answer, I asked if he'd kill them himself, given opportunity.

He held my eyes for half-a-minute without speaking. I'll never forget the precise phrasing used when he did. Hear the plain-spoken honesty in his voice even as I commit the words to this page.

"I'd hope to be able to bring myself to. But what I'd want and what I could do might not be one and the same. I don't know that I could, after you were gone. It wouldn't matter, by then. I'd desire what didn't matter, but with you lost I don't know if I'd take it.'

Not breaking our gaze, I took the question one step further. Instructed him to picture me alone in a room. To envision some person approaching from behind with violent intent quite apparent. To contemplate the sight of such intruder bearing down while I sat thinking, entirely unaware of their approach, lost to my own contentment, and utterly defenseless. Would he strike such person down before they could act had he the power to do so and some implement of death at his disposal?

"In the moment, yes. Were they moving to hurt you, Noor, if they so much as seemed to be and I could obliterate them, come what may, yes. I need to believe I could. Want to believe that, without hesitation, I would."

For all the beauty in your father's imaginings, his ideas were removed from the reality of my experience, in no way influenced how I'd proceed with your defense. To him, the matter was a conceptual dilemma which might be tweaked countless ways so endless questions could be milked of it. If I'd presented the true terms of what I was wrestling with, he'd giddily bend them abstractly all angles.

"One life over five? Some might say there's no question, sacrifice the few for the many. Except it'd need be asked whether such metric applied across the board. Were it a matter of allowing one doctor to die in order for five concentration camp guards to go on living, did the principle stand? Should allowances be made were it down to letting one child perish so the lives of five ninety-year old men might continue? Ought we permit one victim to be victim so five murderers might murder then live on in sanctioned punishment or the pursuit of spiritual redemption? Shall we let them commit their acts but call for them, afterward, to be to penalized with confinement, assure ourselves such mercy consigns them to lifelong stabs of conscience, to the possibility of Hell on Earth, and finally to hellfire, provided such thing exists?'

All good questions. But they were his, never mine. I wasn't attempting to bolster literary *bona fides* nor ranking my morals, wasn't pleading my case or asking permission to do the unthinkable on the dubious strength of an esoteric loophole. It was pre-established I'd be committing an atrocity. Nothing could sanction what I intended. Knew I'd die, thus found myself beyond the reach of criminal justice. As to what dreams may come, I neither cared nor'd be cowed by the most blood curdling prognostications.

I believed in souls. Believe in them, to this moment. But I don't regard them as what most people do or what your father went on about. The Soul was a notion he considered only in the abstract, an element to balance the equation of narrative structure, a tool to roll out in jocular debate. He'd poo-pooh anyone positing it an extant commodity which could be quantified in a uniform way or produce actual impact on life. So far as he was concerned, 'soul' was a word interchangeable with a multitude of others, analogous to a thousand intricate concepts and to utter nothingness, just the same.

I regard souls as Holy things, though unconnected to any God and independent of the tenets of spiritual discipline. They aren't given us any different than breath or blood or cognition. Can be diseased through selected action, the same as a lung, heart, or mind. Are an aspect of ourselves we merely possess. Being possessed, can be affected for fair or for ill by our behaviors or factors external to us. I honestly believe they go on forever, though I've no inkling how they function or what function they serve. Were the soul something granted us conditionally, which an inhuman hand wielded the authority to rescind, I still believe it no more than an article regulated by our decisions, which our actions or thoughts might improve or ruin.

Whichever thing a soul is, however it's bound, such contrivance is the first I'd sacrifice for you. Before my life I'd forfeit my soul. Whichever immortality it might possess I'd trade for the immortality granted me in your thoughts and heart, knowing whichever remnant of me found in you would last perpetually regardless of my life or death. To persist as 'the idea of me in your soul' is preferable to being the whole of me in my own. My life ought be cast aside in a manner which sullied my soul so that yours could remain untainted, except by thoughts of me. I'd gladly be eternally unforgiven by you. Gleefully, gratefully, shamefully exist eternally as the part of you you wished yourself rid of but from which you couldn't uncouple. Since even the grime of me could never tarnish you, let me shed my life, forsake my soul, and embrace an eternity of your hatred without enjoying even one day spent knowing the weight and warmth of you to my chest. You free of me would be worth the forever-minus-that-moment I'd experience. Such moment is one I'll never have, anyway. Were I to fail in what I'd undertake to protect you, all eternity would be spent with no memory of your eyes on mine. What would a soul profit me, writhing forever in purity without your touch, sound, or scent having graced me?

Mitigating the horror I'd enact down to anything pardonable was an impossibility. My situation didn't concern a dark pact being struck, fine print revealed only after the dread document bore my irrevocable signature in blood. I'd not solicited some occult broker for a glimpse of your future, bargained for control over aspects of it, hadn't requested the knowledge I was crushed underneath. Not concerning your life. Not concerning my own.

Had someone informed me before I'd become pregnant that I'd not survive your birth, I'd not have decided against becoming your mother. Once carrying you, if someone said the choice was between dying in order for you to live or your never being born so I might live on, I'd not have chosen in my own favor. Under similar circumstances, or circumstances nowhere near so dire, someone else may have. I'd not begrudge them that. Call for them to face consequence beyond whichever they hung on themselves. Suggest there ought be penalty at all if they felt otherwise. I'd wish them peace. Feel a deep bond to them in whatever they'd done.

The suggestion you'd grow up to take your own life was hogwash. But to cleanse my thoughts of such rubbish, I explored the proposition as deeply as any other. Held myself to it. Insisted I consider the further possibility you'd conspire with five others in an intricate farce to make your death appear accidental in aid of some desperate purpose. You may've become stricken with incurable illness, days spent languishing, twisted out of dignity by the cascading failures of your body. May've succumbed to a psychological malady which'd driven you toward self-harm and, due to such prompt, brought in a cluster of trusted confederates to end your misery in a fashion which'd appear clear of your own hand, ensuring your good name and posterity remained intact so an insurance policy would pay out to your own child. As your father had hinted at the ludicrous possibility of, I went so far as entertaining the fancy you'd become a cultist, willing to hand over your life as part of some profane ceremony. It was of paramount importance I unflinchingly plumb every ghastly What-if, so I genuinely contemplated how perhaps, through a dark quirk of wordplay, you were the victim of five people while also being one of the group at whose hands you'd be slain.

PREPARTUM / 43

Supposing such extreme or unthinkable scenarios were the truth, what could it matter? The reasons behind what'd happen to you were irrelevant. I'd be long dead, never able to know them. Were I to live and discover you'd become engaged in whichever scuzzy situation, I'd do everything in my power to help. If some Machiavellian guru held you in their thrall, I'd extricate you from their clutches even if it meant slaughtering them before your eyes as you begged me to stop. If you fell ill, afflicted with bodily torments unceasingly, reached your tether, could bear no more pain, and there existed neither recourse through palliative medicine to ease it nor exemption carved out to humanely end your life under a physician's oversight, I'd be the party you'd turn to in order that your rest be secured. You'd trust myself or you father with your life. There weren't words you could utter while we lived which'd bring either of us to countenance you conscripting into a murder-suicide club when we could bring you the respite you so dearly sought. If your reason was stripped from you and despair had worked to snuff all spark of vitality, that was another matter. I'd never indulge you seeking self-termination at the behest of a diseased mindset, but to my last breath expend efforts to thwart it. Chain you to the wall, chew your food, force it down your throat with loving fingers were nothing else possible. Supposing you were revealed to be the fifth killer in some Third Act twist, perhaps exterminating the four accomplices I knew of wouldn't guarantee you'd not find another quartet to take their place. If unable to do so, perhaps my killing them would've set the stage for taking drastic measures with your own hand, fulfilling the prophecy in a Daedalian way. But not only would I never believe you'd be moved to so motley an act, were I alive to witness its preamble such scheme wouldn't see fruition without my doing all I could to wrest the dagger from your hands, suck the poison from your veins, or pump from your belly whichever leprous pills you'd have swallowed.

Every one of these macabre considerations bloomed three more which then contaminated my thoughts with dozens of others. All equally meaningless. No string of specifics would compel me from your rescue, so I explored for the sake of proving my convictions against any sophistic springe. It made no difference to me what might happen, it only mattered what would. You'd die in whichever fashion during your thirtieth year. Be it murder, suicide, or tragic accident, that specific death was something I may be able to prevent.

You might die in some other manner, earlier or later than the death I knew of with certainty. Of course you'd die despite any machination I conceived. Your honest life would end in death, as all lives would. It was this prescribed doom, the absolute expiration date you'd been stamped with not by nature but by conscious calculation, I lashed out against. Your murder wasn't your life. I refused to defend it as though it were.

Living as anyone else did, you'd confront any number of obstacles, endure miseries, experience whatever you may. All of this I accepted, embraced, desired for you. But even were I to live, this ghastly act guaranteed you was insult. Not an illness I'd revile yet know there was no choice but to face the irreversibility of, sat at your bedside, our hands entwined while you passed on, however unfair or horrific I'd deem it. Your death was the choice of four men and one woman. Five people who'd no right to claim dominion over your life or any. A handful of fiends I could clear from the board. If I didn't act, your death would be murder for that inaction.

You mustn't exist under the cloud of a death which wasn't an organic dictate of life, rather a perversion of human agency. Little point pontificating how someone else might murder you in a manner ten times as unthinkable as the one I'd have you spared. I didn't know if that'd happen. Never could. What I knew was five specific people would live to take your life. Worthless to parse it a jot further. As I'd no way of knowing if your murder would be the idea of only one of the five, I'd no calculus to determine whether eliminating only that one would be enough to spare others from dying. Didn't and couldn't know if without such ringleader the lives of the other four would alter trajectory in a manner making it impossible they'd be moved to act against you. Perhaps without the correct one of them, no thoughts of cruelty toward you would enter the minds of the remaining four. Perhaps they'd be rendered innocent once the pestilence of the fifth was subdued.

Though this was possible, it was only possible. I'd no reach from beyond the grave. Wouldn't be there to watch over you. My capability lasted no longer than the days which dwindled as you grew inside me. How I might prevent what would happen to you wasn't a business I could treat as theoretical, hedge my bets, adjust any wager as I went. I'd be dead. Regardless whether I promised myself how, were I to live, I'd investigate your killers as they moved throughout the years, attempting to discern which one of them, if eliminated, would stay your execution. Which two. Which three.

The only thing irrefutable was that if none of them ever lived, none of them could ever kill you. If five others then killed you on the day these absent five would've, I'd no method to discover. Nor did I care. I wasn't shooting craps with your life, guessing and planning for what only might be. I could never live with myself were I to trade sparing you having to suffer for the mere theory of sanctity. The principle of what life ought be for everyone wouldn't sway me from keeping you safe from what life ought be for nobody and would be for you.

I don't want you to misunderstand or become confused about why I've done what I've done. Whatever you'll think of me, want it clear what I did and how. That you to comprehend why I'd been able. I write to impress upon you how I didn't proceed haphazardly, awash in a fever of maternal instinct, willing to lash out indiscriminately due to terror or impatience. Care and meticulous planning were required. But under constraints. As your life grew, mine shrank. Less than six months was the most I could hope for, perhaps only one or two of which would find me in any semblance of physical shape to go through with what I'd need so cautiously to arrange.

I knew only generally what was going to happen to you and when. Needed to be certain who specifically I'd proceed against. Nothing was gained from visiting revenge on parties nothing to do with your fate. With it already so daunting to consider killing who I must, there wasn't bandwidth left over to contemplate risking all only to learn I'd taken innocent life.

This need for caution increased the pressure to unmask your killers as soon as possible. I'd require as much time as could be secured to think before moving against each. Had to arrange in advance that how I killed the first wouldn't restrict me from ferreting out the second, eliminating the third. If I eradicated only two or three of your murderers before being found out, whichever number survived might yet acquire life and use it against yours.

By the time only one or two remained vital, care and planning could slacken or be abandoned outright. Toward the end, little precaution would remain necessary, provided I knew who your killers dwelt within and where those people could be lit upon. I might massacre the first of the final duo without quarter, flee the scene, make my way directly to the second, and utilize any means of dispatch I could manage against them. For the last, especially, I'd engage in inelegant slaughter were there no way to keep the deed immaculate. If the mothers needed to be sacrificed along with the children they carried, I'd bring the task off. By then would allow it. Knowing I'd no choice but the choice I'd already not made.

I wanted to spare as many lives as many agonies as I might. The mothers to be spared and myself spared the ancillary horror of their butchery. Desired that you, your father, the mothers, the families of the slain, never be afflicted with the truth. What I'd do ought be left a mystery to those who pressed on in its wake.

No speck of care was reserved for myself, though. No moment wherein I'd considered I might die in an accident or through some health complication. Even the possibility I might be killed while attempting to kill wasn't entertained. That you'd die still within me, your killers' birth screams a chorus of blood wet gloats neither of us would exist to hear or reflect on, didn't cross my mind. I felt invulnerable. As though it were a codified fact I'd give birth to you. You'd live and I'd die only then. Whether my life ended and yours began in a hospital, a prison, or wheresoever, no action I'd undertake in the time before you birth would kill me. There was almost unbearable terror in considering I might be injured, rendered unable to further act in your security, but never so much as a shiver of belief that my broken body wouldn't survive long enough for you to be pulled from it alive. Never a question of whether I'd die too soon, only of how long you'd live. Of doing everything in my power to see to it your life wasn't cut short. You were my legacy. All that remained was getting right what I must before being forever effaced from the ledgers.

I knew how ponderous and varied the avenues before me might wend and fork, the innumerable hindrances standing in my way, the impossibility of knowing a single thing for certain even if I discovered the people I'd need to act against. What was there to do in the face of such variables, though? Lay myself down, bury you with me? I'd no choice but to proceed with the most certainty I could acquire. Fully cognizant no certainty would remain certain. All life was flux. Choice mere component of some further choice.

If I could've waited until after your killers were born, perhaps I'd have followed their development from a distance, kept tabs, made determinations as events unfolded, narrowed in on an absolute truth, and gotten my grip firm around indisputable proof which could be laid out to vindicate me after my hand had been played. The task before me would've been easier, safer. But I'm no longer certain I desired that. When I think back, it seems I must have. But it may've merely been something I knew might be desired. Maybe ought to've been.

What I recall is wondering why I should feel compelled to behave as though your murderers weren't yet who and what they were. I was what I was, after all. A killer of children. Made no squirm otherwise. Was there any sense delaying my move against the five people who'd take your life until ten minutes before they were upon you, when instead I could seize the advantage I'd been provided? If I saw a man drawing a gun and could cut him down before his aim on you was trained final, I'd never entertain the argument he might've changed his mind right up until the moment his finger was flinching the trigger down. In that final twitch, he might've swiveled the flashing muzzle to the side, missing wide his mark due to a strangle of conscience he'd only in the nick of time managed. Would I call such fiend less a killer, absolve him for only having attempted his sickening intentions but overcoming the ghoulish drive an instant before it'd become irrevocable any more than if he'd missed his intended shot on a fluke? If I could've waited, how would I justify a moment of your killers' lives to you?

I felt it a weakness, but often hoped for a definitive sensation to accompany my tangible efforts. Longed for something outside me to assuage the pangs produced by the fog of doubt which swirled in misdirection around all I knew. Feared I'd not find the mothers. Discover them too distant from me to approach. Living overseas, surrounded by loved ones all hours, a million ways inaccessible. How paralyzed I became when considering I'd know precisely who they were and where they dwelt, yet lack means to get at them. Find I'd run out of time for planning their unborns' dispatch. Discover it impossible to take action without being caught.

I needed to be cautious of that most of all. At least while I had the ability, abundant care must be exercised to get clean away with my crimes. Not for my sake, but yours. I no longer had any sake. Needed to take care not to care for myself. To remember I was acting from beyond the grave.

Nothing would be guaranteed if anything were left half accomplished. To begin but not end worse than not to've begun. One amounted to a cowardice I'd not forgive myself but which the rest of the world would applaud. The other damned us both. You to your unprevented murder and a life stained by the knowledge of what I'd done. Me to knowing that, as your life drained away, you might comprehend how your death was something I'd had means to defend you from but lacked intelligence, nerve, or desire enough to.

I open these pages, raise the pen, but any point at which I feel compelled to begin a proper narrative requires contextualizing preamble, that preamble another, that another another still. If I choose an observation from which I intend to move my explanation forward, instead it drifts into its past and can't then work its way back even to where it began. I find my guilt already present, earlier and earlier and earlier. To properly confess it, am required to move forever backward in time, even when from backward in time I begin. There's no moment readily summoned to mind wherein I'm guiltless, though I feel in this one or that I must've been.

My knowledge shored up my resolve regarding whichever face my coming actions would take. If no demonstrable proof your unborn killers lurked within the women I'd search out came to light, I'd act on the strength of my knowledge alone. Even if my deeds were later proved erroneous and I'd therefore failed to defend you. When the hour came, my knowledge was all I'd require.

Such confession, at the start, is necessary. Only knowing the entire truth will you comprehend how desperately I wanted to be incorrect. About everything. Desired everyone be innocent. That no party existed to raise violent hand against. More than anything, yearned to be proven a fool, a worrywart, diagnosed and deemed whatever my knowledge shown false would term me. But I'd only so short a time to allow for such eventuality. Doubted any sign of being consumed by no more than sickening folly would materialize.

But such long, depleting efforts I undertook. Despised myself for the hours such curlicue investigations consumed. Felt weak whenever I'd entertain the notion there'd be nothing to defend you from. Such felt no different than being unable to defend you. Worse, made my need for assurance seem a failing. Because of it, your killers might slip from the gallows stage. Writing allowances meant some part of me wanted to spare them. Which meant some part of me desired their success. Worked to pave the way for it. To kill you, itself.

How can I tell you everything in sequence if it doesn't seem there was a point before the tale begins, if beginnings only lead to other beginnings which demonstrate they weren't the beginning despite still seeming the honest start? Were I to begin with the end, you'd never understand. What I'd write would be a confession expressed in the wrong direction, therefore untrue. To explain so you'll genuinely apprehend what I disclose, you cannot know what I did before I knew myself, only afterward be told why and how. To express myself thusly suggests an attempt to justify what I've done. Even asserting I've no such aim would be brought into question. I can't allow you to incorrectly believe I didn't understand what I was undertaking until it was all over, present this narrative in a manner which proposes only in the aftermath was the past audited in hopes of providing it meaning. To name what I don't wish to justify then explain the desire cannot help but sound mealy mouthed. 'It wasn't justified, but how was I to know?' I don't justify it now because I never attempted to. Never would've. You must understand that my never trying to yet not blithely going my way to whichever carnage I might, specifics be damned, is the heart of the horror I've wrought.

To have you know the end and then hear it explained is the falsest way forward. You must be privy to all that brought me to these words. Only in this way will you grasp that by the time I took action I'd known exactly what it meant, how only through embracing this freely had I been able. If I hadn't known precisely why I functioned, I never would've gone through with anything. I want you to confront the truth. That the principle crime I'm confessing to is the fact that I understood.

Right now, you can only ponder what I mean. So I'll pick a point to start from. The next thing which comes to my mind. From there move only forward, come what may.

I discover already I'm failing in this documentation. I've neglected to state that I knew the names of your killers. From the first moment of knowledge, they were emblazoned on my mind. Even if their parents hadn't yet decided it, they'd be called Nathan Benecourt, Alexander Lowell, Montgomery Lyons, Keith Goaltender, and Marcy Tellwell. From these names I'd search, though I knew the surnames the mothers currently went by might be entirely different than those their children would wear three decades on.

I'd imagine a precise sensation of danger would creep over me, that I'd know precisely which of your killers lurked down a woman's belly, leeching off them to grow fat, ready for lives which'd lead them to you. At times, impulses seemed to aid me, though nothing along the lines of what might be presented in one of your father's scripts. No voice whispered updates or confirmations in my ear. No flashes of night terror woke me in a sweat, shaking from new details. When I was proximate to a possible suspect, my head didn't swim, ears didn't ring, the skin of my arms didn't got gooseflesh, hair standing on end, and no crumb of fresh information spontaneously dawned on me as the days passed. Any suspicions I had might merely have been strokes of good fortune hit upon during a series of unsystematic groping, even if they were seemingly proved accurate.

Exhausting to contemplate even the start of so laborious an effort. All the more for understanding how doubting myself was the only method by which I'd subdue my own doubts. Ignoring misgivings or failing to forever seek new ones meant I wasn't being thorough. Not making certain of anything. Leaving you vulnerable.

With merciless caution and constant second-guessing, at times inspiration I could scarcely trace the origin of landed me on a genuine clue. Fatigued notions concerning how I might sleuth out the mothers pulled themselves cleanly from the scribble of my mind to become pointers which seemed gifted to me from some guiding place. Even in such instances, nothing close to a specific was granted. With no map handed me, I'd nothing but ideas to temper with my knowledge and hope would be enough.

Once I'd settled on a woman I felt could be one of the mothers, I'd approach them. Surreptitiously if possible, directly if need be. I'd leave my name out of any communication, gave a different false one in each nonsense vignette I'd arrange to kick off interactions, never shy about shoehorning myself into awkward introductions, the obvious sight of my growing belly a ready, unspoken allowance to assume camaraderie with strangers. It was an easy enough task to confirm the details of whichever woman's pregnancy. Mine on display often made them the ones who'd choose to make conversational hay of such state.

I'd ask 'Boy or girl?' and 'Have you settled on a name, are there contenders?' Urge them on by claiming I'd never been the sort to enjoy surprises so'd been over the moon to learn you were a girl. I'd always let them know you'd be called Tasha Parsinbyrd. Sing the words. Practically kiss the sound of you into the air as I coyly scrutinized their faces. Sometimes, I think it was envy over your having so perfect a name which'd prompt them to vaingloriously declare whichever drab thing they'd dub their own offspring.

I'd be on guard not to prompt. Took pains to avoid influencing anyone toward the polite indulgence of some made-up remark during an *impromptu* dollop of chitchat. If a mother was undecided or cagey, there was nothing to be done about it. I'd never strong-arm or coax in a loaded manner, pretend to wistfully admit 'I've always thought Montgomery would be a fine name for a son' or 'If I hadn't picked Tasha, I'd have chosen Marcy.'

To prove the hazard inherent in such ploys, I experimented under laboratory regulations. Utilizing only women who claimed they were undecided, clearly superstitious, or expressed reluctance about divulging information of too intimate a nature, I'd introduce names nothing to do with your killers. Muse aloud how I might've gone with Loretta, or with Aloysius had you been a boy. 'Oh yes, I'd thought about Loretta once, too' or 'Aloysius happens to be what my husband wants to name him, that's crazy' and words near to those came from multiple women, all within the same week. Little call to believe so many Lorettas and Aloysiuses had been incubating within three city blocks, the designations only displaced when whim turned their mothers' fancies to Georgia, Lamont or whichever *cognomen* they'd held dear enough to keep from my clutches.

Something about the evidently tentative women made me feel at ease dismissing them as suspects. As effortless to discard those who'd proudly tell me their son'd be Reuben Yeats Jr., their daughter'd be Callie Ana LeTrot, announcing the monikers with conviction enough it was clear neither ransom nor consequence could sway them toward calling their coming brood anything else.

On the other hand, a current of noia tickled me when it came to the women who'd baldly spout evasive falsehoods, struck me untruthful either about not knowing what names they whispered in their private hearts or else by seeming too keen to go along with my Loretta-Aloysius stratagem. No percentage in fixating on them so early in the game, but I'd remind myself to double back if too many avenues turned up dunce. Never lost sight of how the women carrying your killers might be on guard. Perhaps without understanding why, be wary of transmitting sensitive information, seizing upon any excuse to seem as though they were delighted to. After all, if someone were hunting for a child called Tasha Parsinbyrd, the first and only thing I'd call you aloud would've been Loretta Smith or I-don't-know-yet.

No matter what name I was given, or if given none, I nursed the belief I'd intuit from proximity alone whether one of your executioners was before me. Knew equally well that even if I'd found proof positive they were I might feel nothing. Desired to be magical, able to secure my path without effort, yet knew I'd never trust anything I couldn't empirically verify. Some part of me insisted even the unknowable thing I held such conviction in needed to prove itself known.

In the end, I'd have to trust how if I discovered a pregnant woman with the last name Benecourt it'd be Nathan Benecourt waiting to emerge from her. If I met a woman called Tilsworth with a lover called Benecourt, trust she, the child, or both would come to take the father's name. If such mother was confident she carried a daughter, a sonogram had been misread or this daughter at some point would decide to live as a man.

I increasingly believed Marcy Tellwell would instigate the final crisis, striking the fatal blow or holding your head beneath stale water until you'd gone limp beneath her straining arms. So if a Marcy was found in a woman with the surname Lesh who'd a husband called Holmes, I'd postulate the little Marcy, *in utero*, might grow to marry into her Tellwell, the same if a mother called Tellwell carried in her a Lisette such Lisette might adopt the name Marcy only years down the road.

Curious how tangled my thoughts could become yet how tranquil the knot. A kind of pleasure in the contemplation of your preservation. The more complex an equation was to balance, the more it'd feel I was making honest headway.

Of course I'd not simply note a pregnant woman strolling down the street and assume a killer was cloaked with her. My initial thought was typically the opposite. I endeavored to make verification as brief an affair as possible so I might move on. There wasn't a complex checklist or tightrope of question-and-answer. I almost felt I was genuinely engaging in pleasantries with people I might've enjoyed the further company of. A purgatory tour of the community which ought've been mine. One I could only visit spectrally. Allowed glimpses of what I'd been robbed.

I'd approach women who were clearly showing. Strike up small talk. Almost one-hundred-percent of the time learn promptly they were nothing to do with you nor would their children be. Visit groups for expectant mother. Socialize with the participants. Learn names, histories, often be made privy to intimacies I'd never thought to solicit. Almost always within a single conversation, or else by listening to a group sharing gossip, I'd glean more than enough information to unquestionably confirm unborn children were innocent of any forthcoming violence against you.

My free hours were spent in many things of this nature. No call to enumerate them. For the most part, it was empty time. Often seemed precious time wasted. No experimental proof was necessary to conclude the majority of mothers would have nothing to do with my purpose. There'd only be five. Discounting twins or triplets all born Lowell before mutating into Goaltender, Benecourt, Lyons.

If I abandoned my purpose in writing this, changed gears to an audit of the splintered way my every consideration went as I roamed about conversing with strangers, I doubt I'd be able to articulate it. Were the mothers I sought freshly pregnant? As far along as me? Could they be approaching their due dates, already in hospital as I loitered at brunches or scoped out bookstore aisles thick with manuals on what to expect, to do, to avoid, how wonderful, fraught, and precious life would be once motherhood began? Was it possible they'd given birth since my first knowing what I knew? If so, must I expand my search to include the recently born? Starting from when? Utilizing which criteria? My mind drowned in meaningless catechism.

   I'm learning, as I write, certain matters bear explaining while others need simply be told. I'd get lost in the dissection of every nuance I encountered. Find myself out of time. You left with no better understanding than at the start. I wonder if I digress out of hesitation. Don't want you to know me. Put on the guise of revealing merely to run out the clock. Satisfied to give the impression I'm earnestly attempting to explain, all the while knowing my explanation is a ruse. Perhaps I just desire you to know as many of my thoughts as possible, because such will be all you know of me. Understanding be damned, want you to experience the music and incoherence of my heart. Or I might be utilizing that possibility as a dodge. Coyly suggesting I'm something more than what I've done. What else could you learn about me from my words when my words are these? You can see for yourself the full extent of me. If what I've done is who I am, who I am is of no value.

   Though I don't contend that matters. Must stop thinking so much. Just tell you. I'm getting lost. Have gotten lost. Must stop writing as though anything can change what I've done. Especially as I know how correct I was that nothing ever could've.

   For you to understand the calculations I made, the cautions I took, the anguish which roiled in me as I came to terms with the situation, weighing every move against every possible twist of consequence, I need to stop dealing in abstractions. I'll narrate the discoveries of the first four mothers. Through these stories you'll better apprehend not only how I began but why I was able to proceed.

Entirely at random, I found myself interacting with a woman who carried one of the plagued surnames. I'd not sought her out, she'd simply approached me as I sat outside a bookstore café. Out of the blue, asked if she knew me. It was quickly discovered we were utter strangers to each other and had no person or event common between us. She nonetheless became quite affable. Though it was clear there existed no reason whatsoever for her doing so, introduced herself as Lenora Lowell and asked amiably whether I'd mind if she sat with me until her husband, Alexander, arrived. Gesturing vaguely toward some buildings in the distance, she mentioned he was nearby. I marked how the tallest structure included in her broad gesture housed the offices of my obstetrician.

Mark this all well. Sat to a table, on my own, out in the vast public, convinced your killers lurked all around, intent in contemplation on that exact matter, I was approached without solicitation by a woman who 'thought she knew me' but absolutely did not, and this woman invited herself to sit beside me, made introduction with the surname of one of your killers, mentioning offhand a husband who went by the first name associated with it. This was the first encounter I'd expended no energies arranging. Unfolding within eyeshot of the doctor's office I frequented for prenatal care. Such office literally referenced by the woman, however obliquely. I'd clear reason to entertain the possibility one of my enemies had wandered haplessly into my lair. Such preponderance of circumstantial evidence might've urged me to hatch plans against this Lenora, without second thought. It would've been child's play to work up a friendship. Invite myself into privacy with her on whichever pretext. Slay the murderer I'd assume she harbored.

Except she wasn't pregnant. When I inquired offhand whether she'd gotten herself in the family way, suggesting it may've been my belly which'd made her think us acquainted, she'd laughed boisterously. Such a distinct trill of 'Oh no no no no' this Lenora gave at such proposition. No one pishaws so unselfconsciously to sidestep a social nicety, let alone when such question could've been avoided by not striking up chitchat with a random woman eating a sandwich. The response eliminated her from consideration, instantly, despite the confluence of coincidence and my growing tension as your due date inched nearer.

I'd decided to proceed from the assumption all five of your killers already lurked in the world. So if Lenora became pregnant that afternoon, her child would've been nothing to do with what I was protecting you from, regardless what it was called. Alexander might impregnate her, but it'd be with seed only just produced. Perhaps unbeknownst to Lenora he'd impregnated another woman with whom he'd marry. Perhaps their love-child would be the Alexander I sought. If such woman were discovered, I'd slaughtering the creature she carried. But Lenora was innocuous. Innocent of all.

Could she've been wrong? Pregnant but too recently for there to've been sign or suspicion? Would she presently learn of her condition and regard her giggly dismissal during the chance encounter with me as bizarre precursor, craft it into a fun little anecdote?

I couldn't square that. Nor could I venture down the rabbit hole of Who's-to-say. Her laughter, affect, and the tone to her 'no no no no' were indicative of a woman neither with child, wanting to be, nor about to be dealt a shocking whoopsie. Though her demeanor could've been the instinctive reaction of a woman who'd come to terms with being barren despite a deep desire for motherhood, well trained to deflect talk on the subject by means of nonchalant dismissal. Such even explained her approaching me. A little habit. Keeping brief company with someone she'd trade places with but would never play-pretend around.

Were a miraculous curveball pitched, if tomorrow found her plump with a coming Alexander, such Alexander was no threat. I'd made firm to act from the thesis your killers had existed since the moment of my knowledge. Decided as True North how I'd only been able to foreseen the eventual dark deeds which'd befall you because the perpetrators of them were all alive, moving inexorably toward you.

Yet the interaction with Lenora wouldn't leave my thoughts. I reflected on it. Probed every facet. Soon grew convinced there must've been an aperture through which this woman would be shown integral to your fate. To step away from the encounter which most blatantly seemed to prove reality as I knew without exhaustive interrogation was tantamount to acting against you.

In itself, a woman with the surname Lowell and a husband called Alexander approaching me at this specific time, out of the hundreds of thousands of people in the city, was enough to set me uneasy. Her asking if she knew me then dismissing the idea she might be pregnant was akin to the pretext I'd use to become intimate with the people I hunted. Such warranted acute caution.

Could I have been mistaken about your killers already existing? Perhaps some were only potential, would come to be while I retained life enough to eliminate them. It made as much sense to believe my foreknowledge had been triggered by the conception of the first as by the final.

This Alexander Lowell, presently married to Lenora, might not've yet churned the seed of the Alexander who'd kill you. A poison yet waiting its turn in his physiology. The grime containing your killer might be expressed from his loins into Lenora's only between the brief moments I'd chatted with her and the day of your birth. By which time I'd have failed you for dismissing such chance.

Could my first moment of knowledge have been meant only to sharpen my senses, prep me to await encounters such as these, wherein your assassins would reveal themselves? That moment might've fit flush to when your first killer'd been fertilized, setting into motion the entire affair. Got the ball rolling, conditioned me to hunt. From there, all had become a waiting game. This encounter with Lenora may've been the next step. Official indication your killers would make their way to me, evidence their mothers would fall into my lap. My task might simply be to recognize and act unquestioningly when such opportunities presented.

As sensible a belief to act on as only pregnant woman need be sought. The meaty coincidence of this encounter might've been a godsend precisely because Lenora wasn't with child. Her involvement in matters allowed a particular of my plight to be explicated, a more precise path forward determined.

In a peculiar way, the notion of targeting the fathers pleased me. Dispatching Alexander Lowell before he impregnated whoever would carry his namesake instead of hurting Lenora would be a relief. Almost made me comfortable carrying out what I must. Since no child'd be carried by her, I'd be spared having to visit violence on the body and psyche of at least one mother. She'd lose a child, but only in a semantical way. A possibility she'd merely contemplated was all that'd been denied actualization. She'd endure the loss of the man she most likely loved. But better that than suffering the horror of losing a son, an honest part of herself torn away, dying while the two were yet conjoined.

My near relief at such texture lasted half-an-hour. The husband was immaterial. Or rather was material, merely. A cupboard of ingredient. Lifeless lumber. Killing him only killed him. There existed no child until his input fused within Lenora or whichever vessel else. The seed implanted in one woman might produce a son but if imbued into another result in a daughter. As sensible to think Lenora'd become pregnant by another man, unbeknownst to Alexander, as it did to consider Alexander might sire a son with a mistress. If one man could be the cause for the Alexander I was after, so could any number. It didn't reason out cleanly that cutting down the potential instigator for the birth of one of your killers was enough. If looking for them, their mothers were where they'd be. Regardless who put them there, when, or under which circumstance. The only surefire verification was a child already gestating in the womb of a mother who could be eliminated.

Alexander Lowell dying before Lenora became pregnant would be senseless. Murder without benefit. Perhaps Lenora, after such loss, would marry another man. Even a second Alexander. Feel herself urged toward a child she'd never desired before the horror I'd visited on her shook up her sense of self. Might seek such child based on fresh love. The coincidence of her new lover's name a giddy affirmation. All the more reason to pass the name down to their child. Or else might desire an offspring based on increased sensitivity to her own mortality. Merely find herself pressed toward one based on a new partner's desires. Acquiesce to motherhood on account of a depression she couldn't combat. Once with child, feel compelled to carry on her departed husband's namesake.

Something like that. Anything like that. Whichever combination of anything and everything at all. My knowledge was of events thirty years distant. While I considered it inviolate, wanted possessing it to mean I could protect you, such desire didn't guarantee I'd been granted such ability. The morsel of the future I possessed didn't alter the fact that anything might yet lead to anything.

In a blink, the Lenora encounter morphed from certainty to uncertainty to revelation to square one. I despaired at having to again contemplate the bleak possibility I'd been afflicted with nothing more than impotence. Might expunge as many of your killers as I uncovered, but in the end be left simply hoping doing so'd been enough. My passion didn't provide the literal means to satisfy it. I may well find no method of safeguarding you despite the lengths I'd go to and the boundaries I'd transgress. Flawlessly accomplishing all I technically could might yield the same result as failure to act at all.

For at least a week, the meeting with Lenora writhed in my

thoughts. As perhaps you can understand, life seemed to happen atop life atop life atop life during this period. Medical appointments needed to be kept, telephone calls tended to, social events, intimate time with your father, all without showing signs of secret distress or letting my hunting methods grow time consuming enough my movements would seem peculiar. With such distractions, and within the strict parameters I was required to exist, the Lenora matter remaining unresolved caused me to buckle. A cast of unmistakable angst colored my interactions, depleted my energy, sapped my will to so much as think. It was only a matter of time until my sinking soul became apparent. The concern from others would creep in. Surround me. Worry. Fret. Watchfulness. Desire for your wellbeing would tent me to place. A regimented timeline prescribed by physicians. My every activity scheduled, overseen, reported on. My life no longer my own. Right up until it wasn't at all.

I fantasized drastic action on my part to avoid being shackled. I'd disappear, severe ties with your father and anyone else known to me. Leave a false trail indicating I'd boarded a train, rented a room. Cobble up some ridiculous charade I'd keep feeding new blind alleys into, redirecting anyone from looking for me in the area. As I entertained such daydreams, my certainty your killers dwelt nearby eroded. Perhaps running away was precisely what'd lead me to the people who'd hurt you. Maybe that was the reason the idea took root so firmly. I had to trust I knew which parts of myself and which impulses to distrust, distrust I knew which to trust, even while trusting those to direct me toward which ones not to.

In the throes of so beleaguered a mindset I found myself at one of the many group functions for pregnant women I'd made it a point to attend. Your father was relieved I always had someplace to be, as his schedule grew thicker and more hectic, seemed genuinely delighted by the anecdotes I'd regale him with in what time we spent together. Stories built of the trifles I engaged in while seeking your killers. Oftentimes I'd entertain him with pure fabrications, striving to make them intriguing, rife with characters, silly happenstance, and curious remarks allegedly overheard. As always, when I'd relate even the most trivial occurrence from my daily existence he'd become giddy, speak boisterously with ways he'd repurpose such snippets in a forthcoming project, oftentimes riffing his own additions over dinner, in bed, or from where he'd lay on the floor while I bathed.

This particular meeting was for first time mothers. During the proceedings, my attention was repeatedly drawn to a young woman. Slender, lithe, conspicuously perky. Effortlessly lovely in a green sundress and snakeskin boots rising to below her knees. The girl seemed outside of the bunch, as women presented speeches and provided firsthand accounts of how their pregnancies had progressed, all ending in miscarriage, breach delivery, or in children with severe defects necessitating intricate, lifelong medical care. No matter the specifics of any narrative, it'd be presented with an undercurrent of hope and joy. Most women in attendance seemed my age. Went right along with the vibe of positivity. Nothing of what was discussed seemed to alarm them. Almost as though they more than expected such morbid outcomes and would take offense or become dejected at learning their own pregnancies would result in anything one typically assumed an expectant mother desired. The girl was distinctly the exception. Her face instinctively became drawn, pallor overtaking it almost to lividness if she slacked in the clear effort it took to adopt the stolid attitudes of those she fidgeted amongst.

Beyond the fact she reacted in a manner I considered normal considering the particulars we all sat listening to, there was nothing overtly peculiar about her. From what I could tell, no one else in the small auditorium marked her out of place. Just a young pregnant woman, nothing more. They had concerns far more pressing to remark upon than a stranger's fitness, semi-fashionable apparel, and obvious signs of discomfort at the possibility she'd not perennially be young, effervescent, and enjoying a life fancy free. Truth be told, the others didn't appear to possess bandwidth enough to remark the subtle air of embarrassment she exhibited. The touch of shame, bashful unease, or air of ill belonging it was difficult to pin down even as I treated her with increased scrutiny.

To me, she truly seemed not to belong. Even more acutely, seemed not to want to. Would leave in a heartbeat but for being compelled to remain. Nineteen years old, twenty at most. Stuck in a room of women twice that age, several a solid jaunt older. I tried to put my impression of her down to youth. Observing grown-ups dishing the nitty gritty of motherhood, harkening while strangers as old as her mother unpacked candid fears that what they'd worked to achieve in life would be forfeit if their pregnancies were carried to term, what they were yet attempting to forestalled irrevocably, must've seemed exceptionally foreign. I was disquieted, myself, as the speakers rattled off litanies of the difficulties in coming to terms with what swath of life was already behind them, what portion of the slim sliver left they'd now be required to sacrifice, and as they confessed guilt over naming the next two decades 'sacrifice' at all considering the bliss they were certain to experience in witnessing their children's growth, regardless the hardships it might present.

The mystery was solved when I approached her following the presentations, some workshops, and a circle of casual chitchat such as occurs organically near the close of such functions. The awkwardness I'd been correct to note was on account of initially believing she'd attended the incorrect session, then believing she'd been sent to the group in error. Not wanting to take a risk, she'd resigned herself to paying strict attention to everything, taking notes, and participating as she'd been instructed.

Before I could interject a request that she slow down, allow me to ask contextualizing questions, the girl mentioned how we'd met before. Shyly demurred how I probably didn't recognize her on account of the fact she was now showing quite prominently and that her hairstyle had quite drastically changed.

Once she'd said so, I recalled her precisely. We'd met at a playground where she'd been supervising a bunch of kids who weren't hers, mingling with other girls her own age and semblance, babysitters, nannies, *au pairs* or such designations. I recalled her more distinctly with each word she spoke, smile she flashed then subdued, and touch to tuck strands of her now chocolate brown hair behind one ear or the other.

She nodded along to my recollecting her, genuinely pleased to've made an impression. Grinned in that way a young person will merely at having been remarked on. She even laughed and repeated "Babysitter, nanny, *au pair*, such designations, buncha kids who weren't mine" with unselfconscious glee before she caressed, patted, then rested one hand on the bump of her belly while sighing "Though neither is this little guy."

She was a surrogate. It was on principle she'd felt awkward in the group, nevermind when what she termed 'disaster after disaster' seemed to be the only flavor of discussion on tap. The husband of the woman she was carrying on behalf of had instructed her to attend, though she felt certain he must've thought it was a general pregnancy care group, wherein women learned how to healthfully eat, exercise, cope with hormonal changes, and what have you, rather than a session for receiving tips and tricks to brace for the uncanny and topsy-turvy time of it one's every waking moment might become if things took a turn for the medical worst. She confessed to feeling somewhat sick to her stomach. Anxious she'd been sent by the family who employed her as a sly way of being informed they'd received terrible news from her doctor. That the child she carried was afflicted with some abnormality. The clean bill of health she'd recently received no more than a bill of goods meant to keep her unaware of a danger to herself which might compel her to terminate. Even if the group hadn't been a mistake, the more likely reason for sending her was that the family had reason to believe some birth defect or hereditary condition might come into play based on the father's physiology. Not wanting to contend with such grim realities directly, had dispatched her as proxy. The same as they'd done for a peculiar seminar concerning what to brace for if a child were born deaf or mute.

In a conspiratorial hush, she confessed feeling guilty since she'd not have to contend with any of that, would sidestep the perils and pitfalls of motherhood full stop after being duly compensated for services rendered. We both laughed. All the more when she quipped "I'm giving birth to a payday instead of cashing my life out as down payment for a stranger I don't even know I'll be able to stand."

But the ins-and-out of our immediate rapport aren't of importance. What I came to discover is that the woman whose child this girl carried was Lenora Lowell. Such sensitive information wasn't divulged to me that day, but once it had been an immaculate picture appeared before me. Or rather, a picture and variants. All capturing pristinely the same actuality.

It's easy, now, to imagine Lenora may've seen me at the playground where I'd met the girl. Perhaps vaguely noticed the two of us conversing. Additionally glimpsed me in passing, due to living nearby a park it remained my habit to visit several times, each week. However it may've been, it made perfect sense she'd observed me only enough to not quite be able to place me upon our meeting outside the bookshop. I'd been recognized exactly enough for an itch of curiosity to develop. It'd felt worthwhile to risk a touch of social awkwardness in asking if we'd ever met. Even her 'no no no no' took on a precise tang with this context in mind. She'd not wanted to engage in chatter as she was pursuing motherhood in what I might've deemed a less natural, even inappropriate way. Why court a confrontation or tsk-tsk, however mild? Or perhaps she'd deflected because the surrogacy wasn't her idea but a request from her husband, a concession she'd made. After all, it was the father of the child who'd sent the girl to attend whichever functions and who, she'd further explained, generally oversaw her prenatal care, arranging appointments, tending to transportation, so on. Either way, the fact that a young woman was carrying her child might've been the last thing Lenora wanted to dodge around or lie about outright to a pregnant stranger she'd accosted on flimsy pretext.

You can see that as I'd reached the end of my tether, I'd been presented all but irrefutable proof that matters of terrific consequence swirled around me and had been for quite some time. Questions I'd had found direct answer. Whorls of anxiety clear alleviation. The situation which'd both fallen in my lap and been verified by my original technique of walking the beat was a confirmation that, while the specifics of what I was searching for might be as complex as I'd feared, they nonetheless were extant, occurring in the environment I'd assumed they were, under the dictates I'd determined. I'd been correct to've pelted myself with overwhelming What-ifs. Doing so had revealed your protection was a process of learning not only trust myself and what I knew, but that I'd decipher how to proceed from it.

From such discovery, let's reflect on another. Within a twenty-four-hour period I came upon two women with the surname Lyons, both pregnant, presented as though bookends to a demonstrably harmless bunch. The first I approached was the second discovered. Beatrice Lyons. Pregnant but with a daughter. Married to another Lyons, whose surname she'd taken, replacing her maiden name Willet. This Lyon's daughter might've been named Marcy, the mother kept mum.

Based on the convoluted mechanics I'd already encountered with Lowell, a possible Marcy Lyons could marry into the Tellwell name during the next three decades, becoming the Marcy who'd kill you.

This outside chance wasn't given much attention, though. My noia that your killers evaded me through duplicitous means had started to cool. The rote plod of my investigations made such semantic possibilities feel remote, the Lowell affair in particular showcasing how the knowledge I possessed wasn't a game of three card monte. Matters might be tricky, but nothing was rigged. I was being tutored through an educational sequence. If I failed to pay strict enough heed, identities would seem to perpetually fluctuate, my progress forever looping back to the start.

The Lowell discovery had presented as a roundabout series of intricate events which might've come to X might've come to Y, appear correct then be proven untrue, all seemingly designed to convince me your killers' hiding places were too complex to ferret out. But diligent examination had allowed me to isolate the signal in the noise. All possibilities were, and would forever remain, possible, but weren't by any means one and the same. A path to more confident certainty existed. I'd dismiss hopeless iterations of my plight by way of deciphering proofs when they manifested.

Bottom line was I knew enough to protect you, definitively. To place my will subservient to intrusive considerations or accept that my knowledge was no more than a puzzle box constructed to exhaust me either into making a mistake or, through indecision, into madness mustn't be permitted. If I didn't allow myself to become acclimated to the world I now existed within, required myself to endlessly begin over from scratch, I'd accomplish no more than taking blind, random stabs, my choices only choices-so-called. To believe what I deciphered of one scenario in no way aided my ability to more swiftly and appropriately sort through the next was akin to acting on your killers' behalf.

They weren't thinking entities. Couldn't respond to me in real time. I knew what I knew precisely because they were static, inanimate, helpless. If your unborn killers were able to strategize, could through perceptions alien to me foresee which courses of action I'd considered in order to booby trap the world with misinformation so I'd become flummoxed, my cause was entirely lost. But it was insanity to posit the fiends possessed sentience, intellect, and a degree of cunning more sophisticated than I, a living, breathing, rational person'd developed over a lifetime. It'd been appropriate to toy with such a macabre idea when I'd no inroads to make honest deductive efforts from, when anything could've been anything and anything being anything made as much sense as anything being anything else, but I needed to entrust your fate to the few things I knew rather than the countless I could never apprehend. Otherwise it'd become a Mobius strips of could be could be could be could be. A woman might promise, on her mother's life, her son'd be named Keith Goaltender, that she'd be consigned to Hell if she ever allowed otherwise, while another might be dead certain hers would be called Dillon Pitts, yet I'd never gain means enough to determine if Goaltender might change his surname to Williams while Pitts might decide he fancied going by Goaltender and, while he was at it, make his first name Keith. The three empty decades I had to play with could smother me in arguments for inaction.

Care was required. But I mustn't split hairs. Allow whatever infinite number of things were conceivable to erode the few fundamental things I knew beyond doubt. In the moment of irreversible knowledge, I'd learned what your killers would be called when they killed you. But it'd also felt I knew what their names were, right then. Instead of pedantic second guesses, I needed to set stern my faith. If I focused, I knew more than I knew, never less.

The second Lyons was called Violet. Pregnant with a son she proudly and without hesitation informed me would be named

Montgomery. Sang 'Montgomery Lyons' with the same timbre of unmistakable fact I cooed 'Tasha Parsinbyrd.'

I'd surveilled a park for several days, spoken to other expectant mothers, nannies, babysitters, and had marked this Violet several times, but until that day found no occasion to approach her. Dressed for mild exercise, I used the water fountain near where she'd sat down, showcasing my windedness quite theatrically, joining her on the bench with requisite apologies she'd merrily told me weren't needed.

We were shoulder to shoulder, her two toddlers entertaining themselves on some metal contraption, when she gushed Montgomery's name. I immediately clasped my hands together as though in happy recognition of obvious perfection, beaming over how dignified it sounded and enthusing that the surname Lyons on its heels evoked a composer for strings or a writer whose work was meant exclusively for the stage. Was her husband called Montgomery as well, I inquired offhand, the query posed to allow me a segue into remarking it was so unique a designation I assumed it was being passed down from the father. But he was named Reggie.

"Why Montgomery?" I pressed. Laughing, she told me it hadn't been her idea. As though it were simultaneously the damnedest thing and the last to find a sniff of peculiarity in, narrated how she'd been forced awake by headache a week after her pregnancy'd been confirmed, found herself in the nursery rocking chair, caressing a hand in soft circles over her still slender belly, attempting to compile a mental list of all the lullabies she knew and of songs she could repurpose as more. During such drowsy task, she'd repeatedly whispered 'Shh' as though soothing her child to sleep. Soon enough, this altered to 'Shh, Montgomery.' Then, as she'd stirred herself to return to bed, she'd spoken aloud blearily 'Okay, Montgomery, let's go back to sleep.' Would never forget the way the utterance which'd made it official had sounded.

I could tell, when she repeated it to me, it was in perfect replica of how the words'd been spoken to your killer, that night.

Reggie'd been none too pleased when she began referring to their unborn in so definitive a way. She'd not told him she'd settled on the name, simply began making offhand references to 'Montgomery's room' and added the name in blue capital letters to the calendar box designating her due date.

Violet tittered as she related how Reggie had, tongue-in-cheek, asked whether 'Montgomery' was the moniker currently sitting on top of the Leader Board. Clear he wasn't keen on it. But so far as she could see, the poor man was plumb out of luck. 'It's just his name' she told me she'd told him. From that moment on hadn't entertained any talk of other names, even in playfulness. Shrugged with a look on her face illustrating how pleased she was the look on mine indicated how deeply I comprehended the sentiment. Proven by my grinning "My daughter was always Tasha and will always be Tasha, as well."

I'm certain you understand the import of those stories, how the encounters proved I was to honor doubts but be guided by insights, required to follow the dictates of both noiac and prudent impulses, and that excruciating calculations would lead me aright. The overall sequence of the world showcased that doubt could be churned of anything. Anyone was at perpetual liberty to consider whichever portion of their life coincidence, dumb luck, happy chance. Doing so didn't eliminate the glaring truth that one thing led to another. If not for This there'd be no That and, therefore, This led to That, incontrovertibly. Regardless whether hindsight permitted word games to be played, when looking back at ten sequential events it'd appear as though eliminating the sixth would eliminate the seventh, eighth, ninth. But such reasoning also proved the sixth could only be removed or circumvented through elimination of the fifth, the fourth, the third. However, looking forward from the third, it was self-evident the fourth, the fifth, and the sixth would be what they'd been. Altering the past, in an abstract sense, might alter all yet to come, but the concrete past could only be altered while in it, became locked Absolute only after itself. Life proceeded under the auspices of plain dot-to-dot causality. Nothing proved the future wasn't already written, merely that we existed always in the part-being-penned, crafted by all that surrounded us, however distant, not merely the fragments in arms reach.

Through meticulous attention to my methods, I'd been shown the clean, clear truth of who two of your killers were hidden within. Therefore, I possessed the capacity to discover the rest. Events conditioned me the same way a good novel teaches an audience how to read it as they progress.

As time passed, a more confident sensation of understanding bloomed in me. These men, this woman who'd kill you weren't beyond the grasp of my vengeance. The names Benecourt, Goaltender, Lowell, Lyons, and Tellwell would belong to children gestating in local women I'd be able transgress upon. They dwelt or were otherwise present in the area we'd wound up taking our apartment. All five were near enough I could smoke them out. Perhaps in what I'd consider the outskirts of the area, even a healthy drive from it, but never a distance so vast it'd prove prohibitive to dispatching their brood. Even if one resided elsewhere, I'd have occasion to wind up in their orbit and, in sync with such chance, the proof of their presence would be revealed, accompanied by the will to act when I must. I might return home for a period, called to visit an acquaintance in their time of need, or else travel with your father as an unexpected requirement of his work. Nothing altered the thesis I'd proceed by. Your killers would cross my path. I'd discover them. They'd be expunged.

I began to believe the opportunity I'd been granted was presented to many. Women stirred by foreknowledge to protect sons and daughters. Some ignored their stirrings and stood down. Some spoke but were talked out of acting, convinced it was no more than anxiety, nightmare, all perfectly natural yet entirely unreal. No doubt some acted, were caught out in their attempts. Others might've succeeded, lived on in the glow of their victory. Or else all might be slotted to perish as I was. An exchange rate set firmly. One life for one possible revenge.

Your killers were near at hand. Their confluence awakened something within me. So concentrated a threat triggered an instinct, some deep seeded, reactionary mechanism possessed by every mother. Or possessed only by some. The ability might be potential to all yet fail to develop in most due to incompatibility with the circumstances of their lives, traditions in which they were raised, ideas and environments they'd either exposed themselves to or avoided, beliefs they subscribed to, and conventions they'd adopted subconsciously, much like every human might theoretically metamorphose into a resplendent painter, an expert at chess, attain a rarified palette for wine, or else exhibit exquisite musical acumen if not for experiencing developmentally restrictive conditions. As if you'd been a toddler out strolling with me and some perverse cohort had aims on you, I'd been able to sense it. Whichever casual postures the swine might adopt, however they'd conspire to make their presence appear acceptable, whichever duplicity they'd roll out to disguise having a word with me as innocuous, excusable, easily dismissed by anyone I'd tell, I'd know to be wary of who and what they were. Sensible rationale couldn't be provided, but threats brewed against you and were therefore things I could intuit. No matter if they originated from a stranger, a person in a position of trust, an intimate friend, a sibling, a spouse. There'd been some quiver in me. Such things happen to many people, all the time.

This is why I'd felt certain I'd know which mother carried one of your foes. Not only would I sense something in them, they'd perceive danger from me. Phantasmal, ephemeral, a disquiet would rise. Whether they explained it away as nonsense based on their present mood or dismissed it as a vagrant stirring of negativity couched in the past, they'd experience something uncanny. Perhaps not assign it to the stimuli in front of them. Put it off to some incidental, harmless cause else. Want the feeling to go away without seeking to comprehend it. But they'd never subdue it entirely. Might well assign it to me. Recognize my name as I would the names of their children. If I introduced an alias, presume I'd done exactly as much. Seek to catch me out. Similar to how I'd considered the Lowell I'd sought might begin as a Wexler, entertained the possibility Marcy Tellwell was Marcy Tellwell even if not yet called anything. The collision of formless certainties and instinctual rises in alarm would lead to some tell, noticeable if microscopic. It was no matter if we chose to embrace our fears, express them, act, or entirely disavow our tremor of responsibility. A mother would know my intent against their growing child in the exact measure I knew what the murderer such mother harbored would grow to be intent on toward you.

My choice of victims wasn't predicated on whimsy nor dependent on mystical intervention. I'd not wind up wresting the world into contortion after contortion out of impulse and panic as the clock wound down. The nearer the vital hour came, the more peril there was, the sharper my instincts would cut.

I came to more deeply accept how the task I undertook wasn't one I desired. Wasn't my choice. Or rather, it was. My passionate desire to act in your defense. But such desire was predicated on requirement. I'd chosen to perform how I must. Such conditional election wasn't even cousin to proclaiming a longing for any situation which'd warrant it. As it happened, what I'd no choice in was the same thing I'd choose. Something which predated having purpose, material, or need. As was every last thing about you.

To prove me right, the same day Lyons was confirmed came verification of Benecourt. Without putting in a tap of effort, the creature was revealed in the last way I could've desired. Made plain how absolute my knowledge was. How clear my path forward. How dearly you'd cost. Let me tell the story, exactly as it occurred.

I'll begin the afternoon I'd met Montgomery's mother. Returning from a medical appointment, I glanced out the car window, distinctly noticing one of the garish orange dispensers containing coupon circulars which dotted the area. As on a hundred other occasions, this sight made me chuckle, recalling to mind a story my friend Deirdre'd told, ages ago. Such memory, combined with the feeling I'd two of your killers accounted for, had me in fine spirits. There seemed sense and order to life. A quantifiable truth behind the thoughts which'd plagued me for months. I decided to give Deirdre a call come the evening, though she'd already announced her intention to pay me a visit the following week. Beyond the brief telephonic chitchat during which she'd announced this impending trip, we hadn't traded so much as a dozen words in more than a month. Such was our way. We'd go absentee from each other then suddenly get together, falling into step instantly, cavorting as though we'd never been an instant away from each other nor could bear to be ever again.

Less than an hour after my return to the apartment came a knock to the door. I figured the rather business-like nature of the few thumps given were brusque indication a delivery man'd left another package of materials to do with your father's projects. In no hurry, I made my way to answer, noisily chewing a mouthful of cold taco I'd cobbled together from refrigerated leftovers, dressed in pajama shorts, one sock, and a camisole which by then held tight around the growing bump of you. Blinked in astonishment as Deirdre was revealed, putting on a pouting playact of what a benevolent and patient soul she was to put up with the indignity of my lack of manners.

Though well known to pull such surprise arrivals in advance of scheduled ones, I hadn't even considered it might've been her. We spent five minutes in gushy Oh-my-goodnesses and sticking out our tongues while badmintoning off-color chatter at each other before moving into the apartment proper. Once she'd settled into the chair your father so often perched on, she puffed out a breath, crossed her legs, nodded at me earnestly, and said "I have news." I replied "You're pregnant" without missing a beat. She laughed at my matter-of-fact prognostication, cheekily protesting with high-pitched whines of mock-aghastness how it'd been reprehensible of me to've stolen her thunder by "floating such a motherfucking stupid, and frankly insulting, guess," rolled her eyes when I snarked "It wasn't a guess, you slut, just an understanding of cold probability," then burst a guffaw of the words "Yes, I'm pregnant, you trustless cunt!" while trilling with mirth as she threw a small pillow my direction, clumsily enough it didn't connect. Arms crossed petulantly, she snorted "You oughta be more excited I've turned into a knocked up little whore like you," felt the least I could do was take pity, let her pretend for a few more minutes she wasn't "a predictable slob like every other woman who ever darkened a doorstep."

We'd never discussed the possibility of her winding up with child. I'd known her only to voice a lack of desire at the prospect. Certainly she'd said nothing in our most recent conversation to clue me in. Nor had anything so world altering been coded in the look on her face when I'd opened the door. Considering her mercurial nature and the umpteen pipedreams she cultivated, any of which may've finally struck paydirt, even the way she'd spoken the phrase 'I have news' could've been indicative of any number of things.

Once our freewheeling banter simmered down, she beamed at

me, declaring with much emotion how she'd wanted me to be the first to know. Right on the heels of which she informed me that not even the father was aware of the pregnancy. She wasn't certain she cared to inform him. Hadn't settled on whether she would even if it turned out she wanted to. With formless hand gestures, explained "the blessed event wouldn't exactly be taken as good news" or at the very least was something she "personally couldn't imagine being met with celebration, per se." Holding herself to it, she doubted the man who'd gotten her in the family way would urge her to keep the child. If it turned out the fella did want the kid, she doubted she actually wanted him. This wasn't someone who'd be described as a stranger, but also no one she'd gotten to know or cultivated true romantic interest in, nor was it a chap she'd bother putting in elbow grease to form deeper connection with to the tune of hearth, home, and the endless complexities of cohabitating, marriage, or being required to act as though even marginally integral parts of each other's lives. Laughing, she blurted out "To put the fine point on it, he's not the type I'd want to be unable to rid myself of and wouldn't have gotten near the underside of my dress otherwise." Thus, she'd zero intention of "giving the bastard any impression he's got inalienable rights to whoever it is I'll plop out."

Her idiom became increasingly unchecked. So much so, I began to distrust the face of every statement she made. A breathless blush tinted her energy, as though she were spouting off without filter to avoid admitting something to herself, air of protesting too much to an audience auditing her puritanically, piling on distancing descriptors in order to keep from giving vent to her feelings. I became tense the longer she prattled. Bracing for an inevitability.

The father was depicted as a vague colleague. She and another woman had spilled into the same bedroom with him, all quite *impromptu*, after a night of libations and karaoke during an out-of-town conference. As though correcting a grave misimpression, she energetically insisted she regretted nothing of that zesty encounter, but demanded how none of what'd transpired had been intended to have legs. By anyone involved. Least of all her. To use the word 'intended' about any aspect of the affair was quite a misnomer, in fact. So far as she was concerned, it'd been the sort of unpredicted, raucous romp to muse on in private and to entertain thoughts of revisiting only because you knew you never would. The more she regarded the madcap event, the more certain she was the fellow wouldn't be keen for fatherhood, even in the capacity of a shouldering his share of the financial burden. I wasn't to get her wrong, however. The guy'd no doubt urge her in the direction of termination magnanimously. On account of not wanting her to endure the single motherhood waiting on the other end of an unintended frolic. Couldn't imagine him not being flush at her side throughout such ordeal, if she so desired. In fact, probably would do his part for the child, come what may. She grew vehement in her desire I understand how she'd reason to believe, without the specter of doubt, he'd express, flatly and free of malice, how accidents happen but, if given a say in the matter, be forthright that he wasn't cruising for the responsibility inherent in parenthood, thanks all the same.

"But you want the child" I said. Unable to make it sound like a question. Squinted to hold her gaze serious in mine while, out of breath from her lengthy performance, she looked back at me, seeming to only then apprehend how long she'd been yapping and with what vigor. Her expression suggested she wouldn't be able to repeat any portion of it. Might even posit opposite opinions of everything without realizing, were she to make the attempt. Wide eyed, nodding slow, she eventually chuckled a "Yes" out her nose. An expression of bewilderment lacquered on her face. That little affirmative chortle the first she'd admitted to herself what she'd decided quite some time before. After a few beats of silence, squinting tighter at some nuance I felt hidden in the crisp of her gaze, I tilted my head. "You want his child." These words caused her to blink. Demeanor all at once altered. Settling to calm with the words "Yes, I do."

She wanted a child. This child. His child. Was going to have a child. This child. His child. Wasn't of any two minds about it. Abruptly asked whether she was obligated to tell the father. A kind of fear to the question. Obvious terror at how he actually might urge her against carrying to term. Be unable to bear his saying so. Might well abort were he to make such dictate. Equally as obvious was the fact she was reluctant to admit aloud, to me or herself, how she not only wanted the child but the father. Afraid it'd have to be one, the other, or neither, never both. "Martin has some right to know, doesn't he?" she piteously inquired.

The question startled me. A drift of lightheadedness as I repeated the name. Let it leak slow from my mouth as though tentative. Knowing exactly the Martin she meant.

"Martin Benecourt" she grinned after an apology for woolgathering. "I think you met him, once or twice, way way way back." Her features wrinkled into the usual flirtatious smirk she'd often tease me with when I was caught red-handed. Crinkled her nose as though aware I'd seen through her protestations and *faux* nonchalance during everything she'd said before. Twisted her lips. Grunted as though I was making fun of her, but also as a way of admitting I was correct to believe she had aims on the man. Maybe'd even figured the kid'd been a way to secure him.

I'd not given a thought to Martin Benecourt in ages. Once upon a time, he'd been a figure Deirdre and I nursed a potent, mutual attraction toward. Mine fleeting. Hers apparently anything but. I'd drifted out of any orbit which would've kept him a subject of mutual conversation. She'd never mentioned him. But it was clear he'd been maintained as part of her inner narrative. A fixture in her life kept secret from me.

She laughed coquettishly. Bet if I'd been at that conference it would've been my room where the lascivious deed was brought off. Egged me on with bratty flicks to my arm. Winked how there was no telling who would've done what to whom if the three of us had ever found ourselves alone in a discount motel. Then bit her top front teeth into her lower lip. Slowly let them scrape across. Aimed a kiss my direction. Playfully cocking her eyes while she added "There's probably still no telling, eh?"

I won't dwell on the next days of my life. Time became meaningless other than time had become anguish. Each moment subdivided into countless others which expanded interminably despite feeling already over and done. I won't attempt to express the cavity I became. Empty. Lifeless. Your growth seeming independent of me. I was a shell you'd hatch from, nothing more.

To say I despaired makes me sound too appropriate. I was tormented, yes, but possessed no grace which might elicit sympathy. More than suffering the lashes of what I'd discovered and was required of me due to it, I revolted against the task. Couldn't stomach the notion of moving against Deirdre. Unable to separate the thought of her from the killer nestled in her womb. My energies centered on turning my mind away from the absolute need for action. Fixated on finding words which'd convince me there was no cause to proceed.

I'd been convinced to my core your protection was something no force on Earth could compel me to turn from, now such resolve seemed impossible to countenance. Even thoughts of leaving the mothers alive were unbearable when directed at Deirdre. The most horrific aspects of everything I'd been plotting took on palpable texture and contour, were no longer verbiage I could keep at arm's length. I felt depleted. Helpless. It was all I could do to maintain an appropriate façade for daily life. Every ounce of vitality in me was required to remain simply functional. But I couldn't afford to succumb to dolor. Such would trigger those who cared for me. Bind them at my side, twenty-four-seven. Destroy possibilities for tangible, actionable plans were any to dawn on me. In those ghastly days I wanted not to want what I needed to want. Needed not to desire what I couldn't truly desire, to begin with.

After however long being adrift, I abruptly felt desperate to sight land, feverish to make whichever effort necessary to bring myself to shore. On the cusp of submitting myself to inpatient therapy, soliciting a program of treatment specifically tailored to the breed of mania and degree of distress I endured. My reasons would remain disguised. To your father, I'd claim what I was going through had only to do with an agitation of my diagnosed and documented history of anxiety. An onset of acute depression. Listlessness kindled by the pregnancy. A violent hormonal imbalance convincing me I'd never return to the passions which'd been my focus prior to motherhood. I'd take care in the presentation of my malady, cautious it show no sign of being a result of where we dwelt, his work, our choices. A condition no one would question and wouldn't poke for particulars of.

Obviously such venture was absurd. Amounted to slitting your throat. Though I still did consider admitting some of the horrible ideas I harbored to my longtime counselor during our general therapy conducted via telephone. Ached to speak every word of my plight aloud. Confess myself to someone. Hear the change in their voice after enduring my words. Know I was no longer being spoken to as myself but as something I'd become. Overtaken by madness. Disease corroding my wits. If it could be proven I'd gone off the deep end, I might manage to convince myself how I'd responded to Deirdre nourishing your killer was a strength rather than a failing, my refusal to entertain the notion of harming a dear friend proof I was curing myself not abandoning you.

I needed a face to which I'd show myself, not a mirror to stare into. No longer satisfied imagining the aghast mouths, jaws clenched, eyes disbelieving, brows creased with concern. Wanted to be regarded neither with sympathy nor horror, only clinical remove. Impersonal minds clocking, measuring, codifying me. Educated eyes sizing up the quantifiable truth. To address myself to someone who'd know without question that I meant what I said and would do what I claimed unless they could convince me from it. Desired the voice of someone who'd truly heard me, apprehended the danger I posed, who'd listened patiently without comment while I'd admitted the atrocities I contemplated, heard me when I'd proclaimed my motivations weren't commonplace stresses, ephemeral worries, intrusive thoughts brought about by the circumstances of my life, and believed the actions I spoke went beyond transient consideration, were deeds I'd spent every waking hour working up the will to make manifest.

Whoever I spoke with was to understand that revealing myself to them was part of my impulse to kill, comprehend how in order to go on I needed them defanged. Let them tell me I was sick then prove it with lab results and sanctioned psychological instruments I'd not be able to argue around. I'd not stop myself unless they proved to me I must be stopped. Were they to fail in accepting the gravity of what I confessed, or weren't skillful enough to disarm my mind, all the blood I'd shed was on their hands. I'd done all I could. Allowed them opportunity to defeat me.

I couched the betrayal these considerations represented as a necessary obstacle to overcome on the path to your rescue, but knew I entertained the idea of confessing myself in so naked and catastrophic a way because I desired to stand down. Wanted proof positive my progressing toward the violence necessary to protect you was only symptom of a poison brain. Some mechanism ought go automatically into effect, removing from the equation my will and my choice. A legal decision should swoop in to finalize everyone's fate in one irreversible finger snap. Onus ought be on some outside authority. Were they to step up, I'd allow myself to be committed to an institutional setting, kept under strict observation until your birth.

The thought of being locked down was attractive. Volition robbed of me. No way out. Even breaking down catatonic grew palatable. To exist as incubator for the back half of your gestation. My specific torture ended. Replaced by another. One easier to bear. Which medication could sleep me out of. Let the last of my life pass by carefully doped up, enough to believe I wasn't a killer and never would've been no matter how I might wish it were otherwise.

If I couldn't hurt Deirdre, I couldn't kill Benecourt. If I couldn't kill Benecourt, there'd be no point killing anyone. All I'd accomplish for trying was sewing chaos you'd have to reap. A macabre legacy your father'd have to weather and raise you in the toxic fallout of. Except worse than that. If I acted only in part, I'd have caused whichever number of your killers to die in the costume of innocence while knowing you remained doomed.

My cowardice attempted to convince me confession, committal, confinement weren't methods of shirking my duties but tactical maneuvers necessary for achieving my goals. Whichever talk-doctor I laid it all out to would be the foe I must outwit, my misgivings given flesh and intellect then put to the test. If counselors couldn't make me believe myself incapable of murder, my fears of faltering at the moment of crisis wouldn't return. The crucible of such conversations would exorcise the oinkish weakness in me. I tried to repaint my urge to let you die as a deft gambit which'd checkmate your killers. Knowing it was myself I wanted lain sideways on the board.

In the maelstrom of such mindset, I discovered Goaltender. Had never know anyone with the surname. Couldn't think of any historical figure or celebrity who'd sported it. There was no listing in any directory I could access, either. Which wasn't odd. I couldn't find local listings for many unique names I was acquainted with and many common names had little to no representation.

My mind perpetually squirmed as though to press into the underside of my skull the way you writhed against the roof of my belly, thoughts of my hunt undulating in dull headache, but I hadn't been actively searching for Goaltender when I found him. A tidbit of local newspaper caught my attention. The sort of tossaway rag where it's difficult to tell which text is article, which advertisement. The same circular dispensed in the bright orange containers stationed about town, in fact. Halfway down a column, given no prominence, the word 'victim' drew my eye, glance flicking from it to the word 'name,' both near each other in the semi-bold title of a three-paragraph piece. *Victim Takes Name Of Alleged Assailant*.

The air went bad around me. The same sour tremor of gooseflesh, nausea, and pain behind my ear which always accompanied a sickening nuance of my trap. A feeling akin to being unable to keep yourself falling back into a nightmare you'd woken from after blearily assuring yourself you wouldn't. Cold sweat. Parched throat. Paralysis. I felt to blame. Drained and disheartened despite how recently I'd have not only desired the discovery but celebrated similar. Here was my precious 'sensing something by proximity,' my magical ability to know something harmful was near. Even without strict vigilance, I was being brandished those I must eliminate.

It was succinctly reported how a young woman called Cynthia Wilmington claimed she'd been left pregnant after being sexually assaulted by a man named Norman Goaltender. Wilmington was native to the area, Goaltender briefly in town at the time of the alleged crime. Attempts to bring charges against him had been unsuccessful, as had been forcing him to submit to paternity testing.

Wilmington made it plain she'd seek no financial assistance from Goaltender and would permit him to waive parental rights if he'd acknowledge the child. Had gone on to promise no further action once the verification of paternity was in, even if he maintained his position that their sexual encounter had been consensual. If he refused, she vowed to pursue all avenues available under the law to secure his monetary contribution to the child's upbringing. Kicked up a fuss which'd resulted in considerable support. When she'd made public her intention to carry the pregnancy to term, certain communities not only rallied round but lionized her. The latest action in her crusade had been to legally change her surname to that of her alleged rapist. The rationale for such maneuver was to increase public attention on her plight

While reading one lengthier account of the scandal, an uncanny feeling crept over me. I couldn't shake the impression I'd already encountered every sentence printed on the page. When I focused, could swear I'd heard about the sordid business, out of context, before reading any article at all. Overheard the matter being chatted about in my presence. Referenced when I'd attended a get-together for cast and crew of the first of the three films your father'd worked on. The Wilmington incident mentioned in a cursory way, along with the name Norman Goaltender. The more effort I put in, the more the scene built itself. A snippet of stray conversation not even aimed at me, words scrambled amongst a roomful of inconsequential banter. A man's voice, darkly sarcastic, name-checked Wilmington, though its exact phrasings eluded me. But I distinctly recalled a woman's voice replying with a scoff. 'Jesus, the thing with that nut saying the Goaltender guy raped her?' I'd glanced over to see a young man rolling his eyes while another said he'd be tempted to write a script about it, except this or that other person no doubt already had one in the works and was equipped with better connections to get such project greenlit.

Those moments refreshed. Seemed to've occurred only hours before. I recalled how Goaltender hadn't seemed a surname. I'd heard it as two words. Goal. Tender. Then as one, but a descriptor. 'That goaltender guy.' Because of the quip about how a film might be made, I'd assumed some sordid affair involving a *futbol* player of note who'd assaulted his mistress, a fan, or a spouse. But regardless how I'd processed it, I'd heard the name Goaltender. Months before. Soon afterward must've at least skimmed the article I'd found myself reading, again.

My mind turned over, tangled, tightened, went limp. In one moment felt firm as chilled granite, in the next stale and viscous, then like tepid pond water with armfuls of gnats hovering inches from the surface. I sat in silence. Processing. A quality of echo accompanying the moments. Broken by the sudden burp of a single laugh sharply escaping me unbidden.

My next train of thought was sickly with cynical mirth. No need to jabber with the impartial third party I'd been on the verge of soliciting if I wasn't in touch with the entirety of myself. I might as well've been two wholly unconnected people attempting to communicate without a shared field of reference. Would the me who spoke to a therapist be the me who hadn't recalled the presence of Benecourt in her life or overhearing the name Goaltender despite sweating blood over it? Or would it be the me who clearly knew about the names and had once been infatuated with an actual Benecourt she could recall erotic fantasies of?

Two weeks prior, I'd have sworn up and down how all five of your killers' names were utterly foreign to me, asserted with absolute conviction my certainty in the knowledge of your forthcoming death. Such confidence stemmed largely from the fact that the names of those involved in it weren't anything I could've invented or that, even if I'd dreamed up your killers, it'd be lunacy to suggest I'd plucked surnames out of a hat and then found them represented, flesh and bone, within easy reach.

No outside entity was required to pit myself against, because I was thinking, saying, and subvocalizing the words which would've come from their mouth. I didn't need an enemy to sit across from. I was the enemy. Your enemy. Entertaining the proposition of sharing my ordeal with another party proved this. However careful I might've been to make certain they couldn't repeat a syllable of what passed between us, conversation amounted to jockeying for ways to avoid my responsibility and fighting against such impulse only kept myself occupied in dismantling my own arguments. It was no different than if I'd never been of a mind to go through with anything.

Such internal conflict reached crisis pitch. I was unable to sort clear whether what I called proceeding wasn't actually roadblocking myself, calling it progress despite knowing it was anything but. I'd no conviction in my ability to determine whether proffering a defense against staying my hand was merely a ruse concocted by some quirk of my psyche, meant to lure another part into showing its hand. One side choreographing another into letting slip its plan. Whichever malignancy of conscience was working against you might be biding its time, arranging a semantic counterattack timed with aplomb for when it'd be most disorienting. All of my searching and planning had proven the truth of my knowledge, but may've done so in service of revealing the acts required to protect you were ones I'd never permit myself to commit. I'd only verified how I could never trust my trust.

There'd been no choice but to act against myself, though. Doubting essential to overcoming doubt from the beginning. So I used newspaper articles and vague snippets of memory to fatigue my resolve. Refusing to explore the implications of so shattering a psychological instability was to risk striking out incorrectly, with actions based on lassitude. Not putting in the effort to make absolute that whatever I did served your best interests was tantamount to saying it didn't. I'd either step back or else run down the clock until no choice remained except to act randomly, without conviction, and abandoned of hope.

Wasn't it possible I'd dredged these names from my past and tailored a narrative to suit them? Cobbled together some ghastly horror show to combat then diseased myself with obsession over it? I was a broken person, my wits pestilent, that much seemed clear. If so, couldn't every effort in aid of what I called 'saving you' be a step toward enacting some hideous spree of murder, divorced from all purpose? Might I have been using you as an excuse, the impetus for my own destruction, a reason to obliterate all I cherished and leave behind only wasteland for as many people as I possibly could? Was I only pretending you were in danger? Worse still, was I playacting that I cared to extricate you from whichever hazard there was?

Perhaps my death during your birth wasn't guaranteed. A storyline I'd concocted to feed myself, allowance for acting out atrocious desires I harbored, a fever I'd succumbed to which'd end in taking my own life once you were cradled in my arms and the unforgivable deeds I'd wrought in your name overwhelmed me. Perhaps the only risk of death came with proceeding in the macabre brutality I'd been curating.

I asked myself quite pointedly how I'd let Deirdre get drawn into such lunatic notions. Demanded an honest and meticulous inventory of my constitution. The answer was evident. She'd been selected because I knew her, which meant I could find her, which meant I'd have access to kill her. I'd insisted she be included to render my task unspeakably horrific. The requirement to kill Deirdre, or to harm her by way of destroying her child, reinforced how only something as imperative as protecting you could bring me to the actions I felt compelled to take. Her death being a condition of your safety augmented how dreadfully actual the danger I felt toward you must be. Made at least part of what I'd perhaps only convinced myself was necessary seem impossible and therefore imperative to move ahead with. Deirdre'd been conscripted with dread intent because, were she not nemesis, I might've turned to her as confidant. Let her convince me I was in the throes of a psychotic episode requiring hospitalization. I'd have accepted her aid. Banked on her assurances. If she weren't off limits, she'd have stopped me. I'd chosen to brand her hideous to keep her one type of obstacle while barring her being another, more potent breed.

But had I chosen her? It was the names of your killers which'd occurred to me, not their mothers. I'd had to sleuth out the women's identities. Despairing how impossible such investigation had proven. Hadn't it been a debilitating shock when Deirdre'd been revealed a part of my soulless carnival?

Supposing my knowledge hadn't originated externally, there was little point relying on it. It made perfect sense to suppose I'd brought the name Benecourt in knowing I'd desired to eventually have Deirdre revealed as part of the nightmare. Lumped in with all the possible mothers. She had connection to Benecourt. Was my dearest friend. In itself, this was guaranteed to alarm me. Potentially halt my plans. Even without a confirmed pregnancy, the mere possibility of her becoming my victim would curb my ability to treat things as definitively disconnected from personal consequence, present the stakes as irrefutably dire.

I was aware of Martin Benecourt. Knew Deirdre knew him and at the very least moved in his circles. It seemed suspicious, but was nonetheless fact, how this either hadn't occurred to me until she'd brought him up or else I'd kept myself from bringing it to mind in order to best arrange the scenario.

The pregnancy couldn't be overlooked, however. I'd not've permitted myself to consider you safe until there was a definitive fetus in play. Just because it'd taken a period of time to decide as much didn't mean I ought doubt my own principles. If I'd truly set everything into motion unconsciously, I'd have tightly defined matters, insisted conditions be unassailable before I'd consider taking a life. Her pregnancy as a necessity was self-evident, in retrospect. Having no way to've known she'd become pregnant, it was too much a coincidence she had. Proved I couldn't have sorted things out things in advance.

Or might I have had some way of knowing something like that was bound to happen? Or if not bound, have been likely enough? I'd been unaware she'd maintained a crush on him, unless that was another trifle I'd buried the knowledge of unwittingly at some point, knew but purposefully ignored.

Whether or not I'd been aware Deirdre was pregnant when I'd first learned of your death, the timeline of her narrative dictated she must've been. What mattered was, on that day, I'd had no way to bank on her being or becoming pregnant with Martin Benecourt's child. Therefore, in the moment the name Benecourt became irreplaceable, it made zero sense to imagine I'd willfully summoned it.

Though why so steadfastly profess I couldn't have known? Exactly as I'd known many things in life, without magic or prophesy, I might've intuited it. Undercurrents, ripples, and drafts may've led some attuned portion of my wit to savvy Deirdre'd wind up in the situation she had. I might've grokked it when she'd first met Martin, similar to how I'd divined I'd be with your father or he'd augured that filthy vagrant would become an actor in some horror.

I'd long been aware she'd nursed far more than a blithe attraction to Benecourt. Had been attracted to him alongside her. If not for the present circumstances, would consider him attractive, still. I wasn't blind to how Deirdre conducted her life. Considering the type of person she was, some casual encounter between the two of them might well've proceeded precisely how the encounter she'd detailed actually had. Didn't I know the sort of conferences Deirdre attended for work? From there, might I have constructed a narrative based on a long-standing assumption she and Martin were bound to liaison when their paths inevitably crossed at one? Wasn't it possible Deirdre'd mentioned the conference she and her friend had romped with Martin during and I'd forgotten all about it due to the state of my life? Or else might I have been told he'd attended a similar conference the previous year and rightly deduced they'd meet up and become entangled? Couldn't Deirdre've made some casual remark following the tryst but before knowing she was pregnant I'd scarcely processed but which'd caused subtle stirring in my mind?

Such was the madcap knot my mind wreathed itself into. I couldn't disallow anything. Perhaps I'd spent an idle few moments daydreaming the prospect of Deirdre and Martin becoming an item, entertained it no more than any one of those million flickers of thought forgotten entirely, the endless ephemera which comprises the bulk of our lives, considerations scuttled without regret or regard.

In whichever part of me, there must've been brewing some degree of anxiety concerning what your forthcoming birth would mean to my individual identity and personal desires, simmering trepidation over the risks inherent in every breath I took and how such risks were doubled on account of the breaths you'd soon draw. I could name only a handful of those fears specifically, despite knowing there'd been countless. In that same underground of my consciousness, couldn't Benecourt and Deirdre have become a scenario while I'd simultaneously invented four others, each and every one compiled from information locked up within me? In a moment when whichever sub-mind I possessed was riddled with foreboding over what might happen to myself or to you during childbirth, couldn't these haunts have converged, colliding suddenly enough to instigate a jarring psychological chain reaction which'd cascaded through me, thoughts splintering into ideas which fractured into certainties until the smallest and most jagged shard of all seemed an imperative? Terror that your life would cost me mine. That I'd perhaps never know you. Be able to care for you, nourish you, keep you protected. It all might've hit me at once, with weight enough to seem both impossible and indisputable. Searching for proof that Certainty was what I'd felt in that moment, might I have supplied it in place of discovering it, constructed it from buildings blocks disguised enough to make coming upon them seem miraculous revelation?

Had it only struck me that the people who'd be responsible for your death were surrounding me because I'd cherrypicked them from those I knew were around? Every last conclusion, contradiction, and argument my investigations had landed me on prearranged by my own will, the labyrinthine efforts and anguish involved in hunting out the mothers of people who'd seemingly have nothing to do with me crafted to make imaginary villains appear provably concrete?

I could've chosen five names I subconsciously knew could be found. Not easily, but easily enough. Might've done so to lead myself consciously to them. Relieved and prepared to question matters no further.

Let me illustrate how even during the godless throes of exhaustion I'd not permit any consideration without justification. Each turn of the screw was audited, after which I badgered myself into cobbling up further lunacy I'd use to probe whichever conclusions arrived.

As vile a twist as Deirdre's pregnancy was, the event could've been bizarre coincidence imbued with underserved pertinence. My situation omitted, it didn't seem odd her life had come to such a head. Martin being the father might've been so coincidental it'd blinded me to how merely coincidental it was. Failure to treat it accordingly deflected me from exposing the Benecourt I sought. The trap here being I'd settle on an incorrect target, your killer slipping away while I took the life of his innocent namesake. Might erroneously convince myself there were other possible Benecourts just to avoid hurting Deirdre. Perform the mental acrobatics required to find a substitute victim for her child. I needed to think so, resist thinking so, and resist my resistance to thinking so, all at the same time.

For sake of thoroughness, I proposed that Deirdre hadn't been pregnant when the names of your killers occurred to me, despite knowing she had. So far as I'd known, she'd never sought motherhood nor would've been receptive to the idea had some *paramour* floated it. Only ever'd spoken of having children disdainfully. A life path she'd not be suffered to contemplate until distant years down the line, if at all. More comfortable regretting not having offspring than giving up a life free of responsibility to them. When I'd announced my pregnancy, we'd nearly wet ourselves laughing over her hissing that if I thought I was gonna peer pressure her into kerplunking her ambitions so I'd have a buddy to commiserate with when the other shoe dropped I'd have another think coming. Laughed harder still when she'd huffed "As the person you'll eventually turn to to ask where it went wrong, I can state on good authority, here and now, it was here and now your life went to rot and ruin, you cretin."

Whether I'd selected 'Benecourt' based on subconscious whim or the name had been stuffed into me by powers unknown made no difference. From the moment the five names were assigned, they had not and would not be altered or questioned. Perhaps Norman Benecourt was among the quintet because Martin Benecourt was the name of a man I'd been aroused by and had considered a relationship with in the past. Aware of his proclivity for *impromptu* sexual escapades, the odds suggested he'd wind up impregnating some woman, either on purpose or through lapse of precaution. Even without knowing she kept close tabs on him, Deirdre would've served as a link to the Benecourt name. Had she not become pregnant, there'd still exist every chance someone peripherally known to her would've. Someone accessible to me. Who I could track down. 'Benecourt' would've eventually led me to think of Martin and from there to contact Deirdre. I'd have learned he'd knocked someone up. Accepted whichever woman he had carried one of your assassins.

If he hadn't got anyone pregnant, I might've used that fact to convince myself your murderers weren't necessarily *in utero*, his name and character utilized as demonstrable proof my purpose could be served by killing whichever man would impregnate whichever women before they had opportunity. With Lowell, I'd considered something similar and dismissed it. But I'd only done so circumstantially. If time had marched on and there'd been no Benecourt discovered, Martin seeming to suddenly occur to me would've morphed my outlook. In a blink, despair and desperation making it seem unforgivable I'd insisted so fervently your killers were already fetal. I'd have lamented allowing myself to proceed on no more than assumption, woefully restricting your defense by chaining myself to conditions I'd failed to fully interrogate. Proclaimed it incorrect to've taken so militant and unbending a stance. Insisted doing so had obfuscated the obvious. Concluded the Lowell situation had resulted in a grave logical misstep. It would've appeared that all five women being with child and fitting whichever specifications of name wasn't strictly required. Some would present this way, others that. Circumstances and pressure would've convinced me to adapt.

Uncovering several women, already pregnant, who boasted or were in orbit of the infected surnames made it so I'd not had to seriously consider alternative presentations. I'd dismissed countless possibilities, offhand. Why look for another Lowell when I had proof I'd found the Lowell I needed? Why another Lyons, considering the specifics of how Montgomery got his first name? Why another Goaltender when the proximity of the one in my clutches to a duo of confirmed targets made it ludicrous to reconsider? Most especially, why waste time thinking Deirdre coupling with Martin hadn't bred the exact Benecourt I sought? Even were another Benecourt introduced the same week, mustn't I err on the side of the overwhelmingly macabre confluence of events which suggested the one my friend bore was the one to blot out?

That four pregnant women seemed to've been served up to me made it appear undeniable your every murderer already lurked in some womb. Having found so many in such similar condition in so short a timespan allowed me to cast aside the notion any may not yet've been actualized. Such dismissal hadn't been the result of investigation or the compelling rebuttal of specific scenarios I'd encountered, however. Had it proved necessary, I absolutely would've contorted my thought process. The opposite of what I'd incidentally settled on would acquire the sheen of inviolate truth.

Regardless of what'd literally happened with Deirdre, my mind would've wended round to Martin. In any of an infinite number of ways, I'd have lit upon reason to think of him. Whichever train of thought led me to would seem indicative of chance and fate overlapping. I'd have hemmed details as necessary. Found proof in lack of symmetry if symmetry didn't present.

One of your killers not yet existing could be another clever disguise, couldn't it? These three hid in the womb. This one hadn't yet been conceived. Perhaps the last remaining had already been born. Backed into a corner, I'd have convinced myself of anything as easily as its reverse. If need materialized, would've begun fervently believing altogether esoteric varieties of proof I'd never thought to consider and can't imagine for trying. In those treacherous days, learned doing anything to protect you might've meant doing anything whether it'd protect you or not.

Remove Deirdre, entirely. Observe the strict consideration given to details surrounding the Goaltender name. I'd come to remember having read an article containing the surname alongside memory of comments overheard within a din of voices. No longer doubted the name and alleged assault had been discussed in my presence nor that my perusal of the article had occurred soon after arriving in the area I'd subsequently become convinced your killers gestated within.

Laying out a timeline, it could be argued the Goaltender scenario'd seeded everything which occurred after. Freshly with child, still somewhat unnerved by my condition, disoriented from uprooting, and all the more discombobulated for my living arrangement being transient while a permanent change took place in my body and mind, I'd been a fertile soil for disquiet. Comments of rape, pregnancy, and a child never intended being fought for at all costs might've mingled with my newfound semi-isolation, the pulsing anxieties which already strained in me expanding as you did while I attempted to entertain them, coax more out, and subdue however many I could. Nothing was to be overlooked. You mustn't be left at the mercy of unexpected pitfalls.

It was plausible that a stream of thought, buried beneath countless others, had taken hold. Dreadful fixation hidden within banal concerns. Obsessive fret over diet, blood pressure, exercise. Compulsive self-doubt over whether I'd be possessed of the resolve to bear the pain of birthing you naturally without request for a numbing agent. Ceaseless fear you'd reject my breast milk or that I'd be unable to produce nourishing enough amounts. Nauseous unease over what'd happen if your father took ill, his work dried up, if I'd have more trouble returning to my position at the museum than anticipated, discover my desire to do so'd drained away. Insidious guilt I'd resent you for finding myself cut off from self-centric pursuits due to your being born with some physical defect or intellectual abnormality I'd be unable or unwilling to nurture you through. Soul draining terror I'd abandon you. Become capable of wishing you ill.

In such quagmire, a preoccupation on danger might've developed. The desire for a threat I could get my hands around, a vulnerability I could tangibly combat. I might've conjured a darkness, permitted it to engulf the superficial aspects of my life I could act on, the choices I had full control over, the problems with solutions dependent on my will. Knowing what limited amount of things met such criteria versus how many elements of life were beyond my control, an unthinkable horror might've been abstractly patchworked from the innumerable noias I regularly discovered worming their way into my mind. Perhaps I'd manufactured a single crisis to dwarf all others. A nightmare vaster than all fears combined. One I'd be able to convince myself could be overcome by way of accepting my own destruction. Doing so, I'd have freed myself of having to worry about anything except enacting vengeance for a crime I'd never know proof of. Impossible to control the world enough to make it unequivocally safe for you, I'd invented a way to guarantee your protection while at the same time'd kickstarted the trepidation that even constant and vigilant efforts wouldn't keep you secure.

In such state of mind, it made perfect sense this Goaltender-formerly-Wilmington woman and her conspicuous situation had superimposed on my thoughts, my psyche becoming a rough blend of my own perturbation and random actualization of it culled from the world around me. A mixture I'd soon forgot was such. Unable to recognize how my life had become driven by a series of thoughts nothing to do with corporeal existence, I could've confused myself for this other woman at the sub-molecular level, enflamed an instinct in the tight coil of my lizard brain which'd coaxed me to behave as this braver person would, this mother doing everything in her power to obtain justice for her daughter despite the psychic crucibles she'd have to endure. Carrying her child to term was emblematic of reshaping the path fate had written. The offspring would be provided for, given all it deserved, represent a triumph over the insult visited upon mother and child alike by one of the creatures who moved about so freely in an indifferent world. The child I carried would be likewise.

What shook me to the core as I attempted to sort matters out was that I didn't feel I could confidently discern what I genuinely remembered versus what I'd perhaps only invented. Did I honestly recollect the article about Goaltender, or was I simply giving consideration to how I might've come across it, based on its date of publication? Was I recalling the content of those briefly overheard remarks, or had I heard chatter about an entirely different assault which I now shoehorned Goaltender into? Had I not heard anything at all but cobbled together such scenario because it seemed plausible, after the fact? For all I knew, I'd dreamt about the party after my madness began and such dream now felt the same as a vague recollection. If the morsel of overheard conversation existed, I'd paid no attention to it. Peculiar I could summon it to mind, verbatim. More likely I'd convinced myself concentration allowed me the ability to unearth details from half-gone memories. All I really did was craft make believe and tinker with its content until things seemed drab enough to pass for actual. Not too much detail, not too little. Mundane. As with the Benecourt situation, it was further curious how, for all the effort I'd put into hunting down someone called Goaltender, such pertinent trove of personal experience hadn't sprung to mind. Odd that only after reading the article had I summoned up the conversation, only then could entertain the notion I'd been struck deeply enough by the stray phrases that I'd customized my life around them, yet hadn't recognized the name of the person referenced while actively searching them out. All taken into account, I didn't know if the conversation and the article were brief moments of my life which hadn't originally registered with much impact but nevertheless lurked in the soup of my unconscious, or if I'd merely convinced myself they were actual when it became convenient to.

Can you comprehend what it was like to subject myself to the third degree, unsure whether I housed honest memories or if I was asking questions only about what it'd mean if theoretical events were actual? How it felt to contemplate that I might be incapable of discerning the truth while simultaneously urging myself to act on your behalf only if I could?

Since I'd examined several articles, thinking back to a time before I had was infected with information I only possessed afterward. Possible my creeping desire for self-sabotage was convincing me of an unreality, manufacturing doubt so it'd be impossible to sort up from down. If I couldn't, I'd be unable to proceed a step further. Even if I truly had read the article, I'd obviously done so in a cursory enough manner the name Goaltender hadn't explicitly lodged. Or had read nothing more than the name and recalled it due its oddity. Might never've laid on eyes on any text, but recalled the name from the party and convinced myself I'd read it beforehand when I came across it, again. The same in reverse. I'd not encountered the name at the party but seen it in the article then afterward got it stuck in my head I'd overheard it. Perhaps someone had said something on an altogether different, unremembered occasion which'd taken place after the party and I'd transposed the name into memory of the party because the party seemed the more likely place to've heard it due to discussions about film ideas concerning murder, sinister happenings, and fanciful conspiracies of the macabre.

The more I drilled down, the more dubious the entire proposition became. I might've first learned about Goaltender entirely isolated from articles or get-togethers and the name then occurred to me on the day I first knew you'd die. Afterward, might've worked to convince myself whatever the first possible place I could've seen or heard it was the point it'd entered my lexicon. Going from that supposition, it was logical to choose the party or the earliest mention in any newspaper I could've flipped through since my arrival. Supposing I'd bumped into the name at both points, the scrap of conversation occurring so near in time to the date of the article might've led me to select the name Goaltender precisely because it might later appear I'd discovered it while working to prove or disprove my delusion of needing to keep you safe from ethereal dangers. So far into my pursuit, reduced to a state of physical exhaustion, spiritual agitation, mental confusion, self-doubt, finally too depleted to go on and desiring reason to abandon course, I'd forced the two items together. The result was this crisis of belief. The elements deceptively related because in a story they would've been. My mind taking cues from your father's scripts. From the films or novels he'd endlessly dissect. Using thematic ideas, plot holes, and swerve endings pickpocketed from works meant for casual entertainment to stay my hand. Were I a character, my plight would be representational of some larger conceit. One I'd take the clear lesson of to heart were I audience regarding myself. 'Fate can't be avoided. The Future can't be known. It's always a mistake to behave otherwise.'

Easy enough to reverse-engineer my every thought, see the principal concept I'd tarted superficial details atop. 'You mean that girl who's keeping the kid?' might've been all I'd heard at the party. No mention of Goaltender. Perhaps later I'd glimpsed the article about Wilmington's assault and her decision not to terminate her pregnancy. Wondered if she was who the overheard question had referenced. Just like that, pieces may've clicked. From there I could've idly recollected one of a dozen strangers blathering at me about writing a script 'torn from the headlines.' Nothing to do with Goaltender, but I'd inserted contextualizing details into the mix. So despite the article having been the sole place I'd seen the name, I'd become convinced it was the second. That I'd taken note because of what I'd eavesdropped at the party. My attention drawn to the article on account of the headline. *A Mother's Nightmare Conundrum.* 'Goaltender' appeared in it exactly once, while

Wilmington repeated two dozen times. Well within the realm of possibility I'd not remarked the Goaltender bit until I'd revisited the piece after stumbling upon the most recent article. Perfectly plausible I'd come to think it must've been where I'd learnt the name despite evidence proving how it only might've been. I was ready to dismiss the memory of the get-together chatter as being based on the article, but could also dismiss the article being the origin of the Goaltender name, because the same mechanism which allowed me to scuttle recollection of the party demonstrated how my memory of reading the older article might've been based on the knowledge of the Goaltender name which'd come upon me months afterward.

It made the most sense to think of the matter in such way. If I hadn't glimpsed the tiny article in that coupon Gazette, I wouldn't have sought other newspapers. If I hadn't done that, never would've looked at the newspaper I'd marked as the first I could've conceivably read. If I hadn't done both those things, never've recalled comments from the party I'd not given second thought to until reading articles discovered long after. Most importantly, I wouldn't have done any of that if the Goaltender name hadn't appeared in my mind, *ex nihilo*.

The flow worked as tidily in both directions. Accurate to posit how only with the full spread of information I presently possessed did I have access to the elements required to concoct a garden path to lead myself down. Any clean timeline was impossible to sort straight. What had I seen first, thought about first, what second, third, fourth, which of those'd influenced which, which was true, could be true, and which, though it could be true, wasn't? Memory was no better than tossing a dart. Came down to selecting a startpoint as my prompt to proceed or my reason to back away.

Dismiss coming to Benecourt via Deirdre and Martin as figment of my imagination. Ignore the

Goaltender affair because, at a squint, it was plausible I'd doctored things up through the whims of a mental affliction. What was to be made of Lyons and Lowell? Explain how I'd come across first and surnames matching those I'd already chosen, in both cases. Having read up to this point, you must find yourself asking some questions. We can't overlook how I'd known the killers' names before I'd sought out the women. So what of those two?

Uncovering them'd been nothing to do with being painstaking or methodical. You know from what I've related how both discoveries were downright spooky, the specifics nothing I could've marshalled into existence. But I demanded exploration of the chance Lowell and Lyons were the result of my mind playing tricks. What danger? Nothing would alter what I knew about my fate and yours. Regardless of whether I concluded my targets were selected in a fit of abject psychosis or revealed by the breath of God, the only way to guarantee your safety was action against them. Concluding I'd invented the circumstances which led to their discovery left the question 'What if my ability to invent them was what allowed me to save you?' Terming my knowledge 'insanity' or 'presentiment' made no demonstrable difference so far as the underlying threat. As long as such threat might remain, I'd no alternative to behaving as though it did. If the terms of your approaching death remained unaltered, it was inconsequential how I prodded at the thesis of why, how, or even if I knew what I knew. Anything short of acting before your birth was too extreme a risk. If I failed to then didn't live past your birth you were doomed. Were I proved wrong about everything, I'd have killed whoever I had without justification. Nothing short of doing so proved doing so was in vain. The time for reconsiderations would come if I killed but lived past your birth. Little matter whether I braced for recriminations.

I desired what I knew to be an apparition. The only method to convince myself it was involved doing everything in my power to destroy my belief in the possibility what I knew was the truth. This desire to disprove doubts and to prove them alike may've been element of the ungodly trap. Your killers counted on the mire of my innate decency to halt my revenge. If what I knew was an actual preview of a future which could only be unwritten through drastic measures, no purpose was served by killing the incorrect parties. Action required certainty. Certainty demanded my plight be rigorously tested. If I was the enemy, I needed to defeat myself on whichever front. If the quirk of chance which might lead me to stand down wasn't the inability to locate individuals with the correct assemblage of name and physical condition, but instead was an internal current of hesitation which'd allow you to die simply because I didn't want to kill, I needed to excavate it fully. Excise it without quarter.

Lenora'd approached without prompt. A woman whose offspring was carried by surrogate. I'd assumed such child would be male on the strength one of your killers was called Alexander Lowell, same as the child's father. This seemed sound enough, especially when embedded within other queer intersections of happenstance. Lenora'd asked whether we'd met previously. We'd proved to be complete strangers. Our only connection the surrogate I'd originally encountered on a playground with no idea of her condition.

The particulars of this affair were markedly compact. I'd only lived in the area for little more than a month and been shy of three months into my pregnancy when first I'd known all I knew. When exactly could I not only have met Lenora Lowell but learned her husband was named Alexander and gleaned some inkling her child was wombed in another woman? Every last one of those elements had to be in evidence for me to've secretly chosen the name in advance, arranged a breadcrumb trail ending in 'discovery.' Anything less than having been privy to all that information and knowing I planned to commit murder meant I'd randomly selected the name Alexander Lowell and it'd fit faultlessly, entirely by chance.

Lenora's 'no no no no' in response to my inquiring whether she was pregnant came to mind. That curious tone. How it'd struck me immediately there existed an inherent mystery in it. By then, countless women'd told me they weren't pregnant in ways ranging from matter-of-fact to ribald to obscene, but this perfectly innocuous dismissal had piqued my suspicion keenly. Only because it'd been she who'd approached me and I'd come to learn her surname? Or had we actually met previously, her chuckle so pronounced because she recalled such meeting but'd gleaned I'd genuinely forgotten it, amused at my question being one I ought already've known the answer to? Under the impression our rapport'd been more meaningful, has she overcompensated with affability to avoid the awkwardness resulting from feeling brushed off?

No. Lenora and I absolutely hadn't met. The surrogate and I had. On more than one occasion. But I'd been unaware of her pregnancy or its origin. It wasn't until the motherhood meeting I'd learned she was with child and had connection to Lenora. So she couldn't have been the source of my information.

Except as I set my thoughts intently, directly addressed the matter in strict isolation, it occurred to me I had seen the surrogate prior to our encounters at the park. Would've known she was pregnant well before I'd known of your death or your killers. I'd seen her in the waiting room of my obstetrician. In the company of a man I'd thought to be her father, due to the clear difference in their ages and his demeanor seeming more caretaking than romantic. We hadn't interacted. I doubt either'd taken notice of me. But I'd scrutinized them both. Recalled a tinge of guilt for being judgmental. Why couldn't the man sitting beside the young woman be the father of her child? What could it possibly have to do with me?

Further recalled the surname 'Mothfin' being called out by the receptionist working the Check-In station as I'd chided myself for being a prudish busybody. The surrogate'd perked up then slunked down with an almost imperceptible shiver of nervousness. The man'd looked up, widened his eyes, and gave a little nudge to her knee with his. At which she'd stood. Scraped upper teeth over lower lip. Nodded at the nurse who held open the door leading to the consultation rooms. I'd found it curious the man hadn't accompanied her. Kept mistrustful eye on him. A few minutes before my own name was called, a plump receptionist approached him, carrying a clipboard. The two spoke in the polite hush adopted in medical environments, but due to my proximity their attempt to secure privacy had the opposite effect. It was as though I couldn't ignore every nasally chirp from the woman. She'd began their muted conference with 'Alexander?' He'd given a nod of assent. She'd glanced to the clipboard, repeated 'Alexander,' then followed it up with the surrogate's surname, which he'd corrected her about by politely whispering 'Lowell.' It was then my own appointment'd been called and I'd stopped paying attention.

From that moment until the moment I sat actively working to recall such details, I'd not given the encounter a thought. But the name 'Alexander Lowell' had been spoken aloud. In the context of my questioning why the man couldn't have been the father of the child the practically-still-a-child he'd sat beside carried rather than the father of the practically-still-a-child carrying it. The surrogate, 'Alexander,' and a question of parentage, all in a package. That Lenora later bumped into me was striking coincidence. Enough to've cemented the notion I'd only discovered the surrogate after such chance encounter, especially as the initial encounter with the surrogate would've been during a time I'd not've had reason to note it. Had I discovered her exactly as I had at the doctor's office but never encountered Lenora outside the bookshop, my mind surely would've recalled her, just the same. If there'd been no Lenora who'd called herself Lowell and mentioned her husband Alexander, eventually I would've brought to mind the surrogate in conjunction with the name Lowell and found the name Alexander waiting, as well. Such would've resulted in discovering Lenora. Would've been all the proof necessary to strike against her and the surrogate, both. The unlucky woman introducing herself was ancillary. An extra touch of the inexplicable to keep me from doubt, a nuance which'd assured me I'd found a culprit but now furnished me with reason to doubt whether I had.

Though I told myself I'd seen the surrogate and Alexander Lowell exactly as I've just described, the timing made the memory feel topaz. It seemed no more correct to say all those things had definitively happened than to say I merely thought I'd seen the surrogate and Alexander, imagined I'd overheard what I had. So long after the fact and embedded in the context of investigation, I couldn't ascertain whether I was dealing myself a fraudulent hand. An encounter so detailed, textured, and boasting as many glaring pieces of concrete data as it did ought to've occurred to me ages before. Why hadn't it? Considering the intensity of my fixation, how on Earth had I never recalled the Alexander Lowell from the waiting room? Why hadn't Lenora pointing in the direction of the building where my obstetrician's office was located while indicating her husband, Alexander, had business there jogged my memory? Having met the surrogate and confirming she was connected to Lenora, why had it still not? Why only after trotting through all the dressage I'd tormented myself with were these memories reemerging? Why at a time when all they could do was sew confusion and plague me with doubt?

Was it my mind's way of proving what I'd ascribed to wild coincidence was instead reality I'd been able to uncover due to an instinctual acuity? Did it prove I'd noticed innocuous things all around and, without need for conscious effort, intuited a primal threat I'd understood to bulwark myself against? On a preternatural level, perhaps my attentions had been activated, had verified the storm suggested by the rumble behind the cloud cover, precise memories left out to show how a calculus of the threat could be achieved without them, the selfsame memories finally arriving to codify the result.

It was only the conventions subscribed to by those I lived amongst which required assurances before judgment was rendered and action permitted. Left to the animal aspects of my motherhood, the concept of consequences didn't exist. If a dog sensed threat toward its pup, it needn't prove the danger to the satisfaction of any general tribunal. Whatever happened would happen. Life would continue in the wake of its response.

Despite it being correct not to consider certain events connected to my knowledge coincidence, was it yet incorrect to view them as anything beyond repulsive constructs of my perverse psyche? Did the latecoming presence of memories which ought to've been the first things to've occurred showcase I'd always been in possession of abundant raw materials from which to mockup whichever scenario suited my fancy and that there was variety enough to such fodder I could pivot in any direction I wished to best lead myself along by the nose? Did this miraculous appearance of more evidence than I'd ever need do nothing more than prove I couldn't shoo away the possibility it'd been self-manufactured? Proclaiming 'What're the odds I'd find people and situations right in the city around me matching exactly the names my mind knew, out of thin air?' was meaningless if the odds were whatever I'd decided they were or might choose to make them.

As all this hit home,
I demanded still more scouring analysis of the circumstances to date, one which left no fleck of information uninterpolated. If nee-

dling myself with the available evidence of Benecourt, Goaltender, and Lowell illustrated my subconscious was orchestrating reasonless mayhem, what of Lyons? With three-out-of-five names considered my invention, it ought be lazy work to find like origination for the fourth. Except no clever explanation for Lyons materialized. I'd never laid eyes on the woman who wore the surname, lived within spitting distance, and insisted her unborn child chose the name Montgomery for itself. Even if I'd chanced upon her some innocuous way, she'd never personally known or been in the orbit of anyone named Montgomery, hadn't for a split second considered the name, nor found it to have private connection to her. It was without precedent and although it'd caused friction with her husband she wouldn't so much as entertain a substitute moniker. The one and only time we'd met, I hadn't introduced the name. Such interaction lasted all of twenty minutes, during which she'd intimated how her immediate acceptance of 'Montgomery' astonished her.

You see how it never ended? My mind was the schoolyard bully, worked to cudgel me into discomfiture by admitting and emphasizing how the Lyons situation was utterly inexplicable. Reasoning allowed that the conditions under which the name Montgomery Lyons had been tendered were impossible to re-cast as anything with sensible lineage. Nothing short of uncanny, they couldn't even be called coincidence. I went so far as to deem them miraculous.

Here was a new contraption of torture. Was I prepared to proclaim one freakish situation out-of-five grounds enough to accept everything rather than insist it was the rationale necessary to dismiss all my so-called proofs, outright? The other three discoveries had in common how I could explicate where every element of them originated, retrace them to my own experiences. Each seemed to bolster the others. The Lyons situation lacked this pedigree. Perhaps ought be discarded for being the odd duck. On the other hand, its eldritch attributes might be what justified its inclusion. Indeed, such conspicuousness could mean Lyons was the only name properly confirmed. Comparing the four cases, it made sense to posit Montgomery the single killer I'd actually unmasked, precisely because the circumstances of his discovery were so queer. The other three unborn children might've been entirely innocent. Blind alleys and trap streets I'd led myself down to incorrectly dispense my vengeance. There was every reason to surmise the discovery of Montgomery Lyons being so flabbergasting should make it the gold standard for how victims were selected. Being able trace the origin of a name directly to the windmills of my mind might be another way your killers worked to elude me.

Or was I suggesting conditions had changed? That I couldn't possibly kill the wrong people? Of course not. Ending sinless lives wasn't any more impossible than slaughtering the accursed. Nothing altered how I might die thinking you safe while you'd been made exponentially vulnerable due to blunders I'd committed. Nothing could be trusted unless everything could. But if everything could, anything could. By this declension, any certainty both spawned an uncertainty and spit out a new absolute, every absolute proving nothing was absolute, at all.

None of which altered the game. The same pieces sat on the board. Conditions of play remained intact. Whether I argued with a third party or with the clot of the voice in my head was irrelevant. A ponderous string of one-off arguments could mootly parade past. I'd forever be forced to agree with whichever pedantic possibility presented itself for inspection. Any agreement would leave everything the same as it always'd been. I could concur with everything or with nothing, but could only act in one way, ignoring all others. As it'd been since the first moment, it remained. I might kill the wrong five people. The wrong ten, counting mothers and children. Could slay the incorrect twenty. Murders piling up due to circumstances which'd emerge along the way to produce collateral damage I'd not energy enough even to contemplate. Any effort spent couching matters otherwise was misdirection. Neither reason nor understanding altered the irrefutable fact that if the five specific people who'd kill you were never to exist, those five specific people could do you no harm. Only their elimination fully guaranteed they wouldn't. Eliminating nobody guaranteed they would.

You can guess how, by this point, I'd decided to kill the mothers along with their litters. Hopeful notions there might be a workaround had withered. Argument for slaughtering mothers and children alike were devilish, to be sure, but the proposition itself was the only I'd honestly discovered no sound counter for. I also couldn't deny it made my task immeasurably simpler.

Who five women were currently pregnant with perhaps wouldn't grow to be your killers but were your killers, to any degree which concerned me. Supposing otherwise was rhetorical delay. It was also expressible that while these five yet lived there was no way to determine if you'd have other killers were these eradicated. If they lived, you'd live until thirty. If they died at my hand, your life until thirty became lottery. A new five might butcher you at twenty, drown you at fifteen, poison you at seven, kill you and me both before you were born. The mechanism by which the world functioned dictated I already apprehended all I needed to. In one sense, it served to reason that killing only the unborn children meant you were safe. However, if the mothers were left alive they might birth other children. If I'd damaged them to the extent they couldn't conceive on their own, they might yet be able to broker surrogates or else adopt. I'd no guide to what made a child 'theirs.' But however 'their children' arrived, it was possible the names of your killers would be given them and it'd turn out they'd been who I'd known would grow to murder you. Perhaps when these five were dead I'd be granted knowledge of ten more. Learn how despite my best effort no method to wrest you from your unwarranted fate existed. Perhaps it'd require the deaths of the lot for terms to shift. If four lived, four would kill you. Same as if three or two or one. If the fifth was killed and I learned, again, you'd be killed in your thirtieth year by Benecourt, Goaltender, Lowell, Lyons, and Tellwell, how would I proceed? Did killing the mothers only after it'd been proven conclusively that the slightest mercy added to your peril spoil the broth? I didn't honestly believe if the mothers were slain another set with the same names would sprout another quintet of children with the same names, even though such eventuality would prove my knowledge correct. Nor did I believe that, after enacting my executions, a totally different series of names would take the place of the dead. Something along those lines might transpire in one of your father's stories, all theory and symbolism, but my situation being actual made such logic and balance unlikely. Five specific mothers were as central to your fate as the children they nourished. If five others birthed five others it wouldn't alter what I knew. If ten or even fifty new killers emerged, my knowledge remained. I freely admitted every one of the infinite possibilities which might be proposed, but those infinite possibilities meant nothing so far as what I must do. The only indisputable proof that I'd been correct would be my death during your birth followed by your death, thirty years on, at the hands of five beasts who didn't yet crawl the Earth. I didn't need to prove myself correct, because I couldn't be proved incorrect, either. Needed to save you, as best I could manage. Nothing more. Belief that anything mattered beyond safeguarding you was a coward's way of accepting your fate. Refusing my own will meant I believed you'd lack any will of your own.

At times I found myself enraged. There were moments I literally gnashed my teeth in cartoonish anger, seething toward the bathroom mirror or into the empty air above me while I lay soaking in the tub. Hours spent silently cursing the rhetorical existence of armchair theoreticians who'd point out the endless reasons I ought not go on. I cursed everyone. Damn them, after all. If I could admit being unsure of myself, lacking confidence in the success of whatever course I'd undertake, why couldn't whoever I'd tell of it so much as entertain the notion I might be correct? Perhaps they'd disagree with how I was conducting myself, find the methods I was proceeding by reprehensible, but why couldn't they accept what I knew even as a farfetched possibility? Must they so recalcitrantly deny you were in danger and that my failure to act equated to letting you die while allowing your murderers to live? Couldn't they allow there were slim odds I was correct and, from there, accept how my being correct would mean your murderers didn't deserve a breath of the life they'd have decades of?

If these glib, holier-than-thou auditors possessed knowledge of some way I might keep you safe without hurting another, let them spell it out for me. I'd not only humor their scholarship, I'd desire it to be sound. But whatever shopworn morsel of ethics or sagacity they'd dole out would be one I'd exhaustively considered and dismissed. I'd provide them with every reason why and in turn demand they admit how whatever they suggested wasn't genuine guarantee or irrefutable defense. My God, if some notion proffered me meant I'd no need to harm anybody, I'd gratefully enact the edict and die in peace while you emerged from me.

But all I'd hear ooze from their earnest hearts amounted to 'Let Tasha Die.' Brandishing the efforts of my own mind as proof of their abstract conclusion, they'd instruct me how nothing could be guaranteed with unassailable certainty, therefore the only conscionable course was to warn someone dear to me and trust they'd take the sentiment to heart and behave as my agent, once I was gone. They'd tell me to leave it to fate and hope fate wasn't real.

My vehemence over this point became more potent the longer I dwelled on it. What made these bastards so cocksure I was wrong?

Because it displeased them to think otherwise? Due to it running contra to platitudes they'd heard mouthed and held as articles of faith, ideals they wanted to believe but believed only now-and-then?

What would they say were I proved correct? If I died during your birth and you died at the hands of the exact five devils I'd predicted in the exact year I'd promised, they'd not admit I was correct, even still. I knew this, you know this, and if these words find audience beyond you such others know this and have been thinking it every moment spent reading. All would tell me that I'd not known what I'd known. Never allow I'd been correct to've desired to accomplish what I'd failed, even as they watched me flounder. They'd clinically observe it'd happened. As rote as acknowledging a sunrise, the closing of a car door, or a sip of Ginger Ale swallowed. But they'd insist it having happened hadn't meant what I'd said it meant. Wouldn't spare a spec of appraisal in support of my tormented belief. Their admission of the event combined with the dismissal of my account of it would serve the same as mocking me, mocking you, and cheerleading your death. Oh they'd certainly allow it meant something. Everything meant something, after all. But it meant only something they could see and which I was blind to. They'd insist the fact you'd died exactly as predicted was more acceptable by far than were I to've acted to protect you how I'd intended. Without scruple, they'd accept finding you viciously slaughtered at the hands of the creatures I'd named appropriate. To insult us further, would accept whichever reason your killers gave for what they'd done as official. The ugly rationale or commonplace motive floated would be set down for posterity as the exclusive reason you'd died. Your death would be tragic, but not until it came to pass. Yet were I to commit my killings, all would call the act abhorrent. Worse, they'd call it tragic but on account of insisting the lives I'd taken contained potential good which had been obliterated alongside their flesh. They'd mourn lives which they'd say weren't lives because they hadn't been lived. Label the deaths reasonless because of my reason. However insane or misguided the motive your killers provided, it'd at least be a reason they could summarily dismiss the morality and societal acceptability of then never expend another ounce of effort considering. If your killers proffered no reason for why they'd descended upon you, it'd be taken as proof there'd been no reason for you to've died. Were I alive to hear them, they'd say flat to my face 'Your daughter died because there's evil in this world.' Feel their sentiment refined. But were I to've taken the lives of your killers and said to them 'My daughter lived because there's evil in this world' every last one would wish they could've killed me themselves.

There exist infinite ways to urge oneself to go through with whichever atrocity. To coax and goad until an overwhelming pitch is reached. Compulsion drowns all scruples or hope for any other path forward. I'd experienced thousands of pulses which'd pushed me to the moment of crisis. Made myself capable, desirous to act. Felt I'd arrive at such pique more than once each day. Every trail leading to the sensation unique. I'd trespassed into a permanent mindset. The fruition of such impulses was guaranteed were a moment of genuine opportunity to allow them reign. But how does one kill? What were the specifics of undertaking murder? How does one not only kill but kill and kill again? How is the possibility of a second murder arranged by the details of the first, a third act possible following a second, a fifth queued by a fourth? How would I kill?

There are finite ways to take a life. Infinitesimal compared to the methods for building up the appetite. Less for each subsequent killing. Every new method of dispatch required refinement over its predecessor. At the same time, required utter distrust of any step previously taken, however successful. Each killing a total reset. Individual contemplation of death predicated both on what was learned by the act already committed and avoiding the slightest influence from it.

There was no magic bullet to be utilized repeatedly. Repetition led to pattern. Attempting to avoid a pattern became repetition resulting in pattern. Avoidance of repetition generated links between actions which'd be connected by investigators. Such was how killers got pinched. Sequence and causality were impossible to avoid. This leads to This leads to This which leads to This Other to lead right back to the source. If savvy and lucky enough to avoid chance witnesses, a killer's bound to be foiled by the specific steps taken to avoid detection. These build up as further killings transpire. Eventually a pile of non-repetitions becomes a shimmering circle around the perpetrator. Tight as the grip of a noose.

The moment I crossed into the realm of action, I'd have to contend with trained professionals examining what I'd done in preparation to taking that irreversible step. To those who'd dedicated their lives to ensuring no crime went unpunished, there was no difference between me not having killed but readying myself to and me after the bodies were cold. Were I suspected, detectives wouldn't only consider how I presented myself following whichever malfeasance, but pour over the details of my life in the days, weeks, and months leading up. Diabolically intelligent people who'd cite endless nuance in any crumb of evidence I dribbled. Be able to enumerate the zillion ways whichever residues I'd leak could only've been left behind by me. Stains of nobody else would exist for cultured extrapolation. Any effort to eliminate them would leave stains all its own. Authorities had means and time to match any trace found one place to those discovered in another. Prove them identical even if they'd appear wildly different when held side-by-side. Specks of myself littered to the ground by successful heels as they fled the horrors I'd commit would become the entirety of me.

It needn't be physical scales shed. In the preposterous fantasy no tactile clues were available for professionals to paw over, there'd be indications of the workings of my mind. Invisible telltales, more valuable than fingerprints. If I'd hidden in one spot instead of another, exited via a different door than the one through which I'd entered, performed a certain series of actions versus different ones altogether in my attempted cover up. Every decision granted rich insights. Investigators' experience would narrow the field of suspects from 'anyone' to 'likely parties' to me. Seasoned cops would glean more from the aftermath of my first crime than I'd ever be able to foresee. What they uncovered suggesting I'd perpetrate something further. The second murder of a pregnant women would indicate there'd be a third. From the irrevocable reality of what I'd done and the manner in which I'd done it, they'd sniff out their prey. Divine from which techniques I'd employed to stalk, access, kill, and flee which I'd utilize next. What I'd avoid doing to get at such victim would be determined by sifting through the essence of what I'd already tried to avoid. What I wouldn't do would reveal what I would. Once my pursuers had multiple data points to work from, I'd materialize. No more elusive than the elementary image poorly concealed in a children's dot-to-dot.

There was no getting around how everything I'd do had been done before. By many others. For countless reasons. I was nothing but another scourge. Perhaps not even possessing unique rationale to those schooled in such matters. Were I to explain myself when apprehended, those listening would've heard my reasons countless times. Trained on case studies which contained a term for me. Know exactly how to trip me up in interrogation because others exactly like me had been snared in the past. I was predictable even as I'd no idea what I'd do. A humdrum *cliché* my pursuers would scoff. The more precautions I took, the louder I announced myself. Those who'd strive tirelessly to catch me already knew me better than I knew myself.

The most damning element of my trap was that planning each subsequent murder necessitated as much time as its predecessor. To freely continue, I'd need to assess not only what I was going to do, imminently, but how to proceed in a manner which'd reinforce precautions concerning what I'd already done and would do next. More and more time, more and more thought devoted to examining the unforeseeable. How does one accomplish any murder beyond the first when the thought and time possible for each decreases exponentially as the pressure increases in kind?

How could I murder the guilty without also murdering the innocent? I couldn't rid myself of the question. Was such thing possible when both shared a flesh? Were method discovered, could I terminate the guilty without leaving the innocent who housed them as witness against me?

Killing the mothers remained the coldest guarantee. Seemed the easiest sport. Shooting. Stabbing. Strangulation. Poison. Your executioners would curdle in their hideouts. Why had my intention ever been otherwise? Why did the glitch of such scruple remain? I'd die, why shouldn't they? If all five mothers were taken as a whole, the group considered a single target, wasn't one allowing themself to be murdered the formula by which the largest number might survive? If the aim was to defend the group, everyone in it together against me, the best odds for any set of mother-and-child to remain was another set being slaughtered. The requisite investigation of such would yield the most benefit.

An indisputable murder of mother-and-child would trigger vigorous safeguards, no corner cut. Warnings broadcast. A madman targeting pregnant women lurked in the area. Abundant caution must be exercised. Were widespread precautions adopted, all avenues of approach would be closed off. Every mother's guard perpetually up. The lot transformed into hectoring paranoiacs whose eyes would be on each other for their own sakes. I might kill one with only the natural obstacles inherent in such act, perhaps two, depending on how opportunity presented, but after that there'd exist little chance of evading capture or striking again.

Overtly killing one mother-and-child at-a-time would be detrimental to my cause, the first bettering the odds the other four would live. The same wasn't true if I more cleverly dispatched the gestating fetuses, alone. Arranged to seem accidents, my acts would each exist in their own vacuum. Tragically foreshortened pregnancies wouldn't raise eyebrows outside of those immediately affected. Certainly wouldn't lead to an all-points bulletin or a general state of neighborhood vigilance.

But while each mother would sacrifice themselves to protect their child, they'd never sacrifice themselves and their child to safeguard mothers-and-children-at-large. Given the choice, each would sacrifice one of the others and the child within them rather than allow themselves to be the entity made tribute, even if such selflessness guaranteed the lives of the rest. They'd not act against their piglets any more than I'd be moved not to act on your behalf.

Once again, I began thinking all might be lost. Tortured unceasingly with the belief I'd discovered the reasons I'd fail to change anything. The notion that saving you'd ever been possible dribbled away, any previous moment of certainty proving me a fool. Grotesque rationale settled in. If not even the murder of your killers could secure my life, there was no reason to believe those same murders could secure yours. Why entertain hope your fate might alter so much as a jot when I knew mine couldn't?

Except I could alter mine. Simply by denying you any. If I terminated my pregnancy, I couldn't die birthing you. It being demonstrable my fate could be altered, why insist yours was immutable? If one change might upend the future I knew, it followed that other changes must be able to. Even in terms of nightmare logic, the assertion that the only possible alteration was for you not to live and me to go on at your expense didn't wash.

I'd circle through these thoughts until exhaustion took hold. Return without any change to my outlook. It remained possible I'd change nothing, regardless what I knew. That I wouldn't bring myself to terminate you was an absolute fact, after all. I could speak out or write down the words describing how I might, but those made no difference.

No chance to save you'd been awarded. Rather a heartless punishment doled out. A consequence for me to experience in advance. Because I'd fail in so unforgivable a charge but not live to suffer appropriately afterward, I was cursed to endure a torment beyond my death in the hours leading to it. All I'd done was foresee my failure. The price of it.

To resist despair, I re-entertained long debunked notions. Why didn't it make sense to kill just once? Didn't doing so at least prove something could be altered? Wasn't it as secure a plan to trust to the technicality that your fate-made-different equaled your known-fate-avoided? There were moments I honestly couldn't recall why I'd abandoned a course which seemed so judicious. In others, despite recalling precisely why, I no longer felt convinced.

If I killed one mother, only four of the five people who'd kill you could exist. Which meant my knowing five people would kill you may've been true at one time but was no longer accurate. One successful murder didn't make what I knew before incorrect, merely altered 'What I knew' to 'What I'd known.' Such alchemy had always been my goal. Something irrefutably altered by the death of one killer meant elements of what I'd known might be altered, in general. My own death, therefore, might be avoided without eliminating 'the mother who carried the ringleader' or whatever terms I'd put into play when examining the postulate we both might be saved.

One murder was principally no different than five. Five no different than ten or however many more. So perhaps I was incorrect to assume I couldn't save my own life without it costing yours.

Cudgeled myself over why I was so insistent I'd die no matter what. Demanded that if I wasn't absolute in my belief you'd die at thirty, full stop, there was no reason not to expend efforts seeing to it I lived through your birth. Doing so would mean a definitive change had occurred. Invalidate any foreknowledge. I wouldn't perish of magic, after all, but some medical complication. So it made as much sense to bury my doctors underneath every concern I could conjure, sweat them to take extreme steps to ensure my life, as it did to plot murders against strangers over what they were naming their children.

I used these notions to beat myself into submission. Attempted to believe them so I'd stand down. But they were as much nonsense as they'd ever been. Side-streets of mercurial rationalization or rhetoric I'd squirm down. But resetting the stage one moment to the next left the same glaring consideration as always. The one which made moot any other. Never once had I said other solutions weren't possible, only that possibility was no guarantee. In the unaltering face of such truth, I needed to choose whichever option produced the most possible security. Regurgitated thoughts about idealized paths forward were just an aspect of my torture. I'd never cease looping them nor keep from having them lead to my retreading the same impotent hopes. While I'd rethink what I'd already thought better of, the clock would run down, and I'd have done nothing. Why? Because of schoolkid semantics. 'I might accomplish nothing even if I did everything in my power' meant 'I might accomplish nothing even if I did everything literally possible.' But doing 'literally everything' was beyond the scope of reality and there was no percentage in killing for vainglorious failure.

You'd be lost. I'd be lost. Why visit our loss on others? Why not accept what I knew and find succor in the fact you'd live your three decades, do all I could to inspire you toward experiencing as much with that life as you could? I was thirty-four. You'd live not even a half-decade less than me. I'd lived. I'd accomplished. Had I known the precise date of my end in advance, there was no telling what more I would've made of myself.

This quirk tightened my focus. Showed me I'd come to an *impasse*. With only theoretical paths available, I'd naturally begun backtracking for overlooked clues. Because 'everything I could do' wasn't only not everything but was far from enough.

Possessing four of the required five victims rather than the bunch made my limitations acute. Before proceeding, I'd need to meticulously plan. Know all who must die. From that, determine how to ordinate my acts. Each must defend its subsequent. The bald truth remained that the truest way to be assured of success was to eliminate all targets. Ideally within as short a period of time as possible. The absence of a fifth victim protected the identified four from a mindless spree, cut me off from gathering them into a single area to be done away with as a unit. Little wonder all my mind had left was to fruitlessly parse what I already knew, dredge it for inconsistencies which'd reveal some mathematical misstep clouding the vital piece of information. Lacking your fifth killer's whereabouts made it only natural to return to square one. The only point at which hope had ever seemed to exist.

Without the knowledge of who harbored Marcy Tellwell, your salvation was no more than a moot theorem. Supposing I'd immediately killed the four creatures I knew the whereabouts of, murdered the first the moment he'd been tracked down, gotten clean away with the crime, then followed such a trajectory with the others, all it'd mean was more time for investigators to smoke me out. Without a fifth mother, acting on any piece of knowledge aided in the protection of the other four. Any death served to make me the hunted party of a foe with infinitely more resources to uncover my identity than I had to carry out my cause.

As the hours of my life dwindled and the need for aggressive action became definitive, my arguments and equivocations grew.

Reasons not to act soured my impulse to strike. I'd weaken myself into submission. Succumb to complacency by means of pontification. Since the necessity to do one thing correctly complicated the ability to do several, it seemed increasingly sensible to ask 'If I'd not have time to correctly do all, why do anything?' Wasn't there dignity in surrendering if I'd no other option? I'd die. Your life would be guaranteed. No one would be murdered. No cruelty inflicted on countless people peripheral to whoever might've been. Through reexamining the rules of the game, perhaps I'd achieve peace with my fate and come to terms with yours.

Except I couldn't allow myself to settle for sophistry. Even if I only had access to one of the scum who'd destroy you, didn't they deserve destruction themselves? How could anyone argue otherwise? How could I allow myself to? Impotent to save you, I might nevertheless take from your murderers what they'd no rights to. They ought not experience any of the pleasures granted by life if your ability to do likewise was truncated. Supposing I lived until you were thirty and only then were you murdered by five people. Suppose the perpetrators became known to the police, but only four were apprehended and such quartet was set to be executed. Would I shrug, tell the judge 'It's not fair they'll suffer if their missing cohort doesn't, so please let them go'? Or else imagine five people crossing a room toward us, intent on defiling and killing you, while I held a gun containing four bullets. Should I fire one into you, the next into myself, leave two unspent, and your would-be killers alive? My God, were firing such shots a deed which'd grant me entry to paradise, an eternity spent hand-in-hand with you, from such divine perch I'd yearn to fire the two remaining rounds if only to strike down innocent passersby. Anything for the world to know it was a worse place for your killers dwelling in it while you'd been removed. To show that, had they been eradicated, some amount of anguish would've gone unsuffered. In such fairy story, I'd consign myself to purgation to take their lives, even knowing my killings would grant the beasts passage to a Heaven from where they'd spend eternity ridiculing me for what they'd consider my failure. They might've lived as much life as you, but I'd never allow them the paltriest scrap of life more, regardless what bliss they might attain after.

On the heels of these horrendous bouts of disquiet, clarity would return. Logic and rationality rinsed my mind in refreshing currents, rejuvenating my convictions. What I knew for fact would cement itself as though it'd never been questioned. All I'd learned retook its rightful complexion. My plans weren't sickly devices created in secret by my own misgivings and my misgivings, themselves, had proven this. I knew the names of your killers. From those had discovered their mothers. I'd been granted little then put in extensive efforts to obtain certainty. Were I awash in madness, why not set myself to killing only a single person? Convince myself I could intuit killers and move on as little evidence as that? Work led to what I'd uncovered. Further work was required. A technique to apprehend what it meant that the mothers were who they were. These women whose distinct lives I'd end seemed representational. The wrinkles of their individual identities illustrated how the killers growing in them already plotted against you. Had been devising your death since their conception.

How diabolical it all was when I'd try to determine the order in which I'd kill. Was it best to proceed based on externals, such as who was easiest to approach? Was there nothing intrinsic to distinguish one woman from another? Did the ways in which they differed matter? Contain some clue which could limit what I must enact? Something which suggested the best order to proceed? Could treating them not as one entity but five possible solutions yet be an option? I knew four of them, but what did it mean that I knew what I knew of those four? What more did I know than when

I'd known none? Were they differentiated in order that I might discover an arithmetic, see through what was no more than a shell game? Was the puzzle 'These five will kill your child unless you kill one, but can you decipher which?'

Deirdre. My dearest friend. Who I loved almost as I love you. Who, before you, I'd have said I loved most in this world. She was an altogether different breed of horror to consider than the other three. If she weren't who she was, I might've worked harder to've convinced her to terminate the pregnancy when she'd been vulnerable. Poisoned her mind and convictions. Insidiously worked against her newfound desire for a child. She'd admitted to being on the cusp of such decision, even after confessing her desire for Martin to be part of her life. But such conversations always concluded in Deirdre becoming tearfully indebted to me for allowing her an outlet. Being her loving and steadfast *confidante*. Permitting her freedom from judgement as she'd indulged intrusive bugbears. Deirdre'd gushed her affection for my part in bulwarking her against urges to inform Martin of the child. Counseling her to wait. To allow herself focus on personal desires for motherhood, first and foremost, Martin's involvement separately and afterward. Otherwise her will might be overridden by conflicting emotional desires.

Rather than manipulating her toward taking the life of your killer, eliminating from my agenda the most distasteful appointment it contained, I'd repeatedly taken eloquent pains in defense of the unborn. Reminded her how any decision regarding it was hers alone, subject to no oversight or third-party input. These things were spoken soothingly. My intent to make the choice to terminate palatable. All while I'd no doubt the merest negative word from Martin would be all it took to push her over the edge. Bile rose in me each time I'd talked her clear of such decision, but I'd never acted against Benecourt in the capacity I might've were his mother someone else. The vermin seemed to've chosen her because my resolve worked to limit itself so long as she remained in play.

The surrogate who carried Alexander Lowell was a young woman not even nurturing her own offspring. Which presented a peculiar and calculated defense. The surrogacy obfuscated my aims. Seemed designed to split my attentions, enter the realm of semantics, and bring into question the degree inherent to the measures I felt necessary. If required to kill all the mothers, she'd be extra. Because Lenora would need to be eliminated, no question. Otherwise might yet bear a child of her own. No more than an incubator, I'd yet be asking a girl die.

It was peculiar how only the Lyons woman'd desired and planned with love and passionate expectation for motherhood. If the question of sacrificing for the others was put to her, no doubt she'd defend herself with that fact. Proclaim she was radically different. They'd found themselves in their positions due to circumstances not directly solicited or else never meant to be permanent. I ought pick from them, setting she and Montgomery apart from the bunch

So far as Lyons would see it, I ought kill the child within the surrogate. Lenora and Alexander could easily broker for another without marking a difference between the child they'd wind up with and the child they might've. Whatever madness I'd spout about how the new child might be as much threat to you as the current would make little difference. But if it came to that, I ought kill the surrogate and Lenora, as well. Lyons would defend Montgomery tooth and nail. At the extreme, might balk at laying down her life in place of Goaltender, a bastard resulted from rape whose mother was only carrying to term out of spite and a desperate need to sublimate the horror which'd been visited on her. She'd cast Goaltender's mother as diseased for making a choice rooted in the violence she'd experienced, or out of pure zealotry, rather than love for her child, alone.

The mother of Goaltender might twice as passionately insist she be spared for those reasons. Declare Keith Goaltender ought be ushered into this world not on the strength of personal desire but because her position was emblematic of what a mother ought do, regardless of the circumstances surrounding their pregnancy. Hardships and symbolism sanctified the life of her child. It was all the more imperative the two of them be preserved over countless others who'd been afforded the common and natural opportunity to seek children at their leisure and under conditions in step with the *status quo*. The loss of one commonplace mother-and-child out of a million others whose lives no one could tell the difference between didn't matter in the grander scheme. The sacrifice of a mother and child who'd persevered in the face of macabre tribulations would be lamentable due to its relative rarity, if nothing else.

That I could envision the mothers set in opposition against each other was bracing. They'd simply do whatever was required to defend their young. Sacrifice whichever party available if backed into a mortal corner. Weren't against me any more than I was against them. Regardless which moot tactics were rolled out, one versus another, it was certain all would see you as the most worthy of sacrifice. You grew inside a person admittedly and unrepentantly capable of thoughts such as mine. Would inexorably have some part of me imprinted on you. Your origin was damnable. That would be enough. They'd submit how if anyone ought die, it was me. That I was direct threat to you. An assertion I agreed with. But your salvation mustn't be at the expense of yourself. If you could be saved from my being your mother, you ought be. But you couldn't. If you could be saved from living with me as your mother, you ought be. But already were.

Even in some construct wherein they'd believe their children would grow to do what I'd foreseen, they'd reshape the narrative. Your father would've done the same had I confessed what I was grappling with. As I would've, were I on the other end of the spear. The mothers would vouchsafe your life. Knowing in advance to guard against it, swear they'd never allow who they birthed to harm you. Vow to protect you all the more preciously, considering the pernicious belly you'd sprung from. Insist they were to be trusted over me, as I called myself capable of killing while they'd declare up and down that nothing under heaven could coax them over such immoral threshold. Once I was dead, they'd dedicate themselves to keeping you safe. Would sincerely believe themselves capable of it. But even if in their faces I saw unquestionable honesty, I'd never risk them failing in their charge.

These women whose flesh wrapped around your killers were revealed, once and for all, as clever defense. Layers of armor I'd need to pierce. The killers inside were my focus. The gibbonous cabal who'd employ perverse means to survive beyond my death in order to have you in their clutches disgusted me but made my resolve grip more tightly down. If there was ugly communication transpiring between the unborn, I must not for one moment bank on the meagerest respite being granted me. I was convinced they knew of each other. Despite they didn't yet breathe on their own, were a group with collective aims on you. If they lived, they'd kill you. If I killed one, the remaining would kill you worse for it. They'd chosen the mothers they fed on because the women'd seemed the soundest protection. So mothers need be treated no different than children. I must kill not one of them but all. From the start, I'd been given their names so I might slay the whole gaggle, not pick and choose or play jackstraws with your fate. Been made to know all so I'd have no choice. No questions. No misguided notion there'd be a way to make matters easier on myself or on anyone. My mind re-braced itself to the unavoidable task. But there still remained the same questions. How does one kill? How would I kill? Who would I kill first?

Ought I begin with Deirdre? Child's play to get near her. No need for subterfuge. The simplest to manipulate into whichever place or circumstance required to throw suspicion from myself, thus guaranteeing I'd be able to move on to killing the others. Our friendship left her at my mercy. Were I of a mind to, I could assail her while she slept.

In the event I couldn't stomach direct violence, it might be arranged with relative ease to seem as though an accident had befallen her. Whether violence was taken or not, I'd have ample opportunity to doctor up evidence, massage a crime scene in a manner indicating some unknown party'd been directly responsible.

Was it wiser to leave Deirdre until the end, precisely because she'd be the easiest to dispatch? Having her dead from the outset undeniably led to the most acute possibility my name'd be known to investigators. Despite it being undeniable nothing'd initially be suspected of me, best to avoid proximity as long as I could. My friend dying meant as bodies in my area multiplied police'd have the longest time to consider the oddity of a dead pregnant woman, not native to the environment in which a killer was actively targeting pregnant women, having ties to another pregnant woman residing at the dead center of that danger zone. Were I to arrange for Deirdre's death to transpire elsewhere, mounting murders in my area might yet point detectives to it. I had to presume an investigation of all suspicious deaths involving pregnant women within a specific time stamp would be undertaken, regardless of geographic commonality. Any name associated with such report might be cross-referenced. Mine would come up because I'd known Deirdre and presently resided in the city where several like-murders were concentrated.

It made as much sense to leave Deirdre for last because she'd prove the most difficult to kill. The only victim I not only cared for but loved intensely. Insurmountable emotional stakes were involved. A larger chance I'd falter in the moment of crisis. Perhaps if she were left until victory was near at hand, so many slaughters already on my conscience, I'd be numbed enough to proceed against her. Feel I deserved to be as irredeemable as only my dearest friend's death could paint me. It disgusted me to think I'd be tempted to stay my hand against Deirdre as pathetic defense, weakling insistence a soul resided in me, despite all. Sparing her was a playact of remorse. Reason I should be considered human, even pitiable, as I died a coward and a failure. Sickened me further to know I'd delude myself into peace of mind I'd in no way deserve. I was me, so knew as well as you there were no lows I'd not let myself sink to.

So perhaps I ought use her to start the ball rolling. If I could bring myself to slaughter my pregnant friend and her secret child, it'd prove beyond doubt I was capable of anything. Only knowing myself capable of exactly that could I commit the spree of unspeakable evil against the foes who remained. Shouldn't I kill Deirdre without remorse or mitigation, and as soon as physically possible, because only the anguish such deed would plunge me into would steel me for all else, eliminate once and for all any urge toward clever strategy, leave me primed to annihilate heartlessly, without reservation? Only going so far would bring me to my senses, end any hope I'd stumble upon some tip, trick, or tidbit from each murder, piece together a method which'd minimize how many I'd be required to kill, in total. I needed to be prepared for the endless contortions of my own mind.

Killing Deirdre might've been the act to guarantee I wouldn't flinch, turn desperate enough for my own life I'd cut you from me, in misery convinced I'd forget you. Except didn't it seem wisest to leave her for the final, most definitive act, precisely because it'd take having done everything else to prove myself capable of raising a violent hand against my friend? I'd need to be drained to the last whimpers of whichever humanity I possessed before I could finish her off, but would require my full stock of energy at the outset to sustain resolve through the atrocities I'd enact.

Even were it what I ought do, how could I kill Deirdre? Couldn't I kill the others, but only Deirdre's child, present the death as a horrible accident, disguise it as an assault from some vagrant third-party? All I knew screamed that Deirdre losing a child carried no less risk than allowing any of the others to suffer in such relatively limited way. But would she have another child? Her pregnancy'd been an accident, no matter the undercurrent of desire for Martin which'd lurked in her. If the child hadn't been his, she'd never have considered keeping it. Were the bastard wrested from her under horrific circumstance, she'd never again be moved to procreate. Perhaps I could make certain to damage her in some way which'd bar such possibility. Kill the child and Martin. Surely that'd render it nonsensical to entertain the idea she'd get pregnant again, passing her dead one-time casual lover's surname down.

Could I face killing Martin and butchering Deirdre's body to get at her unbidden son, only to leave her a maimed witness to my going unpunished? Leave her to mourn me if somehow what'd happened to her or the others was never disclosed? Did I believe myself built of stern enough resolve to do what I needed to do, knowing she'd perhaps learn it'd been me who'd undertaken such an ungodly act against her child? She'd see me dead, but would that satiate the vengeance she'd both desire and deserve if, in the same moment, she saw you born? Should I kill her outright merely because I couldn't bear her to discover it'd been me who'd visited unnamable horror upon her? Did I require more motive than that to take her life when I could, if I so decided, take only her mongrel from this world?

What of the risk that attempting to kill the Benecourt fetus while leaving Deirdre alive might allow the child to survive? Such ripple was all it ought take to remove the option from consideration. Plain to see how attempting but failing to kill Benecourt might become the reason he'd grow to kill you.

I'd kill Deirdre, then. But how ought it be enacted? Was it permissible to make special arrangements, hold off until the last possible instant, inflict as little torment as possible? Was acting against her too quickly an insult, despicable and unwarranted, when there existed ways I could allow her a moment more, a moment more, a moment more? Oughtn't I grant her every breath possible, every joy at the thought of her coming bliss with the child, every fantasy of forming a family with Martin?

How I revolted at the thought of Deirdre not being cognizant of her final moments. It tormented me less to contemplate her struggling as I hacked at her limbs or my fingers tightened around her throat while her eye blazed with venom and fever for life than it did to envision her throat cut while she slumbered, ensuring she'd never know anything'd happened at all. My despair was almost too pronounced to endure, thinking Deirdre'd have closed her eyes in peace, plump with hope and passion for her future, only to be robbed of waking. My own worst fear'd always been that I'd not have a minute's preparation before dying. A nightmare more dreaded the longer I lived. To visit so reprehensible a fate on my friend, afflicting her with that which most curdled my blood, was unholy. Was I using your protection to unbecome myself to such a grotesque degree? Had I truly twisted into my inverse?

Wasn't the welling of grief over the anguish I'd every moment imagine on Deirdre's behalf reason enough to hold off her murder? Your remaining killers might survive on account of my psyche cratering too early. Killing Deirdre first then failing to kill further might be the impetus for everything. The surviving murderers would learn, sometime well into their lives, how, once upon a time, a madwoman'd marked them for death, slain her pregnant best friend to ensure such end, but faltered before going a step further. The macabre knowledge they'd been spared might fester, pervert their minds, bring them together to enact punitive measures on you for what I'd intended.

Who knows which lives their lives might intersect with or what loyalties they'd develop to whom. Perhaps Martin would have another child with another woman. Such child might become intimate with one of the vermin I'd failed to exterminate. Because of this coupling, the two might feel bound to some fated storyline. Compelled to see it through. Recruit the others. Seduce them with impossible rationale as I was seducing myself. You'd become their target simply because I'd long ago rotted away. In poetic cruelty, they'd insist you never see your death coming, consider a peaceful, unwitting end the one kindness they'd grant you. Cause you to die in the most harrowing manner I could conjure, exactly as I'd made Deirdre.

I'll confess how the longer I considered these matters, the more I wanted to kill Deirdre. In time, she became the only one I actually desired dead. With the rest, the killers they harbored were all I had aims on, the women nothing more than necessary, but ancillary, carnage. But I found myself yearning to kill Deirdre. An actual enthusiasm for the undertaking I despised myself for. Told myself it was no more than a symptom of my hatred for her child. Wanted to leave the smug bastard who dwelt within her no chance of survival, hence my desire to slaughter her became enflamed. Which was true. To an extent. It did seem especially cruel of him to've chosen to my friend, such disguise selected specifically to inflict pain on me. It was tempting to balm the self-loathing I experienced over treacherous thoughts against Deirdre by declaring the sinister impulses toward her were redirected hatred, venom meant for Benecourt, alone. But I'd come to blame her. For her desire to keep the child. Her shy, childish aims on Martin. It didn't seem Benecourt'd needed to trick his way inside, but rather'd been solicited. Granted access. Contracted for your life. If she allowed him safe passage, he'd fulfill her wish. If through Nathan Benecourt's birth she'd wind up in the bosom of her precious Martin, your death warrant would've been signed in a twinkle. She'd have assured herself it wouldn't matter. Regardless of being aware of every circumstance I'd endure. Since I'd never know for certain you'd be protected, despite the foreknowledge I possessed, all was well. I could simply die telling myself whichever tale I chose. Every day I didn't confront her, she'd feel more correct in her stance. Even if she couldn't know beyond doubt that I knew what was coming, she'd assume I did. Divine from my not confronting her that I had aims against her and the child. Justify her betrayal by pointing out you'd receive thirty guaranteed years of life. Fool herself into believing she'd discover a way of saving you, down the line. Knowing she'd never try. Not once Benecourt nursed at her breast and she saw for herself the vile pact was fulfilled. Lingering loyalties to me would dry up as surely as mine toward hers had while I undertook these considerations. Irrelevant whether they were true or more feverish make-believe. I must live as though what could be true was.

My suspicions might easily be tested. I'd merely have to tell her what I knew. Watch how thoroughly she'd work to convince me out of it. Tent her as she looked me in the eye, not only disbelieving but lovingly, not only lovingly but insistent she'd never make the decisions I already had if the tables were turned. Listen as she did everything in her power to see to it I surrendered. Insisted I tell your father. Consult with doctors. Any recommendation which'd make it impossible for me to act against your adversaries. My friend would lull me toward the gallows with heartfelt promises. That she'd see to it no harm ever came to you. Were I not to survive your birth, would look on you as her daughter. Raise you alongside her son.

I won't have you misunderstand. My hatred for Benecourt was fuel enough on its own. I abhorred him for teaching me the depths of depravity I could be brought to. It seemed your other killers had coated themselves in the armor of generic moral conundrum, selected their protective outfits only to lead me into a morass of ethical doubts, donned an assortment of avatars which made it impossible to act against them as a unit. None of their deceptions seemed personal. Lyons asked if I could bring myself to kill, full stop? Lowell if I could, were some nuance considered. Goaltender if multiple contextualizing factors were brought in. Such variants required focus on my would-be victims' individuality. Served to bounce me around intellectually. Exhaust my emotions. But nothing about the core proposition of killing them changed. Regardless of the multifold facts of the lives of the mothers, they were innocent strangers to me. Little matter how sympathetic they were made on top.

Benecourt seemed to relish in the personal stake his presence in the affair imbued. The protection he'd chosen abjectly sinister, indicative of an utterly godless essence. While the others took precautions against my worst nature, he took advantage of my best. Cowering in Deirdre made the proposition of striking against him almost as pointless as asking if I could kill you. Growing inside her was enough I believed he'd be the one who'd eventually plan everything. Assemble the others. Lure or bribe them into hurting you. With threat and pressure sand down their resistance, until they became no more than implements of destruction he'd wield. I hated how he must be called hers. Reviled her for calling herself his mother. Adored doing so. More with each day that passed. A child she'd never sought. A creature the father'd never intended. That such quirk of chance exposed me to the anguish of contemplating losing her was maddening. In this, I almost allowed myself to believe he was the only one who must die. Deridre the only person I'd need to kill.

As my hatred intensified, I attempted to conceive of what'd bring Deirdre's son to kill you. No use expending a flake of energy on such rhetorical investigation, doing so wasted time better spent planning your defense, risked wearing me down to the point of complete inaction, but Deirdre's involvement held a gun to my head. My bourgeoning hatred notwithstanding, every opportunity to see her separate from Benecourt needed to be seized. I had to think about their lives. The years they'd have. The love they'd share. Had to postulate and test what defect in Deirdre'd allow the child she'd raise to act against the daughter of her dearest friend who'd died without ever knowing a single coo of that daughter's voice. Blamed her for either being blind to whichever warning signs her son would display or else refusing to nip the hazards they'd foreshadowed in the bud.

I went so far as to wonder whether the mother of one of these mothers I'd kill had known what I'd do to their child because of the child that child would bear. If so, could they have concluded the reason I'd do so? Was all they'd known a statement of facts devoid of detail, the same as I? Had they repeated and repeated to themselves 'A woman called Noor will grow to murder five people named Benecourt, Goaltender, Lowell, Lyons, and Tellwell, one of whom is my daughter' with absolute certainty, void of rationale? While I'd been a mere zygote, had the grandmother of one of the children I'd kill known of me and what I'd do, decades hence? Had it only been their inability to fathom why I'd do so which'd spared my own mother's life? If they could've answered 'Why?' to their satisfaction, might I never have existed to paw at an answer to this 'Why?' all my own?

Such thoughts led nowhere. Except where I'd started. Deirdre's son simply would kill you. Inability to posit or stomach a single reason why resulted in nothing which altered my position or duty of care. Would knowing why profit me? Such information could only torment me further. Furnish me a slow-motion preview of your coming slaughter alongside a million microscopic snapshots of Deridre's failure to protect you. Yet I couldn't keep myself fixating. Searching out an explanation. If for no other reason than I might glimpse indication of what I needed to do, to whom, and when. All the infinite reasons a person might kill remained. Ricocheted meaninglessly behind my eyes. There could never be a reason to kill you which'd make sense. So to Hell with the senseless multitude your killers might agree on.

During this period of intense contemplation, I began to lose track of day and night, the ability to differentiate between asleep and awake, thought and fantasy, obsession and desire turning corrupt. The superficial interactions required of life were maintained only because they'd become rote. Indeed, I'd grown so accustomed to the patter and laughter, to the serious considerations and soft intimacies, they were a program spooling in the background. I might be in the midst of a deeply sincere interaction with your father, the both of us outlining our hopes and fears for you or scrutinizing the nitty gritty of plans for the coming years, only to realize I'd been speaking my side of the dialogue without giving conscious thought to a word. My focus would drift, mid-sentence, and I'd have to reorient myself, never able to fully succeed. Your father might cheekily prompt verbatim phrases, his face warm and eager to know the entirety of whatever I'd intended to impart, but I remained unaware what I'd been saying, even given clues couldn't fake a sensible or coherent continuation. An unsettling development, because when I'd drift back into these serene moments, it was on the heels of imagining the details of some ghastly scheme or another. With a jolt of panic, I'd feel I must've been coming across distracted, that whatever I'd been speaking aloud had seemed strained, bizarre, indicative of deception, underlying strife, or fatigue. It'd take time to steady myself, lose the tremor of noia that he'd grow concerned, find reasons to keep closer watch over me.

But although whatever I'd say was devoid of conscious consideration, it never came across queer to whichever audience, even as these slips became more frequent. The less I actively attempted to, the better I could appear outwardly myself to the satisfaction and pleasure of those who knew me. Eventually made the choice to give up worrying. Trusted I functioned under some automaton program. Recited a script deft enough to fool whoever needed to be while I leant my entire conscious intellect to the particulars of our revenge.

It wasn't just during the day and wasn't only my waking thoughts which were consumed. Dreams piled up. Night after night, during any catnap, slumber of any sort sneered another out, tactile, olfactory, and more detailed than whichever reality I'd eventually enact might ever be. Lavish fancies of how I'd eradicate your killers if no restraint or consideration were required. Scenarios free of causality and logic stacked upon each other, throttled and intoxicated me with the desire to perform impossible deeds which'd make it twice as impossible to act further. I could lose hours, afternoons, entire days to the indulgence of abhorrent thoughts concerning what I'd inflict on the women who nourished your killers, swept away in elaborations, fashioning morbid alterations in colors and textures which could never exist in the physical world.

There was much pleasure in the contemplation of saving you, intense gratification envisioning, re-examining, and editing the make-believes in manners so increasingly grotesque they turned graceful. Joyous to pretend I'd triumph through measures impossible to enact. It didn't matter that unreality was unreality if even for a moment it made me feel you could be preserved.

I desired the unthinkable deeds I'd undertake to be simple. Ground up pills of an abortive nature slipped into drinks, the mothers ingesting tainted foodstuffs which'd poison the children requiring their portions of such repurposed sustenance as it trickled to them. Glass shavings, shimmering soft as talcum, stirred into whichever substances might be swallowed, throats and intestinal tracks shredded, the loathsome fetuses lacerated as they kicked and rolled in the shards, healthy growth embedding splinters in their still forming brainstems. The women closed in airtight spaces, fed carbon monoxide, released while their lives could be saved but not in time to preserve those they carried. Forced into a choice whether or not to exterminate the maledictions cradled in their guts. Driven to confess to the fathers or their trusted physicians that the guarantee of palsy, brain damage, physical abnormality, impaired ability to thrive, of lives destined to be thick with hardship or shortened to the point it'd be torture to allow them at all, made it necessary to end things before they began. I wanted the bitches to choke out the words 'I can't allow a minute of life that'll be no more than a minute of dying.'

It delighted me to imagine myself possessed of stealth and ingenuity, virtuosity enough to present the unnatural decision these mothers would make as not only natural but compassionate. Sick with bliss, I indulged in the fantasy that I'd know the women believed it'd been due to nothing more than an unlucky turn of the wheel that they'd scuttled their pregnancies and jettisoned private and precious aspects of themselves by doing so. They'd see themselves as the woeful victims of statistical probability. Representations of a quantifiable eventuality they'd taken all possible steps to defend against but which'd touched them through chance, nonetheless. My sincerest pleasure came in knowing the quirk of fate they'd think themselves victim of was one they'd, at least once, admitted to themselves could happen, and how such reality was something they were comfortable with, provided it left them alone. They'd feel hexed by such thoughtless whispers. Think themselves fundamentally flawed, atomically at fault, believe their horrid prayers had caused the souls seeking life in their bellies to corrode.

If the magic of such subtlety couldn't be achieved, I wanted to strike the mothers some physical blow which'd bring them to the same damnable crossroads. Bludgeon them into a choice which'd benefit you. Pictured myself lying in wait on some dark, drizzly night. Low hanging clouds. Wisps of fog. Dank mint green and burnt orange streetlight spread like sour pastel to form a shroud of chill invisibility. I'd shove them down high concrete stairwells. Trauma enough visited upon their taut bellies the viability of carrying to term would be brought into question. I desired them damaged precisely enough that, if they went through with delivering, they'd discover not only their children stillborn but learn they'd been robbed of the ability to conceive others.

If not the blunt edges of cold concrete, I'd envision myself doing requisite violence with a triangular jag of brick, a meat tenderizer, the weighted bulb of a hammer or the fangs of the forked claw at the back of its head. Behind my eyes flickered the cinema of sudden assault. Public restrooms or other semi-secluded spots entered without care. Strike after strike after strike, percussive and deep, into bellies round or oblong. Sounds of larynx crushed under stern pressure from my thumbs. The rattle of bodies expiring in my grip before being resuscitated with the ministrations of my own mouth. Listening as they gasped back to consciousness. Hugged themselves to me in bewildered gratitude. Thankful I'd been there to save them. Senses not functional enough to apprehend their children were nothing but carcasses weighing down on their pelvic bones. I'd flee casually and unidentified. Mirthful clacks of footfalls. Peripheral soundtrack of passing traffic. Camera following me discreetly as I dropped coins in the slot of a public telephone to make anonymous announcement of my crimes.

But such nightmare desires were disenchanting. Couldn't be acted on. Didn't guarantee the imperative damage to the fetus. Not enough they'd be beyond reach of medical intervention. Nor did they promise detrimental effects to your killers if they were born.

While surveying such fantasies, I'd wonder whether it'd be enough reduce your killers to witless entities, little more than semi-sentient objects dependent on their mothers, fathers, and a staff of care nurses employed round the clock to take nourishment, have garments pulled over them, bedsheets adjusted snuggly, be cleaned after soiling themselves. Perhaps I might impair them into perpetual infancy. Leave them not dead but robbed of who they'd have been. Creatures no more than flesh and basic functions. Rusted instruments of breath, ingestion, and voiding. Incapable of clearing their chins of burp-up, let alone acting on grotesque impulses to murder were some scenario to materialize in which you'd share a space with them.

Further nightmares. Torments of how your life might be forfeit even were such relatively merciful precaution opted for. I concocted situations far-fetched and outlandish, enough to seem lunacy, but which nevertheless kept in the realm of possibility, reinforced how anything might yet happen if one of your killers survived, no matter the repellent state I reduced them to. I replayed and pawed over every miniscule detail of such horrors, retooled them in my waking thoughts the same as I had the dreams in which you were saved.

When such anxieties spiked, they were preposterously convincing. To the extent I'd reason you'd be more vulnerable if the fiends were left to subhuman existence. Perhaps you'd be born with a defect, yourself. Grow into one due to genetics or exposure to environmental hazard. Wind up institutionalized in the same facility as the killers I'd let survive. Who, with scarcely a cogent thought between them, might be moved to corner you. Violate you in a braindead spasm of arousal they'd no ability to rein in. Or else it might come over them to set ablaze the room you slept in. Your presence incidental so far as their intent. Your death a motiveless hiccough of imbeciles left unmedicated or unsupervised a few moments too long. They could be deemed entirely innocent. Experts pleading that homicidal intent was beyond the vegetable capacity they retained. Their every deed permissible for being mechanical and without intellect. All might agree it impossible to punish them. Or that it was only possible to do so by allowing them to continue on in the existence they'd always known without consequence or alteration. Human-beings-so-called. Sympathized with. Cared for all the more attentively. Any sign of guilt they might manifest viewed as tragedy. To be extinguished, at all costs, lest they suffer the measliest pang of remorse.

One night, wide awake, your father warm in satisfied slumber beside me, I tensed beneath bedcovers imagining I'd set the four mothers I knew of on fire. Lured them someplace under false pretenses. Fed them drinks laced with sedatives. Doused them in accelerant. Dropped a match. This dream of immolation followed weeks of despair. Occurred when I'd felt reduced to intellectual shambles by the puzzle of committing four acts of murder and then a final one against a quarry yet unknown. I longed to have it all over and done with. One felled swoop. Enacted in an hour. Walked away from. Left behind me, come what may. I added and added dimensions to thoughts of that fire, risible in their conceit. In the throes of pretend, considered how I might go about concocting matters to have it seem I'd been an intended victim, myself. Survived through a miracle of random chance, just barely. I'd allow damage to my body. Even ghastly wounds wouldn't matter, provided I not mangle myself to the extent you couldn't be salvaged from the wreck of my flesh. I'd bask in how wise it'd be to hold off until as near your due date as possible. To strike only when there was no risk of damage for your being premature. Waiting until such moment before orchestrating a horror-house vignette in which it seemed I'd been as terrorized as those I'd killed.

Insane the time spent wishing I had the mothers all brought together in order to act against alongside myself. But knowing I'd caused the situation which led to my death as doctors worked to free your fully developed body from me was a kind of rapture. Let such demise be what guaranteed your safety. Let me relish in advance the elegance of the achievement. I was in love with this outright farce, though I knew it pointless to consider. Even were I willing to go through with such an undertaking, I didn't have a personal enough relationship with the women. They'd not be interested in getting together with me. Nor were they connected to each other, except through me and my murderous aims. For all its detail and emotion, the fantasy was null.

Lacking my fifth victim's identity made all dreams wastes of time and energy. Even if I weaved in the promise that were the fifth target uncovered I'd kill her, immediately, propelled by having already enacted the operatic slaughters I fantasized, it was all so much jabberwocky. Beginning a process and clinging to hope wasn't enough. Any path forward must leave all of your killers dead, no speck of their lives left to chance. I'd need to see them dead, feel them dead, kill them further, blot them out a dozen times over after enacting whichever atrocity I might, rend the still growing bodies to pieces so the impossibility of revival was absolute. Carve hollow the women's bellies, scour the squirming life from within, sever child from mother, portion of child from itself, unborn limbs plucked from plump trunks like the legs of cicada and left strewn across the floor as though spent cigarettes.

As with the fire, I'd insert lurid particulars to the storyline of gathering the mothers in one place. Took my sweet time play pretending absurd dialogues we'd engage in as I corralled them. Giggled at invented salvos which'd indicate they were charmed by me, openly desirous of my friendship or sexual company. Concocted idle chitchat and heartfelt conversations, how I'd advise them on life circumstances, buck them up when their spirits flagged. Cobbled together ridiculous vignettes wherein meeting me was some sort of dream come true for reasons kept private despite they'd be bursting to confess. I'd gloss over the intricacies of how I'd incapacitate them. Doctored glasses of juice. Curt application of cudgel. Imagined there'd be a carbonated scream when my blade punctured the curve of their abdomens, a shrill whistle as it slit the membranous womb. In my mind, their flesh was thicker than bone. Cleaving it required sawing effort which'd leave me perspiring from forehead, underarms, creases of my thighs, a rash prickling my shoulders, annoyance redoubling the butchering pace, peeled handfuls of quivering meat, hair tangled with scalp and groin tissue tossed aside as I hacked at their bones.

Once the children perched before me, I pictured my hands closing around their translucent throats, finger interlacing, palms pressed flush to each other, squeezing their gastropod mass until a slick of gore seeped along my forearms while I wrung what I held, twined it tightly, tugged it into a knot. Or else I'd visualize the sharp corner of a stray crag of cement brought down through the grape-skin which lacquered their wet parchment skulls, jagged punctures spilling bright colored sludge resembling the innards of caterpillars, a scum briefly incandescent as it smeared the floor, memories of lightning bugs sloshed across pavement with the toe of a boot brought to mind. The eyeballs wouldn't fall loose, burst, or bleed, but deflate slowly like wet slippery party balloons while the skin over cheeks shrunk and discolored the way rotted crabapples might. When I'd corkscrew the brick into the wormy torsos, a viscous slurry akin to liquified potatoes would string to the floor, puddles filled with morsels of cartilage and soft tangles of veins. There'd only be bones enough to form the skeletons of kindergarten stick drawings.

I'd grow giddy at the thought of burning the remains, wanting to be certain not even bubbles of them survived enough to be identified individually. Would gather the stale paste of the lot, slop it into a mound with the sides of my shoe, douse the grime in alcohol spit from my mouth in disdain, and watch as all were reduced to a single pile of ash I'd scribble across the unwashed floors with my fingers spread wide. Or else I'd pour further alcohol onto the anthill of corpses, watch it soak to a pulpy sludge, rake handfuls into the mothers' hair or plop them muddy into the cavities I'd furrowed them to, a gluey sediment filling each woman's middle, dampening further, congealing in concert with their thickened blood as it soured to milk curd before scabbing, their gored carcasses caked in brackish shells.

In this hideous fantasia, everything'd been arranged to suggest the six of us had been abducted together, bound in separate rooms, dragged out one-by-one, added to the ghoulish display. I'd claim to've heard the screams of the others, knew my turn was coming, escaped unnoticed while ungodly wailing sang riot from the fifth of the victims I'd been unable to assist, fled nude into the streets, body wounded horribly with violence no one would think, let alone could ever prove, had been self-inflicted. They'd find me collapsed in a telephone booth, malnourished, dehydrated, traces of the same drug which'd disabled the mothers present in my system, ample physical evidence my body'd been kept restrained for two days.

For too many days such macabre theatre seemed not only plausible but sound, not only clever but lovely. Only not knowing the fifth mother's identity stayed me from taking steps to rent out an appropriate space to serve as kill chamber, making plans for abductions, and readying the implements of uneducated surgery. But spectacle wasn't the end goal. Thinking in terms of dramaturgy, tarting up scenography and plotline in an attempt to convince myself reality could ever match the contrivances of narrative or that life could emulate desire, expended vital energy for zero profit. I'd have to kill one-at-a-time. No argument altered the hard fact of it. Even if I came up with five variants and vowed to employ each method only once, properly sequenced, spread over time to give the appearance none were connected, concrete consideration of each seized me up. Alone in my apartment, I'd panic, vision blurring, breath shallow, a high-pitched whine it'd often take half-an-hour to subdue.

I'd no doubt I could kill once. If once, certainly twice. Slash one victim's throat, drive as fast as I could to empty a revolver into the head of a second. The best I might manage was a spree of breathless violence lasting until my inevitable capture. Were I to succeed even that far, it'd be through dumb luck or incompetence on the part of my pursuers. It wasn't novel or cinema police I'd square up against, entities only there to serve a mechanical function of narrative. Real authorities would hunt me. Save whoever they could by deducing from those they'd failed to. For someone like me to kill kill kill kill kill, I'd have to be pitted against fictional dunderheads, detectives tailored with the exact flaws suitable to larger artistic themes, characters written to lack professionalism, insight, or follow-through, strawmen who'd allow for my triumph but not be in service of it. It'd take shortcuts on the part of whichever author to see a creature like me to victory in so Satanic a task, pitiful reliance on shopworn tropes, imaginary witnesses having seen exactly too little, pages littered with clues revealed moments too late, paperback sensibilities infusing events with artificial suspense, a balancing act of coincidences meant to titillate and circumstances which'd stop the narrative dead in its tracks if not for the fabulist sidestepping logic in service of frivolous entertainment.

Were my killings the plot of a story, it'd be one of insanity. However righteous my slayings were presented, no matter how jolly a romp it was to witness a crafty figure accomplish sinister deeds, mine wasn't a tale of heroics. I was the fiend all were praying would be stopped. Even those in the audience who'd enjoy the idea of some wrong-hearted bastard getting clean away with one killing would find a narrative wherein that same person got away again and again until fade to black juvenile.

Reading these words, you think me a beast. Hope I didn't go through with anything. If you've already verified what I've revealed, are reading passages piecemeal whenever you can stomach it, knowing full well I've succeeded, you'll hope reading further will yet prove I failed.

I rewatched the movies your father'd written, the two he'd co-directed, viewed countless films of a similar stripe he'd giddily recommend, many I'd seen before, umpteen I'd never heard of, two a day, sometimes three. Audited every inch of film I could get my hands on as proxy for conversation, substitute for directly addressing my concerns and asking his advice on how best to proceed. From top tier cinema to what he lovingly termed 'dollar bin faff' I'd steal inspiration, templates, librettos I might expand into actuality.

In this way, I'd allowed him to aid me. Except it grew to feel he was serving the opposite purpose. Aiding and abetting your enemies. With each passing day, I found myself convinced he'd always been doing so. Simply through being personally fascinated with certain genres and so often discussing their particulars, he'd conditioned me to love and accept the thought processes of forsaken louts, to place stock in plot contrivances required to balance narratives, all so I'd have failed killers, thwarted plans, and unexpected rug-pull outcomes filed away in my mind, waiting to freeze me up exactly when I most needed to act brazenly. No matter their level of craft or quality, and regardless the fictional outcomes, the films became his voice working to convince me out of doing what I must.

Viewing these entertainments was tantamount to him whispering in my ear, calmly, insistently urging me to see the mistake in imagining I'd hold up under the merest cross examination. I couldn't kill and kill again, coming and going from my daily life without ever having to endure probing questions. Each film was another reason caution was called for, further plea for me to recognize things'd never end well.

I'd sought no more than an innocuous method with which to explore the unpardonable crimes I'd soon undertake, to gird myself, set my nerves steely, wanted to indulge in preparation for the task ahead without my typical idiom or pastimes seeming to shift. Couldn't risk haunting the True Crime aisles at the bookstore, but desired insight regarding pitfalls I'd need to be wary of, a milquetoast way of researching something other than the contents of my fatigued imagination. Your father being actively at work on his second film project, as well as tinkering with ideas for the one yet forthcoming and tweaking the film already wrapped, had made disguising my intent in vigorous enthusiasm for what he constantly thought about seem ideal. His remarks would serve to augment or rebut my considerations, his endless riffs contain nuances which'd never occur to me. Such would be his gifts, baubles I'd filch and pass on to you without having to arrange curious dialogues which might undo my efforts before actual plans were laid.

But his lengthy dissections of the films seemed almost snide. Commentary concerning what he'd have done differently had he been lead writer, which aspects of scripts veered from reality, served no purpose but to develop harmonious thematic arcs in overwrought, amateurish, or derivative ways. His jocular lambasting thrust in my face how celluloid fantasies which seemed to celebrate transgressive scenarios such as my life had become were intended as diversionary, pontification designed to reinforce how what I wanted for you absolutely couldn't and shouldn't be had.

Exactly as it'd been when I'd first cloaked your fate in rhetorical chatter, your father enthusiastically toured me through the reasons there was nothing to do be done. This time, he merrily espoused how in the scripts he wrote and the films I watched, when antagonists or antiheroes were rooted for they'd most often be stopped. When they weren't, the blunt artistic indication was that they ought to've been. Bleak outcomes and outright nihilism might be acceptable as entertainment, but films which trod such ground tended to suggest their hero-villain's superficial success was rotten and that a fate altogether worse than they'd considered would come to pass. Their victories were presented as impermanent. If they found themselves warm in the bosom of family and their communities dubbed them the height of virtue as credits rolled, consequences would implicitly be visited on others and most often those undeserving.

I wasn't a charismatic villain the way thriller flicks depicted nor an amoral soul taking the law into my own hands to visit bloody comeuppance on scoundrels who'd flouted traditional justice. I was just a person. In over my head. Unskilled and frightened. When the audience desired someone like me to succeed, it was for vicarious thrills, the promise they might prevail if caught in some extreme circumstance with no clear way out. They always knew such success was preposterous, on its face. Any film in which I'd achieve my aims was nonsensical pulp, grisly and over-the-top antics presented for puerile shock value, so hyper-specific in focus it might as well be science fiction. Movies wherein diligent attempts were made to achieve superficial resemblance to the worlds their protagonists inhabited were the worst of all, utilized *verité* as excuse for why certain sensible steps hadn't been taken, surface gloss designed to give unwarranted weight to whichever rhetorical philosophy was under discussion, hemming the moral arguments so events didn't get too esoteric.

In films based on a true accounts, there'd always be artful composition and scenography to suggest or outright depict how when people like me brought off some dastardly caper we'd merely enacted an awful delusion, a figment which meant the world to us but was plain-cake murder so far as anyone else was concerned. Characters in my vein had grandstanding philosophies to espouse or else demented perceptions we'd cling to. The films would methodically showcase that no matter how passionately our views might be articulated they remained myopic, incomplete, or irrational. What we'd done hadn't meant or accomplished anything but death, our empty lives onward, and the shame which'd soil all those in our orbits. In the face of these harsh realities, or in psychic defense against them, we'd entrench our beliefs, end our lives to balance proverbial scales, or perform some theatrical gesture to no empirical effect. When someone unlawfully killed to save someone else, it'd be illustrated how lives and souls had nonetheless been reduced to husks, impossible to determine whether the life saved had been worth the price.

Your father fully admitted to his preference. Adored storylines concerning people accomplishing whichever madness only to have it result in the furthest thing from their stated aims. Genuinely loved characters like me. The aberrant, the deranged, the lost. A story in which someone enacted horrors they felt righteous while remaining blind to the error of doing so and unable to admit failure, even in death, seemed to provide him something near to erotic pleasure. Yet at the conclusion of one such film, which'd deeply moved me and bolstered my flagging hope, his commentary immediately eroded any solace.

"No one really thinks of a murderer as an Artist, Noor. They're written that way to represent the curse of an inability to understand beauty. Such lack shows a central component of humanity is missing, so they're doomed to live as entities only able to inhumanely mimic and distort. Our obsessive stalker isn't someone who profoundly apprehends the acute depths to which love can cut, they're divorced from any comprehension of love to an almost horrific degree, incapable of recognizing, curating, or nurturing it in another. They compensate with tortured and torturous gestures, macabre carnivals of adoration, loyalty, and unconditional passion. Their folly binds us to them because, through them, we're brought closer to what we have and that which we are. Normal human beings. Flawed but able to recognize ourselves as such. More certain we might be incorrect about that which we hold most dear than we could ever believe ourselves pure enough to guarantee or receive guarantee of what we hold most dear. Unlike them, we have to renew, reaffirm, and redoubt every day of our lives, and through them we glimpse why. No audience truthfully cheers 'Wow, the killer got away with killing those people so must've been correct about whichever rationale they spouted!' Were you to hear the same words come from a real person as those so eloquently delivered by a mad killer on film, you'd want them put down like dogs if not left in a cage until they'd rotted. What makes our artist-murderers so interesting, why we love our stalker-romantics, is them not being the person sitting beside us. Those people only might be. Each time they aren't, and each time we show that we aren't, we bask in our beautiful normalcy. It's a triumph how we who're so vulnerable possess what could so easily be robbed or made a ghoulish monstrosity by minds incapable of accepting that the beauty of everything is its frailty, its mortality, and its impermanence. It's our never knowing which allows us to cherish what the beloved celluloid bogeymen never could, despite the passion, ingenuity, or drive we imbue them with. The only thing they have in common with us is how, in the end, all they can do is be revealed for what they actually are and always have been."

He was correct. As were the films. It was hopeless. No matter which evidence I planted to give the appearance some third party bore responsibility for the mothers' deaths, I'd wind up interviewed. If I claimed an attempt had been made on my life alongside the others, the lie would be poked at and turned over in every conceivable way. Until a culprit was caught, detectives would be unrelenting. Orchestrating something against myself before hunting down any of your killers, an elaborate scene meant to reinforce how some mysterious entity'd failed in their targeted attempt against my life but had subsequently refined their technique and succeeded with the others before vanishing into thin air, was gibberish. All the effort'd earn was exponentially more attention placed on myself, whichever tale I'd gone on record with meticulously sniffed. Even before suspicions firmly developed, perfectly understandable questions would need to be addressed. 'Why had a stranger to the area been marked and aggressed upon first, when all other victims had ties to the city?' It didn't fit. Alternate explanations would be posited. Precautions suggested. The perpetrator might wend back around to finish me off. I could be the key to unraveling the horror. A guard should be placed, a squad car stations outside, a list of everything I'd done, everyone I'd met in the past months committed to paper, looked into. For my protection and for yours.

Life wasn't a B-movie. Your father couldn't put his arm around my waist and insist 'She's suffered enough,' usher me toward our parked car, the detectives left stammering without recourse or further access. Authorities couldn't be shooed from the door the next day by his insisting I needed to recuperate and a burst of declarative anger of 'Go to Hell' wasn't anything they'd be officially bound by. While it might seem abject cruelty to ask me to relive my experience, despicable to burden me with implied guilt for not helping the families of the other victims find closure, it was tough luck. I was their only witness. Even supposing I aggressively reminded them I'd been bound, blindfolded, possessed no memory of my abduction, and therefore had nothing of probative value to tell, they'd persist. Need to understand how there could possibly be no oddities in my life of late. Why I'd been abducted immaculately then gotten clean away with no trace evidence left behind when clues existed in every other case and no one else'd come close to escape.

With a killer of pregnant women at large, it was preposterous to entertain the fancy I'd be permitted to use my own pregnancy as excuse for hiding away. They'd insist they could protect me. If I rebuffed them would take steps to do so in secret. Any action I took guaranteed to lead into a trap.

Whichever investigators were assigned to the case would find no sign a killer'd made detailed preparations against anyone. Indeed, it'd seem they'd managed to course the veins of the surrounding city, planning, scheming, selecting targets, spiriting victims away without leaving a crumb of evidence. So why were abundant telltales scattered about after the crimes had been committed?

Like in the films, logical discrepancies would be laid out for me. Interrogations defended through the easy guise of detectives claiming they worried I'd be attacked, again. It'd quite correctly be explained that while people do horrible things, it's not without rationale. No killer escalates to the kidnap and slaughter of multiple women without any connection to them or having committed previous crimes which'd left some residue behind. Even supposing the victims had been selected at random, every killer had their own history. Physical artifact of their existence would be discovered somewhere. From it the pathology which'd led to their slayings would be indexed. Targets so specified, activity contained in so tight an area, repeated so rapidly, suggested a powerful fixation at the heart of everything, an obsession passionate, overwhelming. Only one woman out of the bunch might've been the honest target, all the others meant to cover up the directness of such motive. 'It could be you were the target, Mrs. Parsinbyrd' they might say. Only having failed against me were other victims dispatched. To muddy the waters. Leaving me vulnerable to the most horrible intentions.

I'd agree. Same as anyone. There ought be a trail leading back to a point of origin. There would be. There was. Such trail led to me. The only one who'd left signs of preamble or action. Abundant evidence existed. More and more to be uncovered, every day. My connection to the victims would be stumbled upon. I shared a doctor with the surrogate, for example, had interacted with her at a group for expectant mothers, been observed talking outside of a bookstore with the woman whose child she carried. Similar narratives existed for all the others. However peripheral they'd first appear, soon they'd turn damning. A faked attack against myself would be the most glaring example of my preparations. Nothing before it indicating trouble, no stalker or out of place personality, no stranger suddenly in common with the murdered women except me. I'd be proved the starting point because any preparations I'd made for acting against myself were the only sort which would leave no trace.

Supposing I didn't concoct such attack, there was yet no keeping myself out of the thicket. My best friend was among the victims. Peculiar for being the only one residing outside the overall kill zone. She'd been in recent contact with me, so my name would enter the mix. An interview compulsory if for no other reason than it'd set off alarm bells were I to avoid helping out.

If investigation of Deirdre's death never touched upon me directly, my description would come up in conversation with the friends and loved ones of whichever victim else. I'd be identified as a visitor to umpteen motherhood groups, as someone loitering on playgrounds, cozying up to all manner of people, asking questions. Many others engaged in those same activities, hundreds of mothers-to-be might have trivial interconnection with the deceased, but only I'd be common between all, seem to've made interactions habitual, given my wrong name, and only I connected the city to Deirdre. It'd be dereliction of duty not to keep watchful eye on me.

Your father might hiss in furious defense. 'Are you insinuating my wife had some involvement in this? She's been terrified, herself. Preoccupied with thoughts of dying during childbirth. Now these ungodly crimes transpire and you insist on badgering her!?'

The detectives would apologize. Assure him they'd been suggesting no such thing. Take pains to exude sympathy. Wouldn't trouble me a moment longer. But surely it wouldn't violate my peace for them to have a private word with him, out of concern for my state of mind with everything going on. If I was already suffering psychological turmoil, news of these murders must've been agitating. Had I shown any signs of peculiar behavior? Expressed indication I feared being followed?

Your father might recall to them conversations we'd had. About being approached by a madman. Whether he'd kill to protect a loved one against some ill-defined future crime. He'd perhaps narrate all we'd discussed in pedantic detail. Walk them through my seemingly innocuous probing as to whether he felt murder would be permissible were it to safeguard a loved one.

Considering the timing of our arrival in the city and the mounting death toll, the detectives might reasonably conclude such conversation suggested I'd been threatened, witnessed an event, experienced something I was terrified to discuss out of fear for the child growing in me. Your father'd concede to such concerns, no doubt see it all and then some. Perhaps I'd been charged with undertaking a crime and these dead women were proof of what'd be done to me if I failed to comply. Perhaps I'd literally received the note I'd discussed all those months ago, someone I knew named as a possible victim. Perhaps the others had also been named and I'd been told the only way to safeguard my own pregnancy was not to act. It was them or me. Them or you. I might've attempted to tell your father in the only way I'd felt safe, at that time wanted to think it no more than a sick prank, when I'd learned of the slaughters wanted to ignore them out of protective instinct, willing to turn a blind eye to cold blooded murder so my unborn daughter'd be spared.

But were I to admit to such, investigators would be sent on a goose chase, look for evidence, find none, then circle back. Like in so many movies, what I'd actually done would become increasingly likely. Your father'd often pointed out how a killer aiming to remove themselves from suspicion by posing as a victim was the first thing any ten-a-penny screenwriter thinks up when attempting to be clever, found it pathetic how they never seemed to realize what *cliché* such Third Act reveals had become. He'd posit how a more interesting film might have the woman under suspicion be in cahoots with the murderer. After being threatened, she'd begged for her life. Struck a deal to feed the fiend victims. Carried out the stalking and preliminary work so nothing would trace to the butcher. Become complicit in everything.

I wasn't trying to protect myself. Wouldn't even attempt to get away with whichever crimes I'd commit once I'd committed them all. But no matter, a criminal investigation would commence before I was halfway to my goal. The moment something to investigate existed, I'd enter the picture. Couldn't delude myself with hope. The vice grip of justice would tighten around me. I'd not have a moment's freedom until a killer was in custody or they'd satisfied themselves I wasn't the killer, the target, or the accomplice. A preponderance of evidence would amass while I was penned in.

To act against the women individually increased the risk of mistake, might put whichever mother harbored the final killer on guard, hole her up, induce her to hire private security, flee to a country estate, or some other variable impossible to predict or combat. It made as little sense to act against an incomplete group, as such decreased the odds of pulling off a scheme while increasing the chance I'd raise suspicion before nearing an opportunity to enact one.

I'd already failed you. Since the moment you'd been conceived. Was failing you still. Came to hope my death was a revenge you were arranging against me. You'd be killing the woman at fault for your death, after all. The one granted a glimpse of your fate along with her own who'd failed to alter either. I hoped my death was my daughter exterminating the one who should've protected her but hadn't lifted a finger to do so. That I'd been rightfully cursed with knowing what was in store for you so I'd no choice but to never believe myself innocent of it.

Was I unable to find Marcy Tellwell because there was no Marcy Tellwell to find, no mother, no waiting killer, nothing to protect you from? I recalled the long fit of believing my mind'd selected the names, built delusions from phrases overheard, events peripherally witnessed, psychic debris squirreled subconsciously until arranged to suit my deranged pleasure. Three names all but confirmed such hypothesis while a fourth remained nebulous enough it might be tailored to needs, pro or con. In all cases, bodies existed to pin the monikers on. Sorting out whether they were who or what I believed was a crippling endeavor, but at least had tangible substance to probe.

If I could find proof of any Tellwell connected to me, it was such Tellwell I'd destroy. But though I scoured myself for any trace, the name wasn't there. I scrutinized recollected glimpses of television and newspaper, meticulously poured over snips of stray conversation which'd stuck in my head, squinted at every waitress' nametag, and stared at the indecipherable strangle of scribbled surname on sign-in sheets at the doctor's office. The name remained nowhere. Nothing to do with me. All I possessed was the sickening puzzle box I'd started with.

My wits grew feverish, feeble, as though Marcy taunted me into lashing out at ethereal notions, goading me to strike prematurely against only the killers I knew. Doing so would get me caught. Being caught would best protect her. Fearing I'd put her to rout as I had the others, she played desperate hide-and-seek to run out the clock, thumbing her nose at me much as Benecourt'd given me vulgar sneer by growing in Deirdre. But while he'd wallowed in the abhorrent pleasure of forcing me to place loving palm on her skin so I might feel him kick, at least he'd the gall to show himself. Tellwell was an inveterate coward. Disguised herself as the ether. Proved with such invisibility she was the cleverest and most reprehensible of your assassins. My hatred flared so intensely that were I handed a blade and told 'Here stands a row of fifteen pregnant women and Tellwell's inside one' I'd have strolled the line blithely, fileting the lot. My loathing'd metastasized enough I was blind to reason. Any damage acceptable. Lives lost in addition to your killers' of no consequence. Provided Tellwell was eradicated, even the other four going free seemed permissible.

It no longer horrified me that your killers might've been drawn from my life. Benecourt, Lowell, and Goaltender could be found in my past. Lyons as well, were things viewed at a slant. I was a map. One which might lead me delirious lost but, regardless, might see you to safety. Let Tellwell be something to do with me. I'd search with that notion as compass. Embrace the fact there existed a thread of my lived history which, if followed, would lead to her. She must be somewhere near at hand. The more odious the villain, the closer they kept.

What point delaying? Let me relate how I discovered her then move on to the rest. The moment was stodgy. Were it presented in film, your father'd be disappointed. Lambast it as paint-by-numbers. Riff countless ways a script might get the point more subtly across. Even now I can hear him doing so. Grin at how much I agree.

As your due date inched near, we went all in curating the room which'd be your first nursey. Knew it was silly, but wanted the activities of preparation before you were born, the physicality of them, the closeness between us. All four walls were adorned with freehand illustration, the closet crammed tall and thick with quilts, blankets, bibs, swaddle cloths, and enough infant clothes to last a lifetime, as though you'd remain less than the length of a forearm forever. Toys and books you'd neither see nor touch til years later were hoarded, the room furnished with shelves shaped like crocodiles, giraffes, bandit racoons, a crib devilishly heavy, antique rocking chair, and two secondhand chests of drawers. Pictures were hung on the walls, starships and cityscapes stenciled across the ceiling from which dangled only a fraction of the mobiles I all but compulsively acquired. This glut would be ridiculously cumbersome to pack up, both of us joking we might as well pitch everything in the nearest dumpster when it came time to depart. Your father jested that my nesting instinct had run riot and I allowed he was likely correct. Teased him that a few months of keeping me happy was worth the entire payday his first film had earned. Everything was kept a laugh, a caress, an embrace, though I knew I only behaved so devil-may-care because the nursery was one I'd never hold you in. I wanted a lifetime packed into the space, enough of my frivolity and impulse to warm you for eternity.

We'd put finishing touches to one of our amateur art pieces. A toad at a cash machine. Some rubbish idea I'd blurted out when your father'd asked "What else even is there to add?" I stared at the drying artwork as my mind simmered with a dull murmur of hatred for Tellwell. The infection she'd become. Present during our intimacies. Lurking in my thoughts, always. I despised how even inside me you couldn't be free of her. Meanwhile, your father opened and closed drawers, traced fingertips over garments in the closet, and spoke about you aloud as he always did, tone one of awe and What-if. I heard his hushed voice wonder "Who is she?" Of course he meant what would you reveal yourself to be, where would life take you, what would you bring to the world. But in that precise moment, I'd been thinking of the unknown woman carrying Marcy Tellwell and those same three words had flashed behind my eyes. *Who is she*. The syncing of his voice to my thoughts was overwhelming. I stood in silence, your crib blurring in front me, and a despair I won't bother attempting to express in these pages choked me of breath. As your father said a number of things I don't recall, my vision seemed to crackle, I became congested, my lower lip quivered, and a flush of feverish fatigue wormed through my limbs. Soon he stood in front of me. I only somewhat recall him smoothing the pads of his thumbs over my cheeks as though thinking to kiss me, likely having interpreted my tears as a response to his contemplations. His expression morphed to confusion as I all but hissed "Who is she?" and, in a tone beseeching and desperate, repeated the query over and over again.

Caressing my shoulders, his eyes squinted harsh, searching for meaning in the tangle of my face. "Who is who, Noor?" he whispered a few times, increasing confusion, anxiety, and something close to frustration apparent as he attempted to meet my gaze. I hiccoughed painfully, stunted gasps followed by rabbit-breaths, each burst lasting only a chattering few seconds, then finally, mouth salty with mucus, all but squealed "The woman!" "Which woman, Noor?" he asked while he guided me the few paces backward to the rocker, asked again on his knees at the side of the chair, hands curled around my forearm as my fingers tensed the bulb of the armrest. "What woman?" he seemed to plead, eyes waiting soft and fearful. Hardly knowing what I was saying, yearning to confess but terrified how far I'd go were he to coax, through chattering teeth I whispered "Tellwell."

From the first, barely perceptible flicker to his eyes, the almost instantaneous change-then-change-back as they set to earnest concern and patience for me, I knew. For a few minutes bawled like an overtired adolescent. Then simply sat. His hands on my arm. Absently rocking me in silence.

I need you to understand I doubted nothing. Every word of your father's explanation rang true. It was a betrayal he'd every right to purge himself of and I held nothing against him. Wouldn't have even under different circumstances and certainly not to a degree requiring theatrical kowtowing in addition to his proclamations of unerring love. He needn't have gone on as he did, but I allowed him to speak until contented, responded only after he'd unburdened himself in the unfiltered manner he felt appropriate, pedantically detailed lest I doubt its sincerity, a performance of remorse so thorough no lover could ever find solace in it. I didn't particularly forgive him, simply considered there nothing to forgive while I spoke words of forgiveness he believed less the more I assured him they were true.

Tellwell's mother had been called Calista Stuyvesant when she'd first met your father. Long before our paths had crossed, they'd been briefly involved. During their tryst, she'd been in a relationship with the man she'd since married, your father an inconsequential romance with someone vaguely acquainted with the two. Their attraction had been understood wordlessly and never so much as guessed at by anyone else in their orbit. Neither had desired of the other any more than what'd passed between them and if less had transpired or nothing'd been consummated it would've been all the same. Pleasurable simply to know they both knew the other's attraction and that such knowledge existed solely between them. The four occasions they'd been together sexually had been spontaneous then never mentioned. When they parted ways, it'd been without goodbyes or disappointment at no goodbyes. Zero effort to keep in touch was exerted. Neither had left, neither had stayed, life'd merely continued the ten years leading to their recent encounter.

She had nothing to do with any of the films and he'd no idea one of the people involved in the first production was loosely acquainted with a friend of hers nor received forewarning this person'd invited that friend to visit, Tellwell in tow. So far as anyone who'd been in their presence knew, they were strangers whose interactions indicated two people being casually introduced for the first time.

He knew little of her present circumstances and *vice versa*. Even as he unpacked his guilt to me wasn't aware she dwelt in the area. Might've wondered about it after their encounter, but neither'd inquired whether the other was local or for how long they'd be around. Neither'd even made remark about the rings they hadn't removed from their fingers. The entirety of their liaison was related. Miniscule and irrelevant details loaded atop each other, as though to prove he was leaving nothing out. No doubt every morsel of the business was true, a tale as oddly inexplicable as you might imagine. He belabored how, though subterfuge might've been required on both their parts, neither'd discussed it. Explained it was the second time Tellwell'd tagged along to a filming location they'd had their brief, passionate time of it, no one on set even noticing them gone the twenty minutes it'd taken. Post-coital, no interaction'd indicated they'd anything to do with each other, past or present. Once more, they'd parted without fanfare. There'd been no communication ventured by either, since.

Such punctilious transparency about the affair bored me. I needed nothing further from him than Tellwell. Could've kissed the man, I felt so giddy at receiving irrefutable confirmation that all I'd feared was absolutely correct. Soon had to talk him down from his distress, convince him there was no reason to ask after Tellwell through the friend-of-the-friend when he demanded to make a show of proving there existed nothing substantive between them and to illustrate how callously he'd sever all ties. But I required no penance. Almost told him he was free to see Calista to his heart's content. She wasn't to blame for anything, after all, and his involvement with her didn't make him a danger to you. For appearances sake, I might've let him make good on some act of contrition, but instead told him all I needed was to know exactly when they'd been together. Despite being certain of the answer, I posed this condition in a tone suggesting I'd be matching up whatever he'd say to a narrative I'd already been given, that any future with me was dependent on full disclosure. If his story didn't gel, all would be forfeit between us. If what he said fit lock-key, the matter'd be buried, never to be raked up, again.

For all his penchant toward absentmindedness and esoteric digression in most matters, his mind was wired precisely when it came to this recent transgression. The exact date was promptly provided. He fairly blurted the precise time of the closeted deed, in fact. I held my face as though waiting for more. Flummoxed, his phrasings became imprecise stammers, his eyes ticked side-to-side, expression strained, comprehending there must've been something specific I desired to hear without having to prod for it, but at a loss as to what it might be. After a pause, he hung his head, closed his eyes, and seemed unable to let out a breath for a long while. Eventually told me it'd been the day I'd said I'd die during childbirth. This admission seemed to anguish him. He began weeping, the abrupt burst of emotion so genuine I almost put a hand to his shoulder to let him know he needn't go on, but in the end let him be.

Ashamed this hadn't been what he'd replied straight away, he melodramatically confessed how, during the discussion we'd had that day, he'd fretted I'd known what he'd done and that everything I'd said about my fears had been a gambit designed to egg him toward some reaction, a coy preamble to my revealing his secret was out. The timing of my statements, combined with how matter-of-fact I'd been, had jarred him into wanting to talk about anything else. Admitted he'd felt relief I'd been going through some vagrant spot of depression, been keen to speak of abstract ideas, because he'd convinced himself relieving me of the peculiar dread I'd seemed to be experiencing would've equaled good deed enough to deserve a stay of execution.

He'd experienced similar unease when I'd later prompted him into rhetorical conversation about protecting a loved one against untenable danger. For a moment, thought I'd been considering killing Calista to keep her from stealing him away. Of killing him to stop them both from taking you. He felt wretched for such ignoble thoughts, but restated his promise to keep nothing from me. Said the capability to entertain such fancies was a part of him I deserved to have made plain.

I didn't care about any such rubbish. To be honest, I was thrilled, felt near to rapture as it clicked tight how he'd literally been making love to Tellwell while I'd been home that day. Wanted to laugh in triumph as I understood that their bodies would've been entwined, he boisterously driving his orgasm into her, unwittingly conceiving the last of your killers, exactly as I'd stood idly in the kitchen, spreading peanut butter over that cracker. That had been the first moment I'd known of the threat to you and could've known not one moment sooner. Your father's act fastened all into place. Made me capable of knowing. Made it possible to stop.

I lied to your father. Told him Calista'd contacted me. Claimed she'd felt it proper, considering my state, to ensure any choice I made about our future was informed. Promised she'd been unaware of my pregnancy, only found out subsequently, unsolicited, and wanted me absolutely at ease. She'd no aims on him, zero reason to suspect he'd aims on her, and gave direct assurance she'd make no further contact nor accept contact should any be attempted. Glossed over details by stating our conversation'd been awkward and brief. Even added how I'd gotten prickly when she'd said 'You can tell him that' as though granting permission I ought be grateful for, so amused at this ornament I began laughing broadly enough your father almost smiled as though he were a friend in my corner, cheering me up after some other party'd wronged me. Ended the scene by rolling my eyes, saying I didn't give her too hard a time, and reiterated her claiming he'd no direct way of reaching out and couldn't imagine why he would, whether I confronted him or not.

In no position to press me with detailed cross examination, nor of a mind to, he assured me everything I'd told him Calista'd said was the truth. I think if I'd invented details meant to paint the scene more negatively, he'd have agreed to those, as well. Had a posture and affect like begging. Repeated he'd not been in contact since the day of the tryst, hadn't been for the ten plus years since last they'd seen each other, re-vowed to never reach out, and re-proclaimed how he wouldn't have, regardless of his chickens coming home to roost. I'd never found him so unattractive. A current of distaste for him tensed through me. Disbelief such a pusillanimous man could've wooed me, been father to you. To this day, I wonder if it showed on my face. To this day, though I hope not, I hope so.

I allowed our talk to go on for hours. There in the nursey we spoke. First of ourselves, our relationship. Then of how we now had a daughter, requiring care and protection. Our own desires, the whole of our pasts, must be put to one side or else visited only in service of such. I assured him I didn't doubt his love for me, for you, nor question his fidelity, overall. Told him I passionately believed certain ideas he'd often expressed. How there existed connections, currents, urges, imperatives operating outside the core of any individual's control, that such currents overlap, intersect, and we find ourselves at the mercy of elements unknown. Such as what'd happened between he and Calista, we can make choices, but the truly consequential ones are built of situations we'd never dream to construct and which must be responded to, *impromptu*. Some believe the decisions made on impulse, when confronted unprepared with a temptation or danger which had genesis deep in the past, are what most define us. But I'd never subscribed to such. The one-offs, oddities, and stimuli responses aren't peeks into our secret souls. Our calculated decisions, weighted with time and earnest reflection, are the only honest revelations. Whether we respond in the moment the same as we would upon reflection is incidental, even coincidental. With Calista, hardly a thought'd been given. He'd responded to sudden input linked to passionate experience and past connection. Any trust which may've been molested would repair with the natural passage of time. There was no value in assigning blame or dissecting why he'd acted how he had or exploring whether the situation might've gone differently if certain events in his life'd never transpired. I told him nobody's strictly anything and that specific moments don't directly affix to, inform, or indict others. People can only be whatever they are, moment to moment, how true or false of heart dependent on circumstances often beyond their control. What he'd done was extant, but only in the past. It was our choice how it lived on. I promised he needn't fear things between us going the way they would if written in some story. Insisted how, in my view, such make believe never spoke to the full truth of our intimacies or transgressions, which so often share flesh and soul.

"We all have things we do and don't tell, we aren't but pretend, aspect we don't desire so mitigate, and there are countless things we say but never do, do but never say. We sit next to people who're the same. It's hardly important if they admit it, or even know it, about themselves. We're all so very little of our lives, my love, and need to claim the parts we are, not let certain choices infect all others. Actions don't have dominion over the truth. What's true is true and can be felt, can be known, if at all, despite all argument or presentation of evidence which might sway us from thinking it true."

As I made this speech, it seemed a part of me'd been crafting and refining it for exactly such moment. Your father appeared as moved as he did relieved. Said "Things that cannot be known sometimes can."

I told him how things known in such way are the strongest, the truest, and, in the end, are the only. Told him "I don't doubt your love and never will." He told me the same.

Such a scene, such a scene. Another he'd scoff and tear from any script he'd conceived. In a petty way, I took pleasure backing him into the corner or such hackwork.

By providence, the table'd prepared itself. I'd no longer have to choose the day and the hour, instead was being instructed when to act, assured I'd been correct to've waited. Previous argumentation revealed itself a refined courage rather than the timorous indecision I'd whipped myself believing it. You've read how I'd frittered weeks in self-loathing, my instincts to protect you multiple to the point of paralysis but I now apprehended it'd needed be so. Only after plagues of misgivings could I comprehend how incorrect, ineffectual, and ultimately fatal any path but the labyrinthine one I'd trod would've been. As any mother ought've, I'd assailed myself with consideration of every possible harm that might befall you. In doing so, repurposed doubt into precision, marshalled countless options appropriately, and through diligent interrogation freed myself from the morass of faulty conscience. I'd hold firm to my conviction even while staring down the barrel of my own demise, trust myself in ways I'd never thought possible, knowing my trust'd never been baseless.

Not required to kill, cover up, kill, cover up, forever fearful how a misstep would lead to being halted in my tracks while further victims remained vital, I'd no longer fret falling short. Fate hadn't conscripted me into attempting to attain your security on the installment plan. I'd beaten such lie. Had my delicious reward. Such relief to be so near the end and to find myself shut of the intrusive notions that'd stalled me. With resolve sharpened, I could see myself through the horrors I'd enact, all of them in the course of one night, no need to artificially maintain over time what was meant to be a single howl of destruction.

Given proper space, granted audience with those I'd sought, from the start I'd have done what needed doing. Were I stopped, I'd be stopped. What'd changed was how, from this moment on, I could proceed until I was or I wasn't, carry on until I no longer breathed and you'd screamed your first. I'd been whittled to what I'd always desired. An implement. You and my wake would be all I left behind.

It mapped out so cleanly. Due to the start of his third film, your father'd be away, four days in-a-row. He'd made certain the state of my pregnancy was understood, petitioned to stack the production schedule to allow that he'd be able to return with relative promptness were an emergent issue to arise, but even were something to require him back, a half-day of travel was involved. I'd be alone in those hours. Five people would be dead. Eleven people. Your killers, their mothers, the surrogate. More might perish, if need be. But that near-dozen was definite.

The entire episode blossomed in my head, not like a plan, more like an entertainment recalled verbatim, akin to my knowledge of what'd happen to you, though the particulars seemed far more pristine. Unlike what I knew of our fates, the events soon to transpire were cemented in my mind's eye, spooled coherently along like a film which could be sped up, slowed down, reversed, replayed without any spec altering. On each viewing, my intimacy with all aspects deepened. The darkness of the coming hours looped and looped, images sharpened, scents joined one to another and melded with sounds, more unalterable each time around. I enjoyed watching the macabre scenes playing out. Spent hours humming songs of them to you.

I'd begin with Deirdre.
She'd been invited to stay with me in advance of your father's departure. Slated to arrive the day before, she'd spend that night in a hotel then keep me company in our apartment until his return. Her intent was to keep the hotel until I'd delivered, insistent she'd not make herself a perpetual nuisance in my home for what'd likely be weeks. The moment I received word your father'd arrived at the shooting location, she'd be in my clutches. No one expected to hear from her for at least three days. Not contact I couldn't be proxy in providing.

Complaining my apartment felt stifling, I'd entreat her to let me stay at the hotel, claim a change of venue lasting even one night would be a vacation, likely my last for a good long while. I'd taken out another room in the establishment, one floor up, arranged to keep it from several days before Deirdre's arrival until several after, strict instructions of *Do Not Disturb* left with the desk. In it I'd stashed a bag containing the various blades and changes of clothing I'd require as events progressed into the night. Once Deirdre fell asleep, I'd slip from her room to mine. Retrieve my kit. Return. Make it peaceful. Cut her throat while she slept. The carcass dragged to a bathtub half-filled with perfume, her remains covered in bedsheets doused in the same scent, ventilation grates covered, every precaution against odors wafting free during the remainder of the week I'd extend her stay for, front desk informed that staff wasn't to turn down the room. My friend was the only victim I'd be easily connected with or immediately questioned regarding, so such acts seemed appropriate precautions.

You see how careful I was, that I understood any risk of preparations being stumbled upon was to be avoided, wasn't a senseless automaton despite knowing an assured fate guided my way. Care with confidence, each step cementing the next, was how I'd protect you. I was braced to be apprehended for my crimes, but would afford myself the best odds of remaining free and unsuspected until already in hospital.

You'll ask yourself about the obvious mistake of taking a room in my name, something directly connecting me with the grisly events. This was acceptance. There was nothing else for it. My crimes couldn't be left a mystery nor my hand in them a question mark. Any effort spent on that front was effort wasted, attention taken from you. Since I'd soon be no longer, I acted as though I already no longer was. Had abandoned myself in favor of you.

I no longer entertained disguising myself in a bulky coat pulled from some dumpster, donning a wig, a mask, or whichever ridiculous ruse. Such business would only impinge on my ability to travel to and approach the remaining four targets. You were the perfect misdirection. Proudly showing your bulk was the cloak which'd hide my intent from anyone who'd chance to encounter me. Your innocence obscured my guilt, allowed me to move freely amongst the public as I progressed station-to-station, fixed it that I might knock on front doors, beg myself inside with feints of exhaustion or cramp, exit after completing my tasks. Possible witnesses would state they'd seen nothing suspicious enough to match the horror of the crime scenes uncovered. A pregnant woman, perhaps a friend of the deceased, had been welcomed inside then departed in jaunty spirits, showing no signs of distress, only hours before the murders took place. Friends of the dead mothers would be questioned. Had they been over that day? Know any woman fitting so vague a description? Could anyone have had motive to hurt these poor women?

Same as with the addresses and evening habits of the others, I'd verified as best I could that the surrogate lived alone on the third floor of a nondescript apartment complex. A busy enough pile of dwellings, it'd be no bother to enter the lobby, ride the elevator, approach her unit come middle evening. She'd open to my knock, perhaps confused at the sight of a stranger in the narrow, chlorine scented corridor, duffle bag in hand. I'd make whichever awkward introduction would ease me over the threshold or else feign distress were she markedly hesitant, ask could I use her toilet, have a seat, a drink to help a spell of lightheaded nausea subside.

My blade would wait atop the duffle, beneath a folded sweater. As the door shut, I'd drive it cold and angular into the girl's firm belly, shoving her violently off balance, inertia unsheathing the serrations so I might slash fierce across her throat before delving the filthy steel back up her gored womb, twisting my wrist to sever arms, fingers, feet, dicing the Lowell fetus into a slurry which'd leak from between the surrogates lifeless legs, crag like dried porridge in her disused lap. The corpse would be left wherever it fell, dragged even an inch only if the worthless bulk blocked my path out, and I'd move into her living space to strip off my clothing, sundress to undergarments, bunching them into one of the plastic bags I'd packed for such purpose, my next outfit waiting in similar wrapping for me to slip into after the murder weapon was briefly rinsed and left in her silverware drawer or the dishwasher I'd leave running. Breath returned to me and tidied up, I'd exit into the corridor with an affectation of glee giggled over my shoulder for the benefit of any nosy observer.

All of this I saw, crisper, more vibrant with each passing day, each dwindling hour. Parts of lived reality wouldn't match lockstep to what I envisioned, of course. These were my thoughts, not glimpses of our exact future. But whatever differed would be to my benefit. In that absurd way it is, events would come off smoother than I'd braced against. The world wasn't built to prevent acts like mine, merely to sort out their aftermaths. I found it obscene how unencumbered I'd be. Shocked to watch again and again the ease with which I'd be able to operate. Disgusted with the world I'd bring you into.

Goaltender's was a rental home toward the end of an odd suburbanesque avenue, pinned between a blank expanse of unkempt parking lot and a shopping center on one side, on the other showcase shops for billiards equipment, kitchen facades, and a single pump gas station, unlit overnight. Vague pedestrians on their way to or from nearby metro stations and motely pubs about a half-mile off intermittently dotted the brown-lit sidewalks on both sides of the two lane street, vehicle traffic running tight alongside various trucks branded with insignias lining the road shoulder flanked by untended trees, beyond which perched an inexplicable bubble of more respectable residences. All manner of potential witnesses to my arrival and departure, but don't you see how frighteningly little difference it made? A dozen nobodies might glimpse me as I calmly strolled the same rubbish strewn concrete as them, meet my eyes, perhaps even speak to me, but none of it mattered. Goaltender's fate would be as merciless and brief as the surrogate's. A change of clothes, a return to my car waiting parked in the pocked shopping center, then onward to the quaint row house where Lyons dwelt with her husband.

There I'd wait for night to fully descend, serene dark spilt everywhere, roads growing sleepy as possible, windows unlit or else shaded in the faint scribble of televisions and nightlights. My car would've been left in an hourly garage from where I'd taken a bus to the mouth of the neighborhood. Doorbell rung. Alexander would die if need be, though I sincerely hoped Lenora would be alone. At one point, I'd considered leaving her until the next morning, when it'd be guaranteed the husband was gone for the day. The fact such scenario never played out in my head, unbidden, seemed proof the method wouldn't do. The father's fate could be left to chance but yours couldn't. No allowances of any stripe would be made after what I'd have already done.

Sometimes the film in my mind would have Alexander come to the door, dumbfounded to discover a pregnant stranger asking after his wife, explaining they knew each from whichever place or else apologizing for the late intrusion, but could she trouble him for use of the toilet, confessing herself in a bit of a pickle considering her state. He might motion that I could use the facilities if something was the matter, explain his wife had already retired to bed, was occupied bathing, or a trillion things else, none of which would alter what came next. Fourth blade at the ready beneath t-shirt atop duffle, I'd playact a missed step, lean down, grip the handle, and, right in the lit entrance portal, drive it home, bullying the man backward as his lung perforated or as he blankly attempted to process the grinding burn throughout his abdomen as my wrist turned. Either way, the door'd shut. If some passerby thought they'd seen something as they'd peered through their across-the-street curtain or been airing their dog, let them knock, receive no answer, call the authorities to perform a well check. Within minutes, Lenora would've joined her husband and I'd be draped in fresh clothes. For days, my rental car would've been parked in a lot cattycorner the house's rear entrance. I'd cross the covered courtyard, jaywalk the street at my leisure, saunter up a block, and, ten minutes after the slaughter, have air conditioning and radio soundtrack. Whoever may've witnessed whichever odd duck glimpse of me would have zero idea what'd transpired in the residence, whether I'd left, or which vehicle I'd driven, if any at all.

Two hours was all it'd take to find Tellwell, from there. Multiple distinct tracks played out in my mind concerning her. None more dominant. The scenarios never taken in turns. All versions experienced simultaneous. My mind able to treat the gnarl not as cacophony but orchestral composition. In one, I imagined having words with Calista in private. Introducing myself. Met with a look indicating she apprehended my presence and would never dream of barring me entry to her home. In some iterations, I waited until she'd apologized before cutting her throat, letting Marcy expire, unwounded, drowned in her mother's fluids, buried by her flesh. Other times, I'd extract the child from her, hold it aloft while she writhed moaning on the ground, stab it a dozen times while I apologized for having no choice. Sometimes while I butchered Marcy thus, I'd growl how what was happening was on account of your father, other times make certain Calista understood her fate was nothing to do with him, at all. In most vignettes, her death passed in silence. No words spoken. As confusing to her as it was to me.

There were versions where matters transpired publicly. Calista on the street. Amongst a group of friends. I'd approach with weapon concealed. Not a care that everything would end there. Your final tormentor rapturously brought down in naked view of all gathered. I might have at her before a single person could sort up from down, plunge my blade straight through the maggot writhing within her, slash at her animalistic, all directions, grunting as I did, forcing hands into her lacerated belly as though to dig her hollow, find residue of your strangled killer caked under my fingernails for days and days after. Or Calista's husband would lunge to wrest me from his wife. The group of women drag me clear, several keeping me pinned me to the concrete while others screamed and tended to their felled friend.

Always too late to save Marcy. I'd need mere seconds with her. No more than a moment in the presence of her unwitting mother. Let them save Calista, smother her wounds, bandage them, suture her shut, rescue the emptied husk she'd be left. I'd have accomplished all.

What did I see in the film, afterward? The reel continued to unspool, the screen bright with scratches like stray hairs across it, a pleasant rattling sound *fip-fip-fip-fip-fip*. Other than that, nothing. Not even days going by as usual or time spent imprisoned until being brought to a birthing room. I saw no image of you, either. There wasn't need for fantasy of those things. To imagine specifics from beyond the night of our revenge made that night and all I felt assured would transpire during it seem whimsical pick-and-choose.

Two tasks would remain. Would occur in tandem. I'd birth you. I'd die doing so. Provided I did, you'd be protected by the exact authorities I might turn myself over to, who I'd perhaps have waited for the arrival of on the scene of Tellwell's murder, who'd perhaps not've knocked at my apartment door for days while I hummed in your nursery, my dead friend and the killer within her bloating in a fragrant hotel bathtub. Or perhaps while he sat in the rocking chair, years later, singing to you, your father'd be stirred to the front door of whichever house I'd never know you in by knocks I'd never hear and, holding your toddling hand, find detectives somberly loitering on the porch.

I wanted to take it for granted he'd act to protect me were he to discover what I'd done or if I confessed all to him. It warmed me to believe there'd exist only the impulse to keep me safe, help me escape, but knew such instinct would filter through endless rhetorical consideration of how he might and why he ought not. I can almost hear his voice as I write this, undercurrent of merriment as he'd work to assure me there was nothing for it but to move on, bearing whichever guilt, the two of us, a burden shared which, to his mind, was a quaint plaything, practically a gift.

He'd lay out implacable rationale proving no tangible good could come of my being apprehended or unbosoming what I'd done to the families of my victims, that the world writ large was nothing to do with my deeds. Those actions behind me, their ethics reduced to semantics, interchangeable daydreams of ideals which'd crumble if they came to be actualized. Whichever punitive measure could be enacted stood irrelevant. I'd killed only under the most extraordinary possible circumstances, after all. It was immaterial whether he personally believed I'd known what I'd known, thought it chronic mental illness, or blamed transient mania brought on by the pregnancy. Twice as moot to him, because he'd consider it all those things at once. So insane a series of stimuli would never repeat, therefore I wouldn't continue to kill, thus the families of my victims learning what'd happened amounted to the confirmation of a senseless act, which was already what they were enduring. It wasn't as though husbands, sisters, mothers, fathers would earnestly consider why I'd done what I'd done, admit a reaction to it other than horror. My sincerest attempts at explaining would be taken for a performance of clever mitigation, admitting myself deranged as cheap *apologia*, squirming to save my skin so I'd skate on capital charges, wind up under cozy medical supervision. I'd be told I was further victimizing them, plying them to pretend themselves possessed of a humanity above my own, required to show mercy on behalf of those I'd been merciless with. Your father would suss how they'd want my slaughter and how only when barred from it would they deign to set the terms of my continued life, desired my destruction but when unable to procure it would exhaust themselves with seeing me rendered to pieces by torments worse than death, never settling for the sentence this or that jurist deemed appropriate or conceding to any psychologist's authority. They'd no honest right to dictate or decide, but since their revenge couldn't be mortal would do everything in their power to have it decreed I not participate in my child's life, be declared not only impossible to absolve but psychically incurable.

I wouldn't put it past your father to throw himself recklessly behind me, concoct an alibi, venture to Deirdre's hotel, massage the crime scene. He'd lovingly coach me what to tell detectives, but there'd be rising consternation as I laid bare each detail of what I'd done, flummoxing any narrative he'd invent to account for why I hadn't reached out to her, why I'd taken a room days ahead of her arrival, rented a car, so on and so on and so on.

What he'd wend round to was that my hand had been forced. Our unborn child threatened, I'd no viable choice but to've acted as the instrument of an unseen scoundrel. He'd advise me to present myself as sympathetic, claim I'd caved in beneath devilish pressure, under strict orders to conceal my plight even from him. Or else he'd insist I immediately begin a possum act, allow him to have me admitted emergently to a psychiatric hospital, claim I'd been nearly comatose for two days, that with your birth so near at hand he didn't feel comfortable supervising me. Implore me to take to heart whatever role he proctored me in. Whether I'd done the killings willfully, in a fugue of diseased wits, or been strongarmed into aiding some third party was all the same to those kin to the victims, as deep down they'd know the victims themselves would've acted exactly as I had, were the tables turned.

He might take the entire weight of the crime on his shoulders. Say I'd solicited him with my plight. That it'd been his decision not to act. Make false claim after false claim. Go so far as to state under oath that he'd assured me the proper authorities had been contacted, how for all I'd ever known sanctioned steps were being taken to catch out the killer, that he'd gone along with my part in corralling victims but informed me in exhaustive detail how police would spring into action when the time was ripe, save everyone, had shielded me from details, news reports, practically held me prisoner and acted as proxy in conducting the unseen fiend's business. He'd do anything on the strength that keeping me free until you were born was all that mattered. Together, we'd choose how to proceed from there.

Perhaps I'd have let him suffer the consequences on my behalf. Come to believe whichever version of life he charged me to. Talk until he'd convinced me I was merely 'the way these women happened to've died.' What difference to the families or unconnected outsiders if their deaths had been accidents, illnesses, or even five murders by separate perpetrators? It amounted to no more than a handful of examples of what happened every day for every reason and no reason at all, indistinguishable from all other accidents, illnesses, and murders by people other than me which, to me, to him, to everyone, were simply nondescript events in a world ninety-nine percent imaginary for all we cared or could ever prove, nothing to do with us even when we brushed them directly, five random instances of the endless happenings there's nothing to do but accept, no call to understand, process, or even acknowledge individually. What difference if my thoughts were my own or foist on me by your father until I exhaustedly said 'Okay.' Accepted things happened how they happened and thus I was no more of a thing that happened than what'd happened to me, was nothing I'd understand even were some mysterious figure to appear and explain exactly how, exactly why, exactly what I was. Such specter would then have to explain itself. What it was. Who it was. Where it'd come from. How. Where that place'd come from. How. Why. Who'd told it. Why did it believe. I might let you father talk me into an almost opiate surrender. Be glad his words succeeded where mine had failed.

On the other hand, he might've simply said it didn't matter, either way. Believe every single thing I revealed. Profess it morally wrong I'd chosen to act as I had then dust his hands and shrug. If my fate was truly sealed, perhaps the only important thing to him would be to see his daughter safe. To do so would require countenancing no distractions from her, so he'd cast off the burden of acknowledging the pain of strangers, wouldn't bear the intrusion of gawking onlookers, allow his life, your life, to be made into a carnival. I hoped this'd be the case. It ought be. I'd be dead. You'd be either protected a bit more than had I not acted or else exactly as protected as you'd have been were all I'd done unnecessary. For him, first and foremost should be the desire to keep you free of what I'd done. He'd hold my secret. Take on the gruesome responsibility because it kept the virus I was from spreading to you.

He'd be incapable of believing until he saw me dead. Which was the way matters ought find terminus. Me dead, you secure, him relieved. I hoped he'd find himself joyful when I died. Victims out of the equation, their loved ones either unwitting, so holding no grudge, or else left without recourse to justice beyond my corpse. He'd discover the horrific things I'd done in your name, without his knowledge or participation. Learn all I'd kept from him. Shudder at who I was. Whichever guilt he'd weather ought be forever abstract. A story prompt spun every which way. A tale he'd tell you. One you'd ask for. He'd find the version which suited you best, pleased you the most, nourished you properly. Make me a story as loving and decent as you deserved. Speak me into the sort of mother I ought've been, because he'd know what I'd done meant that was precisely the sort of mother I was. One who'd do the impossible for you. Attempted to by inventing an impossibility. He'd give you the story of a world containing me without containing what I'd done. After I'd protected you how he simply couldn't, he'd protect you how I'd been denied.

There was perverse serenity to what I knew would be my last days with your father, our last days together, the two of us, the three. I took special care to display no kink of emotion which might convince him to shirk work duties, was dreadfully aware any disquiet I conveyed risked him asking me to call off Deirdre's visit or else request the both of us join him on location. He'd coo his deception. Not admit the push for nearness was based on concern. Couch it as a favor I could do him. There'd be no rational explanation for denying him so cordial and caring an accommodation. If described as a way to alleviate concerns he harbored in response to some behavior of mine, I might wriggle free of the proposition, with words or gestures set his mind at ease. But an admission of his own trepidation would require a delicacy I doubted I'd have guile enough to bring off. In the event he implored me, claimed himself weak, in need of me, how could I, in good conscience, deny him? Were I to do so, it'd be counterproductive. If I didn't do as he wanted, he'd make me. I'd no power to prompt him not to speak to Deirdre. No way to stop him, in ignorance, taking action which'd upset the conditions I depended on.

But it seems silly, writing of fears I kept primly concealed. They were fleeting and bubbled to the surface only infrequently. Not a jot of distress showed outwardly. Any fretting myself over the approaching task was relegated to my hours alone, showers, or staring at the ceiling during the night while harkening the untroubled breath of your father's slumber beside me.

The days were tranquil for their normalcy. No revelation of tension, no extra displays of passion, not so much as flirtatiously coded goodbyes in the mornings or indulgent I-missed-you-so-muches come evening. The same activities, conversations, arguments, jokes which would've occurred had nothing been happening took place as though nothing was. It was the last I'd experience rote life. I wanted it to be special for seeming anything but.

The kiss I'd give your father as he left to location work would be nonchalant. He'd return it in kind. My 'I love, too' a *blasé* riff to his absentminded 'I love you.' Ordinary, though each were the only kisses like them. One kiss would be the first time I'd kiss him for the last time. One day the first time I'd never say 'I love you, too' again.

As the day grew nearer, I found myself possessed of the strangest idea. That I ought not bother with the hotel. Should kill Deirdre in the apartment while laying beside her in bed. Open her throat mid-sentence as she began drifting off to our casual chatter. Afterward, I'd enjoy a leisurely shower then strike out to slay Goaltender, Lowell, Lyons, Tellwell. The pleasure this thought produced bordered on erotic, as though tending to Deirdre in such a fashion altered an intrinsic element of the deed, imbued it with intimacy she deserved, made it something she could better relax into, understand.

Other thoughts. Bizarre. Many. Only about Deirdre. That I might have her tag along with me when I killed the Lowell surrogate. She'd be kept none the wiser. Fed some story about a new friend I desired her to meet. Slash the girl's throat. Pivot and drive the placenta caked blade into Deirdre's belly. Hold eye contact as I worked the serrations back-and-forth. Sawed her unborn's head off. Pulled the knife free. Percussively jabbed it into her neck till my wrist cramped. Or else tell her I'd some quick errands to run. Claim my duffel was something I needed to drop with the surrogate. Ask her to wait in the car. Butcher the girl. Change into an identical outfit. Drive to see Goaltender. Enact some similar scene. All in advance of having Deirdre walk to Lyons' door with me. Where I'd kill her, Lenora, the hapless husband all in a frenzy.

The best I can surmise is that my hatred for Benecourt made me want to torment him. Rub in his face how he'd failed. Gloat that his perverse colonization of my friend had gained him nothing. But I never considered dragging Deirdre all the way to Tellwell. Making Benecourt witness every death but Marcy's was in service of her knowing she was alone. I couldn't shake the feeling they could communicate, shared a bond, had chosen their dwellings to inflict maximum harm on me. Were this true, using them to torture each other felt appropriate. I didn't bother trying to sort these thoughts. Nothing more than residues of hatred. Prodding me to do what I actually would.

The fantasy of fire returned. As in those ghastly dreams which by then seemed from a different life, I thought of lugging a cannister of accelerant around with me, killing Deirdre outdoors or in her vehicle then setting it ablaze, dousing every felled body likewise, the floors and walls around them, infernos left behind me, crimes made more difficult and time consuming to sort out. All nonsense. What purpose would be served? A grotesque misdirection to guarantee me the time til your birth, alone with your father, his heart not yet burdened, free of all knowledge until I was gone and you were nestled safely in his arms? Such selfishness couldn't be the pulse of anything. The notion of safeguarding myself for any reason besides completing the task was girlish betrayal, the last-ditch effort of some mewling aspect of me wanting to worm out of my charge. Or may've been my last vestige of decency working to disallow blasphemous victory. I must've wanted to ensure that I'd suffer. Perhaps there existed some quivering speck of me wanting to ruin it all. Weak-kneed guilt, long simmering, which knew I'd die before it could be properly felt after-the-fact so desired failure outright.

What the reason for these unprompted thoughts was, I've no idea. But they came. More peculiar and nuanced as they amassed. As though I was addicted to alteration. Thought like your father chattering me past fatigue with poking and poking and poking at make-believes.

In the bathtub, I began laughing, outright giddy at an absurd, cinematic vision of our revenge set as montage to song. Artfully photographed. Images deftly edited to beats of a Bubblegum Oldie. An unmitigated joy to behold, to play back, to recommend, to award. In it I brandished a pistol Deirdre'd felt compelled to purchase and teach me how to use. She'd have chortled at how horrid an object it was, explaining a creeping noia she'd developed, while I inspected, loaded, trained the barrel at her belly. Pranging chords announcing the song's refrain would blurt as the image cut to me driving my car, celluloid red freckling my face sensually, tongue clearing some from my lips with a shiver of juke-joint arousal. Likewise with each woman. For the duration of the song, the verses would display how simply and unstoppable I'd make each approach, the refrains showing my clothes grown increasingly sullied, passersby remarking me but never certain what to do even after witnessing each mother's door opening to the crack of a blunderbuss.

My body was no more than a machine on a circuit which'd end in its capture, our vengeance a gismo nothing could stop until it'd run down its fuel. A suicide run which'd end with your life secured was how things always would've gone. Everything fated. I was simply more cognizant how life was automatic than those around me. Glad to be who and what I'd been created for.

I'd dismissed the thought of writing to you. In the days I'd thought would be my last with your father, setting something down seemed antithetical to my cause. I'd many times considered keeping a diary, chronicling my efforts in real time. Not anything so detailed or long as this, but a few words jotted each evening which I'd never read back. I'd attempted to work myself toward penning a letter, heartfelt, direct, sealed in an envelope, left behind. Considered making an audio recording so you'd have my voice. But in the midst of the developing maelstrom, I'd been loathe to choose words. Any effort was too much. The futility of whichever media I'd create overwhelmed me. My task still in the offing, no sentiment could yet be the truth, merely a litany of notions and *faux* explanations of matters I'd only considered, an expression of love unaccomplished. Were I to allow focus, expend energy, I wanted to leave behind only veracity. In those hours of zero achievement, was incapable of it. Until I'd given you life, it made more sense to write simply how I was sorry. That it was my fault, whatever would happen. I didn't want to proclaim certainty about what I'd attempt when nothing'd been attempted, to floridly promise I'd have done anything until I'd proven to myself I'd at least taken one step toward what I needed to. Wanted no more could-bes, maybes, possiblys, not an instant more spent thinking. Desired my mind decided. That accomplished, wanted it dead. To be the first aspect of me which expired. My body could go on without consciousness, since my body was all that was required.

But intrusive nitpicks ceaselessly arrived, unsolicited. So many words wasted. Nothing but stories your father might write. Anyone might. There'd always be more. But I refused to express myself to only the concept of you. Until there was actuality to make sentiments tangible, I'd write nothing. My love was an action. Your life the result. I was to be gone before it was given to you. Needed the story of you-not-yet to be one you'd never hear.

Much has changed since then. Many things I didn't yet know and many more I would've revolted against, labeled quirks of exhaustion meant to misdirect. Even if I'd understood, in those hours I wouldn't have trusted.

Deirdre'd explained some last minute debacle would delay her an entire day, leaked profuse apologies over the telephone which I assured her in tones of laughter weren't necessary. Your birth was weeks off, she ought feel no urgency. This cordial air of nonchalance was a deliberate overcorrection to my pang of terror. She'd sensed danger in joining me. Unconsciously orchestrated reasons to avoid coming. Ridiculous, I know. My dearest friend needn't be lured into my company. Was delivering Benecourt unwitting. Would call when she was properly *en route*. Arrive past midnight, according to her best estimate. By which time your father'd be on location. If there was someplace safe to stow a key, she'd let herself in. I needn't wait up.

It was very early when your father left. He'd tried not to wake me. I didn't protest when he told me to go back to sleep out of fear he'd notice I'd been awake long before him, note the strain on my face from the contractions which'd stirred me and yet smoldered while his lips pressed to the skin of my belly around you.

I'd been alone an hour when they intensified. The change sudden and marked. No longer a deep, pulsing tremor but a persistent gnarl which seemed cruel, inappropriate, unnatural, nothing like the slim warbles of discomfort I'd grown accustomed to in the preceding weeks, nor a match to the intermittent spikes. These had an urgency radically different than the pain which'd stirred me awake and kept me from drifting off after. All at once, it didn't seem I'd slept. Memory of ever not being awake vanished, replaced by a limbo of soggy thoughts, muted glimpses of conscious time surrounded by a swamp of listless breathing and waiting between breaths.

Pain began in earnest. I thought cold water would be enough to quell it, so ran the shower. Cold became scalding became lukewarm became icy. Each alteration in temperature mutated the contractions into sensations more aggressive and tangled. Dripping wet at the sink, I numbly brushed my teeth, repeatedly. For some reason, the activity distracted me. Watched myself shush the bristles in a reflection first obscured by steam then blurry as the greyish haze cleared. I was unable to focus. A sensation of nausea overcame me, stomach bloated as though with swallowed ointment, my saliva tasting of rust, a crackle of vomit waiting at the top of my throat, licorice scent filling my head from within. I hobbled to the rocker in your nursery, plopped in it, and sightlessly gazed in the direction of your crib, fixated on a pimple I scratched growing hotter the deeper I brought my fingernail back and forth.

I never considered what I was going through an episode I couldn't wait out. Was relieved it hadn't started an hour sooner or during the night. Had it done, your father'd have already whisked me off to hospital, scuttled his work plans without second thought, not on my life entertaining the notion of being away a split second until you were born safe and sound. Even if the pain subsided, the situation was declared non-emergent, doctors waving off any need to remain for precautionary observation, all would've been lost.

Such relief was quickly subsumed by panic that whatever was happening wouldn't pass soon enough. Deirdre'd arrive. Discover me in the throes. Summon help. Were I to halt her doing so, killing her there and then, it wouldn't matter. I'd be in no condition to venture out. Tend to the others.

My mind throttled me next with a relief of betrayal. If I'd not have the strength to kill Deirdre, I wouldn't have to kill anyone. Opportunity'd be filched. Having waited too long, I'd been spared committing violence. Everything would be over. The thought sickened me, knowing myself weak enough to still accept such outcome a torment.

A paste of fever crawled over me. Cotton mouthed, I grew lightheaded. Unable to lock down any train of thought, execute the smallest action. My left arm shivered, tingled from circulation loss, then began to twitch, a cartoonish flop of palsy, every inch of my flesh turning damp and rubbery as a biliousness like carbonated vinegar coursed unchecked, my ears ringing then clogging then both at once, a swirl of tart bile coiling worm-like above my diaphragm.

It's so difficult to describe. These moments seem unreal yet so particular. I'm compelled to have you understand. Will relate them the same as I have all the others, as they happened rather than how I've reflected on them, since. The memory of that morning is akin to the immediate recollection of a nightmare, too precise, too specific, and for all its formlessness too sensible to process or genuinely recall, the remembrance of an experience which didn't happen, wasn't even imagined, the sort of horror one only feels the byproduct of. Except I've no recollection of these moments ending. Their peculiar sensations can be summoned up, intact, but are too hyperactive to be parsed, impossible to pin down their start or their *terminus*.

I stared down at the cavity of the kitchen sink basin, faucet spewing hot water I refused to put my hands in despite an intense urge to slap scalded palms to my face and run raw fingers through my hair. The gushing filled a bowl until it overflowed, then filled a cup I positioned the pivoting spout overtop before it tipped over, and steam belched unrelenting from the disposal's gullet, a dank and humid odor of substances the gears hadn't ground out of existence wafting against my face while I deeply inhaled, the scent peppery like the breath of a dog and bringing to mind thoughts of chewing the stubborn fat on the bone of a pork chop.

I recall emptying cubes from freezer trays into an orange plastic bowl which I set on top of the bagged bread beside the refrigerator, three four five times in-a-row sitting to the sofa, standing immediately, walking a circle of the living room, spitting briefly sucked ice onto the carpet and against the dusty television screen. I thought nothing, registered little, the room around me hollow and gummy, air oppressive, artificial, the space I moved through in one moment vast but in the next moment obscenely confining, a world no wider than the fingers of my ribs, as though I expanded, shrank, expanded, shrank, playful but excruciating, burping in time with your feet, shoulders, and head scouring the inside of me, as though you were pressed directly against the underside of my belly skin, only a thin veil of sodden construction paper between your fingernails and my palm as it pressed down into your clawing.

I recall my forehead to the bedroom window glass. Looking out. Transfixed by a scene on the street below. But what I recollect so vividly doesn't match what would've been visible from such vantage. A postman speaking to an elderly woman, her body bent to the shape of a question mark, the clothing around her limp except for at the distended flab of her middle which clamped part of her sweater between it and the hang of her distended breasts as though bound with sutures thick as unwound wire hangers. It was the most uncanny thing to observe, although nothing of substance occurred. I thought to myself I must tell your father about its every last detail. Grew excited at the prospect of regaling him, of insisting he write a movie depicting the old woman as a detective with personality traits kept the same as any other character he'd written, became manic as I prattled aloud how he must have literally the woman I'd seen hired to play the part, not a word of the script tailored to accommodate her age or bearing. He'd think this was marvelous, declare it the most beautiful idea he'd ever heard, wish he'd thought of it himself. "He will write it!" I heralded, hugging myself in pleasure as though something of consequence had been accomplished after vast effort and deserved celebration. I repeated "He will he will he will he will" while lacerating pain viced me, inhaled rough and salty, mucous cleared from my top lip with the back of my wrist while I raised my shoulders to my ears, lowered them, hands dangling limp at my wrists, bumping over my breasts as they were brought up toward my chin, caressing my breasts purposefully, gripping, kneading serenely on the way down, raising, lowering, raising, lowering, as though I were posing as an insect cleaning itself or in the fashion of a schlock cinema creature. I pretended your father was pointing a camera at me, laughing too boisterously to depress the shutter every time I changed position, until I became irritated, told him to stop laughing, to be silent, be serious, bullied him to take the damn picture, as it'd been his idea to begin with.

So many formless patches of memory. Real and unreal. Purposeless. It strikes me how long I could go on relating them. Filling volumes if I felt like. But little need for that.

My water broke. Abrupt and absolute. Horribly aware of myself and what was happening, a spitfire of abject terror rattled me to attention. I don't recall if I screamed or merely wondered if I ought to be screaming while wondering what else I might do, instead. Screaming seemed ridiculous, despite my comprehension of the danger I was in, head throbbing the bold print of a symptom list I'd once read in a pamphlet, the bullet-point directions of what must be done were labor this intense to begin so far from one's due date, how imperative it was that immediate medical attention be sought, the odd syntax 'Everyone will be relieved if it turns out a false alarm' weighing me down while I teetered in place and scratched the top of one foot with the untrimmed nail of the other's big toe until blood had pooled on the kitchen tile deep enough to splash in.

Needle cold, an ache spread over every last inch of me, inside and out. I caught myself mid-faint against the counter side. Again at the sofa back. Breathed according to various methods I'd halfheartedly practiced. Insisted what was happening wasn't. I hadn't finished what I'd planned. You weren't protected. This wasn't safe. Shouldn't be, couldn't be, how children were born.

I recall the telephone ringing. Having it against my ear. Don't remember speaking. Remember very clearly not. Your father's voice in my ear. Then it was later on. The telephone was ringing and had rung before. Its receiver slick in my tightened hand where I stood beside the bed. I felt as though I'd made preparations. Appropriate clothes and toiletries packed. Was ready to go. Simply awaiting the arrival of a taxicab, an ambulance. This feeling relieved me, despite I knew I'd done nothing, called no one. It confuses and chills me to think on the moment, in particular. I'll attempt no further description.

The phone was ringing again then the phone was ringing again and then again and then later and still later and later still your father's voice and then Deirdre's voice in good spirits before being anything but.

My mind wrenched shut. But I must've been speaking. Terrifying those who were trapped listening. Must've said endless things I don't recollect while I bawled, hung up the phone, had it to my ear again, incoherent pleas blurted at your father, at Deirdre, to medical personnel, or at least to myself, to you. But I couldn't get one thought to catch, not one idea how I ought behave to grip firm.

I don't know if I recall shaking in horror while wondering if my mind was obeying how I'd begged it not to think ever again. Perhaps I remember considering this only much later on. I'd no mind, in those moment. Not even enough to think I had none. I can summon these disconnected moments, but lack any conception of their duration, ordination, or if I attempted to help myself in between each. I can't honestly recall even wanting to.

I don't recall when I collapsed. Don't recall when the apartment was breached or by whom. Have no memory of which method I was transported from the apartment following whichever duration I'd been there alone, conscious, semi-conscious, or out cold. Your father's since explained it. Deirdre has, too. I've had it narrated that medics were dispatched. They'd found me responsive and communicative. I can't bring a word of what was said to mind, but have been told I begged for your life, pleaded with anyone who'd listen to save you, am told I screamed 'Find them!' and became aggressive when told your father was nearby and that Deirdre was *en route*, as though they were who I'd wanted found. The story goes I grew violent and erratic, bellowed that I'd not meant your father, that Deirdre could rot in Hell, and had to be restrained when told I'd be with the doctors, soon, and was promised my daughter'd be saved.

Entering the hospital, being rushed to the room where I was attended has all been described. From time-to-time, I've attempted to picture my body working in desperate cramp to expel you while I'd muttered "Hide her, hide her, hide Tasha, Tasha, hide!" Am told I rabidly insisted you needed to be hidden, kept telling you directly you needed to hide.

I've no memory of you dying, being taken away from me, no recollection of what noises I made or which words I babbled while doctors and nurses flurried with vain efforts to make you draw breath as your father choked both my hands in both of his, face reeking of brine as he pressed it into my hair, the bulb of his leaking nose grinding against the divot of my delirious ear. I've no memory of calling for you, demanding to be given my baby, pleading to hold you before I died, to have you with me as I did. I've no memory of being told you were dead. Had died. Had never lived. Was told later that it'd happened. Those moments I'll never forget. Being updated with a feeling I'd already been imparted the same news before.

Peculiar to think how swiftly everything altered. Or rather how immediately it unaltered. As though in a blink, life returned to an almost precise approximation of what it'd been, no different than how any one day when met with the next is distinct yet seems the same. In this case, felt new but so alike to something which ought to've passed and been impossible to replicate its similarity became its primary difference. Time isn't meant to flow backward. Never does, regardless how often it seems to. But for awhile, time acted as though it'd die trying. People attempted to convince me the world as I knew it was yet the world as it'd once been. Perhaps did so to convince themselves.

As I walk my mind back, I'm unable to find proper footing, never certain I know anything about what anyone did or how any circumstance felt, what I or anyone desired life to be like or supposed it ought to or could've been. It's as true to say nothing felt strange, nothing seemed altered, nothing returned or progressed, that time staggered sideways. 'Continued' might be the best word to express it. Life could do nothing but continue, yet how peculiar it was that it did. As though a confusion which claimed to not be confusion simply because it knew it was confusion and recognized itself.

I was no longer pregnant but also had no child. A common enough occurrence. One of the two standard outcomes. Neither more inappropriate than the other, each to be equally expected, no matter how fervently one might be preferred. The temporary state of my pregnancy had always been meant to lead to a permanence. For anyone else, the after-state would be having their child or having lost it. For your father, life raising his child alone or with whoever else life might've found him. For me, the most permanent state of all. Nothingness. Instead, I'd been led to what'd only be temporary, again. What was the nature of this repetition? What terms dictated its duration? Which hand, whose will, decided when or if it would end?

It occurred to me that everything was choice. No element of existence could simply be, rather some decision sets into motion the choiceless parts of life's composition. I don't know how best to make myself clear on this, but shall attempt.

It isn't a stretch to say breathing seems consciously decided, despite our lungs functioning without any regard. At some point in life, though we've always breathed with no conception of having thought to, there's a moment of deciding to breathe. Glib to say, but I believe such elections, seemingly moot and fleeting then instantly forgotten, exist in service of permanent objectives. There's a particular breath in one's life which was particularly breathed. Such allowed that all other breath might return to being automatic. Some thought or realization occurs, is felt profoundly, and from it our unthinking reality goes on.

The moment where I understood this is gone. Didn't last long enough to be remembered. Unremembered, it can't be explained. It feels as though I'm jotting down make believe. Trying to describe what never was in terms other than 'it never was.'

Almost the instant I knew I was alive but you hadn't been born, a fixation began, equivalent to how a painter'd become struck by the notion of what to adorn a canvas with before any specifics of the composition coalesced.

A presence in the mind. Desire to render, to express something never experienced, never known, and which might not exist in the strictest sense. Not time, place, person, situation. Some abstract notion. Love, confusion, passion, fury. Compulsion to invent something intangible, which language couldn't describe but seemed like it ought be able to. Artists no doubt draw on matters overhead, witnessed, or merely imagined, images or scenarios recalled from dreams blend with personal experience to produce something they won't apprehend the full scope of until their work is finalized. The build-up to creation can be recollected, but never explained, as creation isn't beholden to the method leading to it.

I pondered whether painters thought in terms of creation or of re-creation, though felt wary of discussing the philosophical speculation with anybody. No doubt it'd seem a frivolous and esoteric distraction meant to wile away my grief, but I was cautious it remain as unknown as so many thoughts had for so long.

I couldn't decide if painters who'd experienced whichever event or emotion they attempted to render had a leg up on those who hadn't. If they'd looked into the eyes of someone they loved or of someone in the throes of falling in love with them, could they express the feeling to canvas more honestly than if they'd never witnessed anything of the kind? Or could the painter who'd only desired such experience, but never lived it, get the features down correctly? If it was the face of another being painted, the emotion being rendered wasn't their own and thus an emotion merely surmised, perhaps simply imagined. Would there be tangible difference between the two compositions? Wouldn't the painters be the last people consulted regarding which attributes their renditions possessed?

The thought'd begun while in hospital but wasn't spoken aloud until perhaps a week after being back in the apartment. The second communication I'd ventured beyond mechanical response to whether I was feeling alright or needed something brought to me.

The first had been a quip to your father about how quickly they let someone who'd entered a hospital pregnant leave it without a child, after which we'd rotely discussed how, in our private thoughts, we'd both acted out the conversations we'd imagined would've taken place after your birth, bewildered chatter wherein we'd have joked how odd it was the hospital'd allowed us leave so quickly with a child in tow, but had never let each other know of such rehearsals. This muted banter had been in service of earnestly confessing how curious I found it he'd already removed the child seat from our vehicle. Knew he'd already made decisions. Considered you dead or lost or never to've been. Settled himself on things I didn't agree with. While I was still alive, decisions about you were mine alone and I ought need never explain or defend them.

As what would've been your due date officially passed, we'd been back to the apartment nearly three weeks. My disorientation at being alive had increased almost hourly. No doubt your father was unfooted as well, but his situation was opposite mine. He needed to sort out how to continue living with life's details temporarily altered, find a new rhythm for existence. For me, the fact I still breathed was out of sync. It was antithetical to my existence to yet exist. I'd no purpose having failed in what my purpose had been.

What was I doing alive? What meaning could my life have, what function? Was it punishment? Had I been denied death for failing you? Was death now to be my choice, an unnatural act undertaken despite I'd accepted it as natural while working to keep you safe?

If I'd thought I'd yet had time, had made preparations, brought myself to the moment of crisis, how had I failed? Considering what I knew, how could it've been unreasonable to've waited as I had? Why call it 'waiting' when it'd been time spent planning, any seeming lack of action far from stalling out, rather a conscientious method of making certain my chore wouldn't be left incomplete?

Finding myself alive, would I prefer death? Was I denied it because it'd allow me to join you? Did I want that? I'd never known you individually alive, you'd only ever been part of myself, and in that we'd never not been joined. Hadn't we therefore been as close as ever we could be? Death wouldn't be shared, after all. Yours was yours, mine would be mine. If dying meant we both went on being, knowing, I might as well say living with you dead was no different than living with you in my arms.

Another torment of wordplay. A poetry of doublespeak. Concepts parsed to hide behind. I couldn't join you in death due to my understanding of what I knew. You hadn't died. You'd simply never been. We'd been. You and I, as one. Now you weren't, but I was. If growing within me was part of your individual life rather than a state of moving toward it while still being component of mine, how had I failed? Your life had been guaranteed until thirty, I'd fretted to preserve it that long and to arrange for it to persist longer, so while inside me you must yet have been you-and-I not yourself. I couldn't meet again what never was. The only way I could be alive was if you never were.

I looked on as your father's life returned to some earlier iteration of itself. He seemed resistant to allow normalcy back, hesitant in a way I was incapable of, having known no life would exist past your birth. Whenever I'd spoken of how things'd be once you were with us, it'd been out of mercy to your father, speeches and daydreams and going along, keeping up an illusion, concealing my continued belief in what was going to happen, deceptions in service of no one thinking anything amiss with me and, because of it, acting witlessly to restrict my ability to defend you. When I'd spoken of myself as a mother to Deirdre, my therapist, whomever, voiced thoughts of myself as a living entity who'd nurture you, it'd all been calculated make-believe.

Based on what you've read up til now, you understand I'd made concerted effort never to allow myself the indulgence of picturing the life we might've had if I was incorrect about our fates. I wanted to know who you'd be and who I might become for knowing you, but hadn't let myself pretend I'd ever be able. Cordoned such thoughts off. Out of fear they'd be too overwhelming. Instructed myself that allowing so much as one hour of mollycoddling would weaken me, become an avenue your killers would take advantage of. Musing that I'd ever hold you was a fantasy I couldn't afford.

But your father'd pictured it. Spoken of it with humor and passion a thousand times. Had prepped to change, evolve, a new creature down to the atom. He'd longed to become a being utterly unknown to himself, incomplete without you present, desired it for fair and for ill. Everything he'd been doing, feeling, thinking, whether shared with me or kept private, contained you. His daughter was to've been the living center of the rest of his life. He'd tether himself to you, even when unnecessary or irksome, live embracing you as the most meaningful thing he'd ever have hand in, would 'bask in his obsolescence' with the same fervor I'd prepared myself to die knowing mine. The 'down-and-out realist-romantic' he'd dubbed himself back when we'd first met apprehended the hardships of what having you in his life would be on many levels. Too many. He'd weave speculations about every variant of every day of your life, how he might react or not react, wish he'd reacted but hadn't, to X Y and Z, would spin yarns about regretting things he'd do or say, grow to no longer regret them, then grow to regret having grown not to regret whichever miniscule failing he'd wistfully ding himself with, go on so much that all he might do or might say was as real and unalterable as its inverse. He turned and inspected your coming life from all angles, every which way, the same as his stories or whichever films he'd take in. Except, with you, his pontifications were even more boundless. His daughter was an entity still dimensionless and therefore provided him infinite surfaces to twist and regard from vantages imaginary through apertures extravagant and theoretical. I remember he'd once spoken unflaggingly for three hours straight, postulating on what he and I'd do were you born a goldfish, a mushroom, a wine glass, the Letter R, or an unresolved geometry equation, while I'd listened, alternately in hysterics and alarmed that he might never stop, might be unable. He had it all mapped out yet none of it concrete, every day of your life and every alternate of what he'd do or not do for you or with you, be you healthy, ill, or entirely abstract. Never cared which manner of life he'd have or what'd come of it, simply desired it be with you, for you, of you.

Now I observed him grappling with having become only almost-your-father, every step toward the identity taken but robbed of the full metamorphosis. I wondered if he'd lashed himself for thinking it'd be the same to have you in the flesh as some abstract idea, if picturing you being born as a handful of pine needles or a few ounces of sugared water had led to your being born nothing. Wondered if he heard Fate mocking him, thumbing Its nose. 'Since it's all the same to you, there she is: your daughter the not-quite-a-poof, your daughter the fizzle!'

I never asked if he'd seen your body, witnessed what'd been removed from me but never birthed. If so, wondered had he felt, even for a flicker, like a father-in-full, granted his change for an instant, if holding you in his eyes had transmuted him. A father who'd lost his daughter after having her less than the length a blink, never knowing her weight rested along a forearm, her slumbering head in the crook of his elbow. Did he feel you'd never been real enough to possess aspects not merely imagined, never more than our hopes and our trepidations? I never asked if you were still multitudes. If all the millions of things you might've been had been pulled out from under him, too.

I felt peculiar and lost when observing the man. I'd only thought of him as 'your father' for so long that recasting him 'the man who would've been your father' was something my mind wasn't equipped for. You were our daughter. More than an idea which hadn't been realized. You were Tasha, just weren't Tasha, yet. He wasn't your father, yet. I was the mother who hadn't yet made you either.

Remaining on my guard, I spoke very little, did very little, felt unable. Silence, stillness, could make me appear sunken, unreachable. At the same time, I was careful not to give an impression of being 'too recovered' for fear it might translate as volatility. The things I said remained performance. Any pleasantness not laced with a pinch of gloom or exhaustion could be deemed a blip of mania, indication I teetered on the verge of an outburst. Everyone who spent time in my presence tensed for my expected, deserved collapse. I sometimes think there was disappointment in it never arriving. Judgements whispered and kept concealed from me.

What I desired was time alone. Privacy in order to think. It felt unnatural to be always surrounded, blockaded from access to solitude, kept from myself. As though by unwritten decree, seclusion was deemed hazardous. Carefully disguised precautions were taken against it. One month prior, no such thing had been a consideration let alone a condition so artfully maintained. I had my thoughts to myself, but thinking while alone is an entirely different proposition than doing so while sitting next to someone, subsumed by company, or jarred from contemplation by whichever well-wishing tap. When the content of one's mind feels as though it must be kept hidden, they can't feel truly alone. Alone is where thought's most alive, existing full bloom, not even personal will able to corral it. In company, however intimate, unfettered thought isn't permitted. Worse, has to be requested, considered, then allowed.

I thought of you, but if I spoke couldn't divulge the full particulars. The presence of others wouldn't relent. Made me feel present, but as though I was without context of my own. Wondered if that was what it'd been like for you while closed in the womb. If being so utterly surrounded by another could ever be life. Even in your languageless way, had you never been alone enough to have a thought all your own? The idea tormented me.

One matter I couldn't broach aloud, desired silence and space to sort out, was why I'd wound up experiencing what the mothers of your killers would've suffered at my hand. I'd lost my child under circumstances utterly mysterious but seemingly natural. No one could offer precise explanation for what'd happened to me, illuminate the matter more than stating how losing you as I had was something inexplicable which happened all too often. The doctors admitted they'd no specific cause to name and there was no indication given the matter would be probed.

I couldn't help thinking back to my early desires of cleverly arranging the deaths of your killers to be brought off without direct violence, their mothers coming to no permanent harm. Plots of surreptitious poisoning, tragic accidents orchestrated deviously enough the five women would be none the wiser there'd been human agency behind their losses. Is that what'd happened to me? If so, I'd never know. The same as I'd fantasized would happen to them, I'd been doled out drab medical terminology. Were I to suggest foul play, I'd be talked down. Were I to insist, my assertions would be dubbed ludicrous. Were I to demand anything further, it'd be treated as suspicious. An eye would be kept on me.

Suppose one of the mothers had become aware what I'd do. Perhaps they'd bided their time. Managed to outplay me. As I would've, might've been stealing private moments to gloat how the endeavor to protect their child was accepted as 'part of life' or 'the way a child had died' the same as it would've been for me had I acted more swiftly against them. I'd have preened and cock-crowed, even if I'd butchered you killers and wound up in chains for the trouble, proud how whichever way I might've maneuvered the outcome had amounted to no more than concerned brows, hapless shrugs.

I can't help finding perverse amusement in contemplating this. Consider for a moment how if the content of these pages I'm filling were ever made known, I'd without doubt be marked aberrant, ungodly, inhuman. On the other hand, pretend I'd been targeted by one of the mothers, had lost you due to their machinations. Simply for never opening their mouths, never moving confessional pen, they'd be seen as innocent, no investigation undertaken even were I to make outright accusation against them. All they'd have to do is what I would've done. Say nothing. Feign ignorance were something said. It'd be deemed appalling to suggest they were anything but undeserving targets of a grieving woman's slander. I'd be looked at askance. If I came clean about what I'd been planning, detailed my preparations, deemed degenerate and locked away.

The lot of them may've known as much as I had from the jump, every step of the way been cognizant of the menace approaching. Our interaction may've been as much part of their reconnaissance as mine. Were this the case, defending their children would've been easy as pie. As a collective, they might've surmised my head was as full of cautious misgivings as their own, but would've known my task was exponentially more daunting due to navigating it alone. Simple enough to conspire. Even if they'd known what lay in store for you, they'd justify it, mitigate, finagle the concept of morality. If they'd apprehended the full picture, would kill you to keep their children from becoming killers. That's how

I'd have couched the matter, were I one of them. How difficult a decision would it've been for five expectant mothers? All of their children or just one of mine. No hesitation would've been required. Knowing you were slated to die, regardless, they'd annul the thirty years of life you'd been otherwise promised.

If they didn't know I knew, what on Earth would've prevented them from supposing I did and acting in their own best interests? They'd be securing life for their children. Guaranteeing them freedom from prison, bare minimum. Hopefully barring them from arriving at whichever macabre crossroads led to taking your life in cold blood. How was I to know what they knew, any more than anyone knowing me would know or even accept that I knew what I did? It might've been revealed their children would collectively die at thirty-five if you weren't eliminated. Or their children may've died in the aftermath of your murder. Executed under the law. Succumbed to the pangs of conscience. Turned on each other. Taken their own lives. This mother might know one tidbit, that mother another, each presenting their case in the most favorable light, even were deceit required. They could've been privy to a great deal more than me, had their knowledge tailored to them, pooled resources with every advantage and insight.

From their perspective, you might be deemed the reason their children would act how they would. Without you, after all, they'd consider there to be no issue. Whichever mental acrobatics were required to paint you the cause would be performed with aplomb. Numbers were on their side to soften the blow. Their decision to offer you up as sacrifice would read five times as palatable as mine. All they'd require was one little thing not to happen. Your life. One invisible death meant the hearts and souls of their children would be secured safe transit.

They'd not desired to hurt me, had only vilified me to work up their nerve. Killing you was a guilt they'd believe could be forgotten, a one-time heinous but utterly irreproducible act they'd have their entire lives to make up for. Would promise to show penitence and behave forthright, forevermore. Litter enough good deeds here-and-there to eventually balance the scales. Think one day I'd no longer see you as the child I'd lost or the child taken from me, just the child I'd never had. Perhaps their lives would bring more benefit to the world than ever they'd dreamt. Not killing me might've been a valuable act of deep conscience, one that'd do good for countless who'd otherwise have gone by the boards.

Not that I could afford to overlook the alternative. That they blamed me as I'd never blamed them. Saw me as responsible for your fate along with the fate of their children. Despised me. Desired above all it be me who suffered. Might've never considered you a living entity to weigh the guilt or the innocence of. You'd done nothing yet, hadn't even lived. Your death may've been coded as a stab I deserved. Were this so, the lot could've calculated to let you grow almost fully before tearing you from me. The more imminent you became, the more satisfactory their vengeance. Perfectly reasonable to suppose there'd never been a wink of hesitation on their part, that everything they'd done'd been curated, a purposeful, well rationed torture. If they were aware I knew what I did, it served to reason they'd goad me toward action as a torment, coax me into confronting the depths to which I'd gleefully lower myself. Relish me regarding my true face, never acknowledging it wouldn't be what it was if not for the killers they nourished. I'd be left alive to comprehend the scope of my failure atop what I'd already endured, to apprehend how they'd known all along, succeeded where I'd blundered, brought off their dark deed for the sake of their children, so they wouldn't need sully themselves, know the danger they'd been in, or confront what they'd be capable of. It would've tickled them to see me driven to know what a beast I was, to rub in my face how I was the opposite of them for being the lesser. They'd something to find peace in, had killed for their children as anyone would, as so many do, while I'd been too feeble. It couldn't even be overlooked how they might be animals who wanted you to die, me to die, fiends with membership to some occult cabal such as would be the gobsmacking twist in one of your father's scripts.

Though it was also reasonable not to malign them. After much soul searching, they may've convinced themselves my being permitted to live on was beneficent. Possible they were aware I'd have died during childbirth, concluded that your never being born secured my continued existence. It might've seemed quite an elegant solution. One life for five. Plus my life. One life for six. Less than a life for six, depending how they regarded you. Added into which, my life yet stretched before me to fill how I deemed fit. Having another child was a reasonable possibility and they may've believed only you, the child who'd been growing inside me at that exact time, could be the cause of their children's future actions. Their collective guilt spread out to statistical innocence. Five had become killers to arrange for five others to remain nonkillers. All the same horrific tabulations I'd worked out they had, as well, and it summed that my life being spared amounted to more life in total.

Perhaps they'd thought I'd understand that. How could I not? Perhaps they thought my understanding meant I understood what they understood exactly as they understood it and that, since the inverse situation wouldn't result as favorably, I'd be satisfied, even grateful they'd taken the driving seat.

In such train of thought, I posited they knew that I knew what I knew and, from there, had assumed I'd known what they'd known, as well. Such'd seem proven each time they'd watched me introduce myself, taking steps to get nearer and nearer. At the start, each may've imagined their individual knowledge a sickness of the wits. Then I'd come calling. Stirred them to defense.

Or had they discovered each other, earlier on? Spoken, plotted, decided never to approach me, of a mind that I'd convince myself whatever I felt I had foreknowledge of was psychological ailment, nothing more? If so, it served to reason they'd taken my approach as justification to act. I was stalking them, circling their children. What purpose could I have, if not the one they'd been made privy to? If I'd desired some way other than the obvious to protect my daughter, why had I made no attempt to communicate that I shared their understanding, was caught in my own plight, and wanted to work together toward some method which might safeguard everyone?

Perhaps each and every one of them were going to die. Perish while giving birth to your killers. Wanted you dead to spare their children making a horrendous mistake. Were this so, telling them I'd also die might've brokered an accord, made plain an entirely new way of approaching the dilemma. Though my telling them we were all in the same boat might've been irrelevant. Like me, they could see no guarantees existed, no absolutes prevented what was to come, no safeguard except for certain elements of an equation to never exist. I'd have no argument. Would be the one pitching them to leave it to faith, to fate, beseeching them to let the future be ignored and pretended unknown.

Only by there being no Tasha would there be no death of Tasha at the hands of their children. If I were them, wouldn't it be just so childishly apparent? Once you were dead, hook or crook, I'd conclude there was no reason to act against anyone, even if I knew what they'd done. I was alive, wasn't I? All permutations of what else might've been could be pawed at, leisurely discussed, but would always conclude in the question 'Why would Noor Parsinbyrd have reason to act?'

Around and around went the bloat of half-considerations I drowned in. Too surrounded to give true attention to any, more and more had opportunity to seep into my thoughts. The best I could manage was foothold on some specific, but with never more than five minutes silence, all was for naught. Hours lost to chitchat or hugging your father when he needed comfort, to putting on a brave face for some anonymous auditor. Whole new considerations waited to superimpose over what'd been left unexamined, my mind a palimpsest, ink from stroke after stroke of possible-consideration never fully dry before hurriedly written atop, impossible to test any notion posited as none could be fully articulated.

Soon enough, I'd no way to decipher if I was thinking back on something or having it occur to me for the first time, no tools to determine what was a nuance to or wrinkle in a previous line of reasoning versus the starting point of a new track which'd required examination of nuances and wrinkles its own. Anytime I found myself alone for an hour, each second was a laceration. All I wanted to think about seemed untrustworthy. I'd second guess whether I was thinking about something I needed to or else something I'd forgotten had already been dismissed. Life dribbled away in valueless retread.

Inwardly, I grew somewhat bitter toward your father. Nothing broke surface, lasted long, or reached particular sharpness, but after we'd returned to the apartment, it grated on me that he could behave how he desired, the particulars of existence his to pick despite the underlying quality being anything but. Still subject to what'd happened, he couldn't possess that which he most yearned for, and I knew he mourned under the brave face he donned, but the display of grief was something he held dominion over. Unfiltered sorrow wasn't permitted around me, would be destructive. That's how he'd have diagnosed matters. Would've been correct. But correctness did little but amplify tension. He'd been cognizant I was aware he'd crafted his performance for what he deemed my benefit and that I knew the gesture wasn't purely magnanimous. Had determined I'd be of no help to him. Decided this wrote him allowances to rob me of agency, unilaterally call shots, exert control in my weakness, and mark me recovered only through protocol based on his whims.

I imagine he grew bitter, too. Been able to suss that I'd no desire to aid him. Intuited how fervently I wanted to be alone. Such would've reasonably been interpreted as my wanting him gone. He'd likely been aware I sensed his discomfort, confusion, and believed my failure to address his feelings justified them over and over again. I wasn't only what cut him off from living his anguish, but party to it in the most insidious way. With no means to comfort him, my presence put in his face how he lacked ability to properly be the presence of comfort he felt I required. What he wanted to think about he couldn't, or could only in the brief stabs of quiet filched here and there, same as me. As he came to terms with how he'd lost the life he'd wanted, he grew convinced regaining his own equilibrium would never be a priority. Every stolen moment spent thinking of himself might've tasted of betrayal. Perhaps he'd loathed himself for things I'd never fathom. Loathed me for how I'd never try.

On the surface, his trap might appear to be no different than mine. Comparative to me, however, he could navigate the aftermath of losing you in his own time, retained ability to structure his days, construct how he'd cope, make definitive declarations of his headspace and from them dictate courses of action without pleading his case before experts. No one exercised direct authority to urge or guilt or coerce him to behave this way or that and he'd no adjudicator apart from himself. Meanwhile, I was scrutinized. Every unknown thought in my head considered volatile, every professed emotion seen as no more than a clue, stimuli not to be believed or acted on as I requested it might, but rather turned inside out, conferred upon, responded to like a tea leaf. I was suspected of things, though no one would say what. Asking why I was handled with kid gloves was marked as a further symptom.

No word from me was taken as honest, therefore no word to me from anyone else seemed sincere. Interactions were probing, tentative. Whoever addressed me kept poised to alter their demeanor or professed point-of-view on a dime based on kneejerk perception of me, justified in reversing positions without being labeled manipulative because before they could tell me what they thought they needed to know what I did and the only way to learn this was whichever game of cops-and-robbers they arbitrarily deemed clinical. I was touch-and-go, a jigsaw to guess at, and if I moved to assert I wanted the opposite of what'd been proposed, a duty of care would be cited as though irrefutable dictate. They were sorry if they were wrong or if their choices discomfited me, but better they be wrong than I be wrong and they learn they'd failed to protect me.

However horrible you may think me for couching it so, you nonetheless must admit it was your father's choice to suffer in one fashion versus another. What he'd lost and presently endured had an almost semantical nature to it while I'd no choice in the matter. I was your mother, *de facto*. Had been, continued to be. He was, *de jure,* your father. Had never known, never nurtured your flesh. This distinction permitted the face of his life to be presented as he dictated. He might well say he was grieving but that he wanted to look at it as though he hadn't lost anything apart from a potential life, calmly explain such was something he hoped and believed might be reobtained, and which would directly replace what'd been stolen. Were he to say this, no one'd argue the point, suggest he reconsider, or assume the words were spoken with ulterior motive. Indeed, he might impart the sentiment in a tender whisper, filter it through intimacy, mention how it'd be all up to me if we tried for a child again. Dependent on my recovery, my state of mind, whether I could bear it. People would whisper back, agreeing, empathizing with how difficult it must be for him to not tilt me toward such decision, that no matter how passionate his desire was he must abstain from articulating it, not rush me even if I broached the subject.

Reading this, you think I ought be more reasonable. That it's in bad taste to reveal these aspects of myself with regard to your father. I love you for this and agree. But we're too far along. Remember, I expect nothing of you.

I pleaded with him to return to work. So I'd have the apartment to myself, but also so I'd not feel I was his reluctant duty. But he was deaf to this, grew belligerent. The request was cast as needlessly whipping myself with sacrifice while failing to appreciate the sacrifice he'd made. I proceeded gently, utilizing calm tone, reasoned verbiage, expressed my rationale in perfectly logical terms, but he'd rattle off a litany of justifications for refusing to budge. Needn't even mention me. Could demonstrate both theoretically and concretely how his presence on set made no difference to the film, that boot-on-the-ground participation served no purpose, and his absence left no one in a lurch. Rendering the situation thus left him free to consider my insistence preposterous and himself correct in talking me down from it.

Moreover, he had abundant call to side-step my urging a return to our established patterns. I'd express genuine desire to spend my days as near to how they'd so recently been spent as possible, nursing a normalcy which'd be granted only through life pressing on as it had. As though having prepped, he'd cite personal concern over re-experiencing what'd happened the last time I'd been left alone. In his dramatic yet entirely earnest manner, declared the third film project felt cursed and its set was the last place he could endure being. No need to address how a recurrence of what'd happened when he'd 'left me to be on the project, last time' was impossible. A wave of his hand and a "Jesus Noor, you know I know that' spoken in the cleverest, precisely suffering way would suffice.

Facts other than his own were irrelevant. His stance perfectly correct. My itch for solitude indicative of illness. What he wanted was to be with me, nothing more, and was permitted to say so, unchallenged, even in the face of the clear truth he'd nothing to do when with me. I wasn't bedridden, had entirely recovered from the insult to my physiology, and required less tending to than a potted plant.

If I pressed him, any conversation might swiftly pivot to his asking why I wanted to send him away. I'd have to put up with his self-flagellation, petulant outbursts, whining silences. He'd make it clear that were he to go anywhere it'd be on account of me tossing him out. Things never came to such head, but he'd surely have done so if I'd brought myself to literally tell him to shoo.

Doldrums of his refusal to compromise droned on. Impossible for him to accept I wouldn't perpetually be in the state of invalid shock I'd only legitimately experienced for a number of hours while in hospital. I attempted further tactics. Reminded him he hadn't planned on being present, all day every day, following your birth, so oughtn't he look at the 'being away' I was suggesting as something easier to weather than the 'being away' he'd have suffered had all had gone to plan instead of to pot? I was cautious with these overtures. Took care to present my case lovingly, in a tone near to jocular flirtation. Tried to showcase myself witty, confident, fit enough to express opinions and emotions through the same mixture of lightheartedness and *gravitas* I'd always been. We'd planned for stretches of time wherein he'd be absent from the apartment, hadn't we? Our life was supposed to still be our life, wasn't it? That's exactly why we'd moved to the city, taken the apartment, why he'd worked so hard to arrange these jobs, all in-a-row. I still desired the life we'd planned and knew he wanted it, too. Couldn't we retain as much as possible?

All to no avail. He'd warp the proposal into a tacit accusation of something or else rework the queries into an overall consideration he'd deem 'irrelevant.' Doing so would rekindle my animosity, salt the wound of having my part in any process of healing considered appendix. Though I couldn't rightly be hurt when he morphed my performance in this fashion. He was correct. I didn't mean what I said. Just for reasons nothing to do with why he thought.

If I pointed out how he'd benefit from counseling, ought unburden himself to someone independent of me, he'd agree gamely, then reveal he'd been waiting to say the same thing to me, professing with passion how curative he believed therapy would be. Didn't I understand that if he knew I had security in place, was heeding the advice of trusted professional with my best interests at heart, working through what he couldn't imagine the half of via a constructive methodology, it was all he'd need to allow himself off the hook? He'd secure a talk-doctor, too. We could find the same one, visit them together or back-to-back.

He'd admit I was right about so many things, but artfully segue to explaining the reason he didn't want to return to 'what life would've been like for him, even in part' was that, without the link of the child he'd known it'd be so difficult to be away from for hours each day, time apart from me felt all the more distant. He wanted to stay because he needed my help. We needed to help each other.

But if he desired my help, why was he refusing to listen, why couldn't he leave me to fend as I saw fit? Why'd he assigned himself gatekeeper? Seeing all we had left, and that to alter everything only for nothing to've changed got us nowhere, why insist we behave as so lock-key a unit, reciprocal to the Nth? Couldn't we share the emptiness without breathing the same air?

There were realities I could never share with him, aspects of myself I daren't confess, so I finally had no choice but to become confrontational. Such unwarranted cruelty in how I did so, but as I proceeded, I knew I'd later apologize it all away. Return all his assumptions to him. Act as though what I'd said had been a regrettable but exorcising outburst brought about by losing you. Proffer admission he'd been correct about every incorrect thing he'd believed.

I screeched that his unending presence, day-in-day-out, even when he allowed me my closed bedroom door while keeping to the rest of the apartment, made me feel punished, held prisoner, blamed for what I'd let happen. Viciously reminded him it hadn't been my idea to take these jobs of his, hadn't been my plan to've traipsed away from home for my pregnancy, full stop. Life having transpired as it had, his relentlessly being on hand presented itself as a perverted aggression, an accusation I'd failed him, failed you, our family, our future, shown myself not to be trusted, a deceptive problem to be solved. I growled how his treatment of me in the aftermath of my tragedy was manipulative, overbearing, calculated, unnatural, that being held in his eyes made me feel inhuman. A ghastly violent outburst, performed in exactly the manner I knew'd do the trick.

I honestly couldn't, don't, and never did hold a thing against him. Didn't even feel anger over being needled to the point of so lovelessly attacking him. It was just another thing I'd been forced into because of what I knew, another lash to my back because of what I needed to do. Time alone was a necessity. No interruptions, no doctoring myself up in sugarcoated pretense of healing. My time must be for the benefit of nobody except you. I had to comprehend what'd happened to you, understand where you were, how I was to care for you, protect you. Needed to find you so that I might, even still, counter what'd happened.

'To find you.' Those words stuck like a burr to my forebrain. Were the ones which finally

prompted my insistence your father be anywhere but the apartment. It didn't matter a whit what he did. He could spend the days drowning in self-loathing or in hatred of me at some pub, frequenting brothels, could call up his precious Calista to commiserate. I went so far as to issue an ultimatum. If he refused me time on my terms, I'd take it for myself. Disappear until I was good and ready to rematerialize. Did he truly desire to be my jailor? Because if he were so far gone as to think his love or compassion could be demonstrated by subjugation, I'd not just lost my daughter but my husband as well.

That time is so difficult to fathom. Let me not have you misapprehend how I'd been reduced to so ghoulish a state. Don't think it'd legitimately been anything your father'd done, don't believe it'd been my own mind contorting the texture of intimacy into garish caricature. It was never him, never me, but your killers. Benecourt, specifically. Flagrantly trotting his victory before me, illustrating how your not being born wasn't near enough to satisfy the macabre lust churning in him. The fiend lured me to such abomination, weaponized me against your father. Demonstrated how, if you remained lost, much could still be destroyed.

Deirdre'd stayed on in her hotel. I'd asked her not to. She'd understood why. Made no attempt to insist her presence on me. No invitations, loaded tones, or feeling out whether it'd be permissible to stop by or meet at a café for coffee. Did nothing more than leave one brief voicemail, every other day. Letting me know I was in her thoughts. Available were I to summon here. That she loved me, always.

I'd felt positive your father kept in close contact with her and was proved correct. Despite his entreaties there be full candor and open communication between us, he'd used her as secret confidant. This comforted me. That he'd poured his concerns and frustrations out on somebody close to the both of us rather than to some clinical third-party.

I want to tell you things in order, but see I haven't quite managed, have see-sawed between events and thoughts which occurred over the same span of days. In doing so, I've failed to render the disorientation caused by the compacted duration of events. It's confusing to tell of this time exactly as it transpired because I want you to understand how it unfolded for me more than I care to harp on linearity. What happened immediately after the hospital has no order. Even thinking back from such a distance, I discover no before, no after, nor any all-at-once.

On the day before her departure, I agreed to meet Deirdre at her hotel, to keep her company until the taxi arrived. I'd suggested the venue, because the thought of Benecourt roaming the space where I dwelt, leering victorious inside Deirdre as she relaxed upon the rocker in your nursery, was revolting. She did her best to treat the occasion with nonchalance. Chatted blithely on no particular subject. Laughed as I synopsized a lousy television program I'd watched the previous night. Groused about her forthcoming travel and even chided me for putting her through it. She held off any mention of her own pregnancy and kept wide berth from even cursory reference to mine. Two friends getting together. A little snapshot from another life.

Eventually her eyes met mine. I knew a *façade* had been slowly cracking for some time, her face a melting wax mask, revealing the true self beneath. I saw Deirdre, not Benecourt. My dearest friend, who'd no idea the horror she'd been appropriated by. A victim. A woman ruined and unaware. Seeing this, I couldn't impede her true heart being spoken after having so patiently waited, chained and starved of herself.

She'd told Martin of her pregnancy. An act she neither regretted nor felt relieved by. The details of the story were milquetoast. I didn't know how to posture myself in response. He desired no relationship with her, she hadn't requested one. He'd no interest in being a father and was, in fact, set to be married to a woman he'd known and claimed to've loved deeply for years. But he'd not shirk responsibility. On the contrary, he'd be financially supportive to whichever extent she requested. According to Deirdre, he'd come across as though shamed he'd not be able to make the child a financial priority, imploring her to understand his being made privy so far along into the pregnancy put him in an awkward position. She hadn't pressured him in the slightest when he'd requested his lover not be made aware of the child, instead tenderly assured him she'd never strong-arm or disrupt his life. Nevertheless, he continued to plead his case. Told her, had he known from the jump, he'd have proceeded differently, would've pursued alternate paths and so forth, but when it came down to it, changing directions now seemed purposeless and uncompelling. She'd promised that she felt the same.

On and on she blathered about this rubbish, as though wanting me to understand every crumb and texture and subtext. If I spoke in a manner which seemed judgmental of Martin, she pivoted to explaining she soberly conceded his points, insisted she ought to've taken precautions the night she and her friend went to bed with him, or else went on how she could've come off as conniving since she'd kept her condition a secret. Went so far as to chastise herself, urging me to agree it'd been cruel to inform him. Was he expected to react as though she wasn't foisting terms on him in an attempt to corral a relationship? Looking back, she felt atrocious for letting him think she'd risk his present happiness or require him to cast off his lover.

I listened to everything. Relaxed into the understanding my input wasn't required, though my prompts seemed appreciated as tools to help flush her system. If I took the stance Martin's lover ought not be brought into the matter, but also shouldn't be the man's fulcrum of consideration, she'd agree, then immediately admit, if the tables were turned, she'd certainly treat a woman like herself as a sworn enemy. On and on, on and on, on and on the snakes and ladders of guilt and relief twined. It became clear she'd spoken so nakedly in order to segue to discussing your father. It was then she revealed how often and to what extent they'd spoken. Detailed the confessional manner he'd adopted concerning all he was going through, the floggings he doled himself, the blame he invented to shoulder alone. He'd confessed about Tellwell, related their entire strange history, their recent brief and regretted liaison, explained how I'd promised I'd forgiven him but that he couldn't understand my moving on as though none of it mattered. My reaction'd been unsettling. He couldn't help feel what he'd done'd been harbinger to my current pain. That if he'd told me sooner, or at least spoken of Tellwell's existence ages ago, other roads might've forked, events playing out radically different. He was terrified that, in my private-most heart, I held him liable for what'd happened to you, that his selective erasure of the past had poisoned the air. He'd no right to've chosen what was right and was wrong for both of us, what I was permitted to know or wasn't, shouldn't have decided what he said meant This versus That instead of simply relating what Was and letting our life flow accordingly. He'd even divulged how he'd thought I'd found out about Calista and had actively hoped to've deceived me into dismissing whatever suspicion I'd harbored, utilized our intimate conversations as inquests, calculating every word. Owned up to speaking with me in such a manner on more than the two occasions I was directly aware of. When I'd finally blurted out my question in the nursery, it'd struck him how painfully long he'd carried on a charade, maneuvered me into not speaking my mind, and understood how little he'd allowed me to know him. With no idea how to broach the subject again, he yet longed to. Felt my forgiveness disallowed the matter being fleshed out. That to attempt would be painted an act of revenge. As he saw matters, I'd kept knowledge of something imperative from him in order to display the depth of my loathing, therefore would never hear him if he explained the shame he felt. He'd aimed to keep me safe, keep you safe, but had convoluted the world around all three of us into a tangle he couldn't help believing had led to our losing you.

Sharing no spec of the consideration with Deirdre, I wondered if he'd ever thought I'd harmed you, on purpose, ended the pregnancy so dramatically as a method of torturing him. If he'd broken his vow, contacted Calista, learned she was pregnant, thought I'd discovered it, he might've concluded it possible I'd undertaken so abhorrent an act against our own child in some fugue of rage. I didn't honestly think so. The intrusive query simply mingled into the quagmire of my thoughts while I listened to Deirdre relate your father's anguish. To this day, I assure myself the thought was a necessary reflex triggered by proximity to Benecourt, another grotesque falsity he'd thrust upon me.

Deirdre's emotion became so pronounced I couldn't keep myself from moving beside her on the hotel sofa, grasping her hands in mine, our eyes meeting while the world blurred through tears. It'd been the conversations with your father which'd prompted her to reach out to Martin. The torment she'd witnessed, contemplation of what terror I must've endured upon learning what I'd thought meant my life would be abruptly upended, made her realize she never wanted to cause similar suffering in another. Time robbed even the Truth of certainty. Knowledge visited on a person at the wrong moment left it open to interpretation, falsehood, and every last gnarled interpretation might seem more plausible than what was real, honest understanding or action therefore impossible, and what may've been embraced left irrevocably mutated to delusion, faith, or willful ignorance. It was the worst fate imaginable. She wept while explaining how she'd reasoned that protecting herself, her child, or Martin by concocting alternate realities was insanity, that forcing herself into the role of decider, sole arbiter, all others subject to her impulses and insecurities, was a path which could only end in catastrophe. All of life would become clandestine. Even if the world didn't rot because of the daughter she kept to herself, her concealment of all she knew, all she'd done, all she was, allowed the possibility of personal annihilation. Such allowance was tantamount to deeming it permissible. Encouraging it. Causing it even if there'd never be effect.

In all of this talking, she'd begun reacting to the movement of your killer inside her. With no thought to the gesture, her hands removed themselves from mine, fingers encircling my wrists, and both my palms were pressed to the fabric of her thin cotton dress where it covered her belly. I felt the undulations of the vermin growing strong off her nourishment, plumping into a vile knot, and heard her unconsciously giggling at the insect sensation even through tears and mucus thick breaths.

As she told me how brave I was for believing your father, how she knew him well enough to never doubt the words he'd shared with her, and how she loved me boundlessly for the way I understood the world, apprehending what was of it and what was beyond, grasping what was true despite all appearances otherwise, Benecourt nuzzled into my hands. My friend, your killer's mother, sniffled and sighed in a lovelorn pitch toward him, cooing how she knew all your father'd ever wanted was to protect you and how I'd done everything in my power to vouchsafe the same end, so mustn't ever blame myself.

I wanted to wrest my hands free, brandish one high, bring it unforgiving across her weeping face, tighten my fingers into lacerating claws, scratch a hole into her middle so I might throttle the life out of the giddy tapeworm writhing against me, wring its wet neck, grind it to paste underfoot, laugh and scream and point at the slop of him smeared across hotel carpet, cackling for Deirdre to look and see what I'd saved her from, wanted anything other than to sit there, nodding in silence while I was told I hadn't failed, your father hadn't failed, that everything I'd done had been correct.

I'd done nothing. Such phrasing was foreign. Related to nothing Deirdre could know or be talking about. But it wasn't her speaking. I knew from a cramp in my blood it was Benecourt. Leering how I'd done nothing and been correct to. The fiend was speaking directly to me. Wombed in love and life, tended to with honesty and adoration, he had a vile hand up his ventriloquist doll's backside, Deirdre's mouth opening and closing to his application of levers like some dinner theater vaudeville.

I betrayed no sign of what was in my mind to my friend. Easy enough, as I no longer saw her as such. She was another thing taken from me. A soul reduced to mechanism. Her love for me repurposed and set loose as its carnival opposite. A woman reduced to putty then sculpted into torture. There wasn't Deirdre, now, just a means to punish me. Perhaps since she'd gone to bed with Martin those months ago she'd been eroding. Fully dissolved by the time she'd arrived a day earlier than expected to tell me with laughter and giddiness what she'd done. Deirdre'd been overtaken. Was Benecourt, since that day. Waiting on the most theatric moment to approach me. Now, on a beige hotel sofa on the day Deirdre'd leave to return to her home, had his stage. Used it to perversely showcase how deeply the tendrils of your killers worked into the people I knew. Into any life I might live. Every one of those lives one without you.

I couldn't have been being punished. I'd not lifted a finger against anyone. How would what I was suffering be justified as punitive? All tallied, I'd done nothing but protect your killers, kept vital the lives of the unborn children and their mothers, alike, guaranteed your death would transpire on schedule. I'd rebelled, hadn't condoned your fate, but no matter the content of my thoughts I hadn't acted. That I'd stayed my hand even in thrall to my desperation pled a strong case on my behalf, did it not? Prodded and assailed, anguished repeatedly past exhaustion, admitting a willingness to transgress in unthinkable ways, I'd never gone through with anything, merely considered and reconsidered, planned and daydreamed atrocity after atrocity, called myself capable of them, confessed myself inhuman. There was a chance I'd have done the unnamable, but only ever a chance.

'They weren't even born so couldn't have thought of harming your daughter.' Is that what I'd be told, any claim of foreknowledge on their end brushed off? I'd accept that. If Benecourt, Goaltender, Lowell, Lyons, and Tellwell were innocent on account of they only might've done what I knew they'd do, such outlook philosophically shielded me, as well. If they grew to have thoughts against you and such thoughts became known, I'd be told they could yet change their minds, hadn't acted against you so mustn't be held to account. I'd accept that, as well. So how was I made to suffer when, having considered depravities, I could yet have changed my mind? If they weren't guilty, neither was I. Yet here I was, whipped as though in retaliation for being the malediction anyone'd call me. Make no mistake, if I were to let myself be known, that's exactly how I'd be regarded by even the most charitable of auditors. Even if jurists didn't condone my being punished for the mere idea of the crimes I'd contemplated, they'd never consider me wholly innocent or trust me to roam free. I'd be observed, at least, and, at worst, confined. As I ought be. Had I acted, would have accepted punishment as I'd accepted my foretold death. Accepted punishment all the more if I'd so much as harmed anyone and discovered myself still alive after you'd been born.

I was an abomination. Had admitted as much since the start. All I demanded was an answer. How was I a devil but they weren't? This notion was incongruous. Who'd say that because they might grow to be the killers I knew they'd become they ought be treated with suspicion all the days of their lives, observed hawkishly, kept tabs on? Who'd concur there ought be periodic interrogation of them, bedrooms turned over in their absence, privacy forfeited because of what I'd claimed? No one.

They were innocent simply for having wit enough not to speak of what they'd conspire to enact? Doing so meant all anyone else be permitted was hope that, if they'd planned something, they'd yet reconsider? Did this mean I'd be innocent had I made the choice not to reveal all I've revealed, that my confession is the defining aspect of me? Should I've blurted out everything the moment it crossed my mind and let some third party dictate the particulars of my existence? Is the same true for every thought I've ever had about everything I've done or not done? Is my secretiveness alone to blame for my anguish? I'm to throw myself on the mercy of the people around me, my primrose peers, take it on faith the person I confess myself to doesn't harbor the same thoughts but keeps savvy enough not to reveal them? Is that the best I could be guaranteed?

Let's play one of your father's games. Suppose I seek treatment or counsel. Unbeknownst to me, the person I turn to has association with the family of one of your would-be killers or else will come to at some point. This confidant sweetly, genuinely, empathetically talks me down from my ideas, everything kept between the two of us. They never suggest I be confined or treated as a pariah, rather believe in the possibility of psychological healing, and conclude that my thoughts were a passing episode brought on by whichever outside pressure and would pass harmlessly. Then say I die birthing you. Imagine this party let's slip what was spoken between us. My confession gets brought to the attention of one of your assassins. Becomes the germ that brings them to act against you. Or imagine the person I pour myself out to is a professional sicko, overjoyed to hear my macabre fascinations, believing all the time that I'd die as predicated and, when I do, takes it on themselves to orchestrate your killers into action, five people who, without such intervention, never would've known you existed. Or if not that then something else something else something else, every last else wending me back to where I began.

All that'd happen were I to've revealed the workings of my mind is I'd have been assured the facts I'd planned against were phantasmal and nevertheless have been judged over my reaction to them. If I spoke the full truth, didn't agree to mitigation or allow in falsehoods such as conceding I was scared so had tried to work through my fear while never intending to act, the deeds I'd again and again kept myself from undertaking would yet be seen as things I would've done. My intent was an action, itself. What could be, in fact, was. I'd wanted to act, had been going to, desired action, still, despite not comprehending which to take or how to proceed.

Was I to believe in the countless coincidences I'd been pelted with, occurrence after occurrence which I'd doubted, probed, and found actual, then see the fact that you'd been taken from me mere hours before I would've finally moved to preserve you as just another peculiar bit of timing in a string of curious happenstance there was nothing to apprehend meaning in? Ought I graciously accept that if I hadn't become fixated on my plans to avenge you, you would've been born healthy, free and clear of any connivance, and I would've lived an unmolested life alongside you? That my psychology had tainted some aspect of my physiology, turned me toxic, led to your never existing in the tangible way you'd been meant? Was it to be taken as read only now, after the fact, that nothing could've been done to spare you of not the fate I'd been promised you'd suffer but the one you actually had? Was I to believe your never being born was proof such end had been ordained, that whatever had happened to me and whatever I did going forward all would've transpired, regardless? Was it a sign there'd been another path I'd not comprehended, so had trod the wrong steps? If your father hadn't taken jobs in the area, if I'd stayed behind, if I'd dismissed my knowledge when it'd come to me, if I'd convinced myself it was madness to think you had definitive killers yet unborn who I might eliminate, if I'd chosen to wait and see, leave things to nature and chance, then nature and chance wouldn't have decided you'd never exist? Should I accept all was predestined while denying I could've been granted a glimpse forward? That what I knew was only potential while your end had been unalterable since the moment of your conception? The names I'd known proving true, the mothers dwelling in the area carrying children in such wildly variant manners, and all the insane confluence of my knowledge meant nothing? That myself, your father, Deirdre, the mothers, their children, were all cogs in a watch ticking around which no hand could adjust, dismantle, rebuild, set right was one thing, but who'd say a clockwork couldn't be predicted, what was coming next easily dissembled? Why should I only accept contradiction in hindsight?

What I knew, and what I felt I still knew, was three-fold. The names of your killers. That they'd kill you at age thirty. That I'd perish while birthing you. I'd been on the money about the names. I'd been incorrect about dying in childbirth. But that the children I'd known of would come to kill you wasn't definitive, one way or the other. Even playing fast and loose with matters, some things were known, some weren't, some remained up in the air.

If there was no you to kill, there was no way five people could kill you. What remained was whether there was you or ever had been. To judge on the same terms as anything, that wasn't absolutely determined. A strange thought, but also not so. One which grew more consuming as my mind reeled back through everything I'd experienced, more potent as I inventoried my justifications and doubts, resurveyed your father's rhetorical constructs.

I'd considered Lowell might only 'not yet' be pregnant. How I might spare the mother by killing her husband before he impregnated her. Recollected the surge of relief which'd briefly washed over me at such possibility before I'd dismissed it. There'd been no need to truly excavate the notion, because I'd discovered the surrogate and, at that time, had felt your killers were already extant. Soon I'd seemed proven correct on that front. Investigation of where your killers might come from became moot. I'd found them, no matter their origins. Would it've been the same had I been granted my knowledge six months previous, two years sooner? In that event, I might've earnestly kept on considering the possibility of murdering Alexander. I'd thought of that already, but again had found cause to dismiss the notion, concluding how if I'd slain the surrogate, already pregnant with Lowell, it did nothing to eliminate the possibility of Lenora conceiving another child who she might call Alexander and who'd be the one to kill you at thirty. Hadn't I shown myself how, if the mothers were left alive, I'd never know whether the children they might have would be the killers I'd been given preview of? Only because all five of your executioners had been discovered *in utero* had there been no requirement to sleuth how else they might come to be. As it was proved I'd found the correct mothers, it followed that if I obliterated them I'd eliminate not only your killers but the chance they might produce more. There'd be no other woman called Benecourt, no second Goaltender, replicant Lowell, replacement Lyons, or alternate Tellwell. The women'd I'd hunted were the ones who'd conceive and birth your adversaries, the same as I was the woman who'd conceive and birth you. Tasha couldn't come from elsewhere, so Tasha's killers would come from one source, likewise. Your being already inside me when my knowledge descended made this inarguable. The child I'd birth and name Tasha would be killed by the children of these specific five people, as ordained. I'd simply taken it as read there existed the strict timeclock of six months because if I'd die birthing you what else was there to've considered? I'd assumed the child inside me would live. But that hadn't happened. I'd assumed I'd die. But I'd not. I'd assumed the child I'd had in me would be Tasha. Would be you. But perhaps it hadn't been.

If what I'd known was true, it meant I wouldn't die except birthing you and that you couldn't die except after having been birthed. In essence, you weren't you until you'd been born. Only the Tasha who'd been born could be the Tasha I knew would be killed. The child I'd carried had been someone I'd thought to call Tasha, but I'd been pregnant with someone other than you. I'd not died in childbirth because you hadn't been the child I'd carried. That child had never been born, couldn't die at thirty at the hands of five others, because that child hadn't been you.

Your killers lived and would continue to live, despite the fact you hadn't yet been conceived. Clarity returned with this consideration. The equation balanced. My child, your namesake, had been marked for her end before ever knowing life. You'd be born, called Tasha, I'd die, and your killers would grow to cut you down three decades from when first you drew breath. It was precisely how I'd suggested it might've been if Lowell, or Goaltender or anyone of them, had been left alive to conceive another child after I'd killed one they'd fostered. Would that child have been another child or the same child finally realized? Would such thought-play and convention of title matter? Having lost the child I'd have called Tasha, would calling another child that name make it not another child, at all? Why would it be another? It would be you. The same as the child I'd carried would've been. You were the same Tasha. You, growing inside me now, were the same. You were Tasha. Are Tasha. Whether you father or whoever else might consider the child I'd never had 'not-Tasha' or you not 'the same Tasha' but 'another child called Tasha' and go forward into your future without me, such future remained the one I had knowledge of. I knew and had known only what'd happen to you.

Did I imagine your protection could be secured simply by calling you Trisha or Lexi? Ought my first wily thought, when met with my knowledge, have been a deft arrangement of alphabet across birth certificate to spare you? Same as I'd thought concerning your killers, you might choose to call yourself Tasha later into your life, regardless. I'd no way of knowing for sure. For that matter, it might be said you were Tasha despite being called anything else by whoever for whatever reason. The unburied names merely pointed me toward your killers, saw me clear to embracing the truth of what every thought in me'd wanted to declare impossible. Names were the least tangible aspect of anything and were, in the end, devoid of meaning. I'd considered many times how monikers might be altered, first and surname non-binding. Only because I'd discovered the known names in conjunction with other evidence had I curtailed investigative pathways I'd have probed were said names left unfound. I'd not ventured any further than seemed necessary in the moment, had turned stones over only until I'd discovered the requisite information to secure your life beneath one. If one of the mothers had lost their Montgomery or their Nathan due to my ministrations, would they think the Montgomery or the Nathan they later conceived was a new person, a different one, see them as the same or as a continuation? Such was irrelevant. Whatever they thought, believed, or desired didn't dictate what was. It's no matter how I worded it. I could say you were the same child or a different one. You are my Tasha. You'd been Tasha, never born, were to be Tasha, in these moments of thought I'm describing, and remain Tasha, pressing against the walls of me while I write.

All of this I could know for certain only after enduring what I'd endured. Losing you but not myself was the alchemy of transmuting theoretical to absolute. For a metamorphosis so severe, the price needed to be commensurate. I'd been correct not to act, but it would be a mistake not to act, still. My hesitations, questions, and wariness had been instinctual, a process of culling possibilities so nothing might be left to chance. The strangulation of confusion had girded me for what was ahead.

I'd need to wait until your killers were born to protect you from them. The loss of my child had been waiting in the wings to illustrate that my foreknowledge hadn't been a paradox, would always have happened so lingering doubts might be removed. Tasha had needed to die so I'd understand what it meant to lose Tasha. How protecting her was unerringly worth any fee I could name. I'd needed the child which'd grown in me but never drawn breath to perish so I might comprehend the emptiness of living on without her.

Once your killers were born, they'd be at my mercy. Until you were born, you were safe from them. The task before me had become a genuine choice. Not only to bring you into the world at the expense of my life, but when to do so. I'd eliminate as much danger as possible, before. Had all the time I'd ever require to consider, settle on, and execute the strikes I'd make. Both children and mothers removed from the board, I'd become pregnant, carry you to term, and let myself die.

All the same considerations as before assailed me. Alternates, wordplay, What-ifs. I had to dismantle each in turn. Did so curtly to spare myself growing *effete* from reassessment. With so much uncertainty gone, final uncertainties seemed fairly quaint.

I know it's you in me as I write this, Tasha. I know it was you in me, before. That's become evident. What relevance could it have to anyone else? Nobody knows what I've done except you. Nobody who might would be concerned with parsing such matters. But I did. Felt a touch of maternal shame, though supposed it was harmless. Utilized the pouring over my every thought as a strengthening measure. Needed to know my mind on the matter. Understand exactly what I thought'd happened before rousting myself to the final solution.

For sake of investigation, I entertained the possibility the child I'd lost hadn't been you. Doing so led me to humoring the notion it might not be you, this very minute, kicking so powerfully while ink colors these confessional pages. It amounted to the same. Perhaps you, who are in me now and to whom I write of this dark business, will be born and I'll live through the birth. Knowing what I've done, I'll torment myself with the same questions, same doubts, and come to the conclusions I already have. I'd still have no choice but to've done what I've done. Eliminating your killers and their mothers remains the only guarantee of safety, even if it's no guarantee. I'll wonder if you aren't my Tasha, but you'll be my Tasha and I'll have protected you, all the same. Perhaps you, the child I keep, aren't the Tasha whose fate I'd been warned of, the same as the child I'd lost hadn't been. It could be my next child will be the Tasha who'd have died if not for the actions I've taken. Actions I'd have taken, regardless. Actions I've taken for you, your lost sister, your possible sister to come.

Your father could no doubt write hundreds of drive-in features from such a libretto. I can hear him, even now, regaling you with the million ways such grindhouse life might go. I die while birthing your older sister, who I'll have named Lisbet. You die through some accident and, at seventeen, Lisbet takes your name to honor you. In doing so, would always have been the Tasha I'd protected, though wouldn't have been Tasha at all if not for the Tasha I'd lost. Or he'd explain the name makes no difference. You'd be born, called Tasha, and your life would move into Lisbet after you died some unexpected way. She'd never be aware of the change. Live on as Lisbet while being Tasha, as well. The Tasha I'd known to protect, nestled in my Lisbet who I'd died giving birth to.

Only once I die will everything be known. The child I usher into the world while perishing is the child I've protected. That body, that vessel. Which name, which history, how all of it works, links, interacts, will be known or won't be. I've done what I've done.

I know it's you. Was you. Is you, still. Were I to discover, in some unexpected way with absolute certainty, it'll be my fourth child who'd have been victimized by the people I've killed, it'd change nothing of what I'd needed to do or when it'd needed to be done. Because I might vanish while bringing you into the world, I've needed to act on that possibility, as I'd been prepared to act on the same chance for your lost sister. Now is the same as then. No guarantees. Which pleases me. I've been made to act as I now know I most honestly always desired. To never allow your five killers to experience a truly conscious moment, be permitted years enough to grow cognizant of their thoughts, gain honest comprehension of anything, be possessed of a single memory of experiencing the pleasure of their mothers' love.

I know who the suckling and thoughtless creatures I've killed were. Death grants them no innocence. If it does, let them possess it in nonexistence. Let everyone pretend who one becomes isn't who one was while becoming who they'd be. To me, nothing has changed except the words which describe what I'd always have done anything to achieve. You're now safe from them.

Please remember, I never aimed to forgive myself or to deny who and what I was while I progressed. I've confessed self-hated for the moments I wanted to be something other, but never did so in the belief that desiring to be something else ought earn me pity. I don't ask you for pity, now. Only that you apprehend who I am, what I am, and how. I wasn't the person who killed the people I've killed only after I'd killed them, just as your father wasn't the man I loved only after I'd met him, and wasn't your father only after he'd held you. As you weren't his daughter, only then. Or my daughter, only after I leave you.

Such thoughts often came to mind in the moments before acting against your killers. Always in the hours immediately afterward. I was the person who killed all of them even when I'd only killed one. When I'd killed a child but not yet a mother. A mother but not yet a child. When two, four, seven were dead, while others yet lived, I was no less than what I am now and no different.

I know some would argue with that. Can you imagine being burdened with the sort of mind that'd litigate what's so obvious? To suggest I became, step-by-step, what I am now, was step-by-step less than it at point-X versus point-Y, a killer but less a killer, damned but less damned? How could one function, who'd look at their lover and say 'You loved me less yesterday than today,' turn to their daughter to impart 'I didn't love you before I did' or tell both how the degree of their love is dependent on duration, sequence, and that love exists only in one direction?

I can think of nothing more ghastly than believing love can't be predetermined. I never thought so, therefore never thought myself less than my end. Only casting back to write this do I bother considering the question enough to point it out. Had I been caught when I killed Lyons, I ought to've been punished for killing Benecourt, Goaltender, Lowell, Tellwell, and their mothers. That's what I'd been caught doing when bad luck and technicality kept it from becoming true. I never thought of myself as only partway what I was while on my way to it. Which doesn't matter at all, except I want you to comprehend how I didn't write any of this until I'd killed everyone. I'd never have done so, though certainly could have. More-or-less every word.

Sometime around Montgomery Lyons' first birthday, the happy Violet learned the child had a sibling *en route*. This brother or sister was one her poor husband Reggie likely thought he'd be allowed to name. Maybe he had. Perhaps it'd been agreed upon long in advance. If it's a boy, such-and-such, a girl, so-and-so.

Alexander Lowell was born to the surrogate who, from what I've discovered, had no rights to so much as visit the child nor desired them. It was strange having to kill her. Just to be certain. Was she the mother or was Lenora? I couldn't take chances.

The Goaltender woman bore her assailant's child and made him carry the name Keith for his brief time on this Earth. He'd no thoughts on the matter, but I wondered if, had I allowed it, he would've worn the name proudly or shamefully, shared his mother's view of what his life represented. Would he be grateful to her pride for allowing him an opinion had he existed long enough to form one? If he'd grown up, would he have considered taking violent revenge for his mother as I'd taken revenge against her alongside him for you?

Marcy Tellwell would've lived to believe her father was called Hubert. Hubert lives on with no reason to know his daughter shares a father with you. Your father will never know, either. Not unless you tell him. If he's still with you when you read this, I can't imagine you'd want him to be made aware. A man nearly seventy? Why punish him with what he'd never known he'd done?

Deirdre gave birth a year ago, today. Called her son Nathan. Had become Benecourt, herself. After Martin left his lover. He'd seen the light. Understood what he 'needed to do,' was how Deirdre'd put it to me. I was present for the delivery. In the room as your killer emerged from my former friend. She'd asked for me over Martin. Insisted it only be me and the medical staff. I'd held her hand. Encouraged her to push. To scream. To not give in to requesting the epidural she'd dreaded she'd beg for. During her labor, and in the four days she remained in hospital after, I fetched her popsicles from the Maternity Ward pantry, buttered the toast she was ravenous for, and watched a mute television while she slept.

Due to some complications, she was for awhile unable to fend for herself. Had lashed out at Martin quite viciously. Claimed only I prepared her desired meals to her liking, so I cooked for several weeks. Helped as best I could during the tormenting days when your killer had difficulty latching her breast to suckle. At first, scary to ever love you enough" the monster he'd painted to watch over you for me had declared. I like to think maybe you'll declare back "You love me too much to ever scare me." Though you'll be wrong, it won't matter.

By now, you'll have known yourself thirty-one years. Perhaps will have seen me as that monster every hour of them. Does seeing me as the monster I am change anything? Does it alter who you are, who you were, who you'll be? Have I left you a choice in the matter? If not, why not? If so, what nature of choice and how is it exercised?

If I'm that monster still, please forgive me for being this monster, as well. If I'm this monster, now, please don't forget I was that monster, too. I'd be any monster for you, Tasha. But I could never be none.

forever. Instead, I let him speak to me unburdened. Unaware he's speaking to me about what I've done, what it means, closer and closer to the last time. He doesn't need to know he's protecting me, as he'll protect you, simply by speaking as though what really is isn't.

I wrote none of this thinking you'll love me. Write even these words knowing, after them, you'll not spend one minute more wishing you'd heard my voice. By the time you open these cruel pages, you'll have loved me far longer than I deserve. I write these words so you can think of me as I am rather than the dream of what I ought've been. Without them, you might be able to know things which cannot be known, but without them I'd be keeping you from knowing the one thing about me which can be known in no other way. You'll know I loved you without these words, but could never know I loved you not nearly enough.

I've no desire to justify my actions. Please understand I'm not so cowardly as that. There exists no justification for what I've done. I won't pretend I required one. I am, and have always been, a monster. That's why on the painted wall of your nursery you'd seen one. I'd asked your father to come up with the image. He'd laughed despite being pleased to. "What kind of monster?" he asked. I told him "Any monster will do." "Do you think it'll scare her?" he'd teased. I told him "It might." But you'd grow up loving the monster. It'd protect you. I made him promise to promise you that your monster'd protect you even if nothing else could, even if there never was any need. He'd winked at me how, if that were the case, he'd make it look like me. That he'd never want you to believe there was a monster more necessary. So I'd told him "Make it look like me, then." But was glad when he'd stuck out his tongue. Glad it'd turned out to look how it did. Glad what you'd loved wouldn't resemble me. As I'm glad the words he'd painted coming from its mouth were his words, not mine, and that you'd only ever know them in his voice and in your own. "I'm too

I think back to what I was told concerning that day in the hospital. How I'd begged the doctors to hide my child and how I'd begged that child to hide. Was it you I'd told? Did you hide, Tasha? Did you wait? Is another Tasha hiding from me, now? Because if she hadn't hidden but been born and then died, wouldn't that mean she'd been born into failure, locked fast to its contours? Had she hidden herself from me, as perhaps always she ought to've, to spare me doing what I've done, to show me that since I'd not acted until then there was no need to act, at all? Perhaps she'd spared herself suffering the death I'd foreseen by sparing herself being the daughter of someone who'd have done the unthinkable in her name.

I don't wonder such things often or for long. Know you're my Tasha. That I'll not be aware of the moment which proves it, whether that same moment proves anything else or not. You're my Tasha and I only ever think otherwise to feel close to your father, who I know sees you differently than I. Who I love for seeing you exactly that way. Whichever way. His way, not mine.

I turn my mind to other possibilities. That the Tasha I lost was the Tasha I'd been meant to protect. That because she was killed, I'd lived on. I can't speak such thoughts to your father, even playfully or disguised as storyline banter. There's no place for those words between he and I. Just as there was no place for so many others. If I could, I'd tell him everything. Let him spin me the thousands of things what I've done might mean, permit him to surprise me again and again with interpretations I'd hotly disagree with. He'd work to convince me a million times over that I won't die. How even if I die, it could be said that I didn't. Might be so maudlin as to float you as proof. I live on through my daughter. Death's not the end, just the place where I'm waiting for you as I'd waited all the years previous in life. He'd find words for the things that don't matter, bury me in them to be certain the few ones that do had been said and were said again for the first time, you not knowing who I am. For the thirty years you would've lived regardless of my interventions, I'd never want you to've been burdened. For that time, I'd find it abhorrent to be anything to you apart from what you and your father invented me into. But to only exist as your joint imaginings, thereafter? I'm too weak. Too selfish to burn down what I am. To let who I am expire with my body. I can no more do that than I could've let you exist only as dreams of what you may've been had you never.

I sometimes wonder what it'd mean were I to live. Find myself holding you. Listening to you laugh the first time. Being the one who nurtures you to the ability to read these words. It'd mean I'd been wrong, in a sense. That you'd never been in danger, the way I'd thought. You'd not been in danger, but I'd protected you, nevertheless. In another sense, it'd mean nothing at all. Indicate you technically weren't the person I'd needed to defend, but through moving to defend you I'd have defended that person, regardless.

Other times, I idly consider whether living would mean I'd definitely have another daughter. This becomes a puzzle. Would I have a choice? I whisper to you "If I lived and you, therefore, weren't the Tasha I'd known the fate of, would I be compelled to mother children until I'd created such Tasha? Or would you be Tasha enough for me? If I knew there could be a Tasha I'd killed to defend, would not bringing her into the world be committing her murder myself, despite all I'd done to prevent it? If I live and never have another child, what would it mean? Are you my Tasha in a way beyond how you are? My same Tasha, the one I'd protected, though I'd been incorrect about everything leading to you? If there was nothing to protect you from, had I protected you? Or would I have protected this other Tasha by having you in her stead? If that Tasha had never been born, never conceived, was I keeping her safe or was I killing her without letting her live?" Sometimes I pretend you hear me when I lullaby these questions aloud. But I never play that you answer.

them alone would've been deemed in the eyes of investigators. Their murders would've seemed brazen, ugly, and glaringly unforgivable. But some short time after, those same murders didn't even seem crimes. I doubt fear of foul play was entertained for a flicker.

Unfortunate deaths of strangers, spread over time, remote from each other in location and happenstance, were called 'Things that happened to other people.' Even the victims would think so, were they still able. I'd transmitted no indication of direct, vindictive agency in what I'd enacted. A dozen deaths nothing more than background hiss in the roiling flux of the world. I find it transfixing to consider this, fascinated perhaps because my death looms so near and my death, itself, is related to these others so intimately yet will never appear connected. A mother dying in childbirth is merely 'something that happens.' No reason to associate it with any outside event. Even if one knows to look for the link, wants to look, who actually would? Even you, who know not only to look but possess the means, will lack the desire.

Those who've lived on won't be pleased if you show them what they never thought possible. I doubt they'll accept it. If anything, they'll dismiss every word, cast you as some ghoul tormenting them for no purpose. They've more than settled for there being no reason for the losses they've suffered. That's the same as it is for anything anyone suffers, so far as they care. I've never had to speak one word of what I've done to anyone. Will never need to. Not even because I'm soon to die. If I were to live on, I'd never be called to account for what I've done. Whether I could keep myself from doing so is another matter, but no one else would prompt me to. I write all of this down, knowing it's my choice to do so. Nothing compels me. I'm free to set these pages aflame, leaving who I am and what I've done unknown. I'd remain who everyone believes I am, what I've done what everyone concerned has settled into accepting. I could yet I couldn't. Because of you. Can't bear with actions behind me so unthinkable, horrors considered not only not mine but no one's. I've never been suspected. Life has moved on. I've watched my hand in events remain invisible, fading even further than that through becoming renamed and accepted as something else. The sadness I've caused is simply sadness, same as any. Multiple things else could've caused it and do, every day. The questions I've seeded in the hearts of a handful of people are no different than rhetorical queries which are feared and considered many times in even the most typical of lives. 'What would I do if ..?' 'How would I go on were ..?' 'What would it feel like to ..?' The only difference is these people have answers. Ones they'd probably discovered they already knew. Interesting how such answers are the same as to questions they don't know to ask.

Were you to search, you'd find little evidence beyond my own words that I'm what killed these dozen people. How much easier it was to bring the tasks off, already knowing the full truth, never having to doubt what'd keep you safe, what wouldn't, or if there truly was anything to protect you from. How vulnerable your killers were without the sheath of their mothers around them. Vulnerable and weak, susceptible to everything. All the easier to have my crimes appear random. Various methods of dispatch employed, nothing to directly associate one child to another, one parent to another, one parent to child, or the lot to each other. The deaths of your killers and their protectors were each individual happenings, not a string of connected events as they would've seemed had I acted too rashly. Five pregnant women dead raises eyebrows. But five dead children, six at a squint, plus six dead women become part of a larger construct, lumped in with dozens of others, hundreds, none more specific than they need to be, no one asking for them to mean anything more than they seem to.

The tight of their mother's wombs had made your killers a unit, their unborn state made the mothers a grander entity than any of

I've no need to write out the particulars of what I've done. I doubt you'll want to know, though don't hold back simply because you might be distressed. Could a handful of horror stories disturb you more than what you'll have read up to here? Details wouldn't help you understand why I've done what I've done, how I was able. Failing to, they're meaningless.

If you research the deaths of people you'll have lived your entire life without knowing a whisper of, you'll find only questions. Wonder if you ought answer them for people or let sleeping dogs lay. What difference to you, how some dozen people died, three decades before you were born? What difference to those who knew the victims, who'd be as old or older than your father? Most anyone directly associated with those I've killed will have faced down their own mortality, the mothers of the mothers long dead, the brothers or sister perhaps holding grandchildren. Will you appear on their doorsteps with this journal, share with them the confession of a woman who's been dead for as long as those they'd have lost? Would it provide justice, solace, any value at all? Why re-write their past for them, show them the futures they chose for themselves and the fates they believe they'd accepted were constructed by me?

You'll question every word I've written. These pages and pages and pages of nothing you'll have desired to know. The thoughts I've attempted to make clear, set down in my hand which I try to keep steady. You'll wonder all the things I wondered, as though along with me, except so far after the fact that, for you, all that can be done is to wonder. You'll only be able to treat as irreversible all the thoughts and actions which, to me, there'd been endless choice in, despite the no choice there'd been. Be able to choose for yourself whether to reveal or keep secret the irrefutable truth no one's ever once sought.

It's so interesting to be an accident. To've lived this short while meant. Circled his hand once over the fabric of my shirt, lifted it with a tight grip almost high enough it exposed my breasts, gone to his knees, and kissed you through me. I'd told him "She already knows that." He'd said "I know, I just wanted to tell her for the first time for the first time." I didn't tell him 'You already have' but did say you were to be called Tasha. After which he'd stood up, kissed me, and said "She was always going to be called Tasha." I kissed him again. Instead of correcting him how she already always was.

He thinks of you as someone else. I could tell it then, can tell it, even now. To him, your 'Tasha' is a namesake, a reminder, a continuation of sorts, a life picking up in celebration of another. You're the daughter he will have, not the one he never did or the one he already does. He sees a difference I don't recognize or understand but which I can't for a moment begrudge him. How could he see you any other way? Why would I ever want him to?

In truth, I find a serene beauty in him not knowing. In never finding a reason to think back on losing you. He has his daughter and would always have loved you enough for several. I hope he has no need for his past. Desire that he think of you as another or as his only. When I'm gone and you're in his arms, he must regard you precisely that way. I never want him to wonder who that other child might've been or to wonder, if she'd been born, would you not have been or, if you had, would you be somehow different for her having been, too. He must believe life is only what he believes. That one cannot know what cannot be known but can say they do, all the same. What difference is there in phrases that're used to mean the same thing? He'll always demand different words, three million alternates, even when he knows the correct ones have already been found. Will say knowing the right ones doesn't mean that there aren't others, just as right or far less right, as deserving of being heard.

Martin seemed to appreciate my presence. Soon, I think he came to resent me. After Deirdre'd requested it be me who helped bathe her and fetch groceries to suit her mercurial cravings, after I made her laugh even during the bouts of intense depression she suffered while her body convalesced. I was glad he took to disliking me. Certain he could sense something wrong. Stayed out of the apartment the entire last day I spent with her. The one during which I said 'Perhaps' when, through grateful tears, she told me what a wonderful mother I'd be. More than a month later, I told her 'That's ridiculous' when she further beamed how she'd never have been the mother she was without me.

I waited almost another month, until after the first time Nathan Benecourt, cradled in my arms, had smiled at me, to look your father deeply in his eyes while telling him "I want to try again." That smile from Nathan Benecourt. That smile which squirmed and boiled in me and has continued to every day since. That smile in which I saw his terror. That smile I returned with my own and a gentle 'Shh.' That smile was when I knew I couldn't go on living.

It makes me laugh when I think back on how Deirdre told me she'd never seen him smile quite like he had in that moment. "Like a real smile, his first honest expression." Makes me laugh how she'd added a teasing shove to my shoulder, ribbing me how jealous she was that 'the little bastard never cries when you hold him.' "He's too proud to cry around me" I'd replied as he'd smiled, again. Comprehended how he'd miscalculated. That there was nothing to do but accept his fate. I laughed after making love to your father, that same afternoon. Remembering that smile. Already feeling you in me.

I'd known I was pregnant for three weeks before I revealed it. Told your father "It's like she never left." Never loved him more powerfully than when he'd said 'I love you' to my belly, right after, without even asking for direct confirmation of what I'd

www.ingramcontent.com/pod-product-compliance
Lightning Source LLC
LaVergne TN
LVHW031611060526
838201LV00065B/4805